The Mental Traveler

Also by Stephen Kessler

Poetry

Burning Daylight 2007
Tell It to the Rabbis 2001
After Modigliani 2000
Living Expenses 1980
Beauty Fatigue 1978
Thirteen Ways of Deranging an Angel 1977
Poem to Walt Disney 1976
Nostalgia of the Fortuneteller 1975

Translation

Desolation of the Chimera (poems by Luis Cernuda) 2009
Eyeseas (poems by Raymond Queneau, co-translated with Daniela Hurezanu) 2008
Written in Water (prose poems by Luis Cernuda) 2004
Aphorisms (prose by César Vallejo) 2002
Heights of Machu Picchu (poem by Pablo Neruda) 2001
Ode to Typography (poem by Pablo Neruda) 1998
Save Twilight (poems by Julio Cortázar) 1997
From Beirut (poem by Mahmoud Darwish) 1992
Akrílica (poems by Juan Felipe Herrera, co-translated with Sesshu Foster) 1989
The Funhouse (novel by Fernando Alegría) 1986
Changing Centuries (poems by Fernando Alegría) 1985
Widows (novel by Ariel Dorfman) 1983
Homage to Neruda (poems by Eight Chilean Poets) 1978
Destruction or Love (poems by Vicente Aleixandre) 1976

Prose

Moving Targets: On Poets, Poetry & Translation (essays) 2008

The Mental Traveler

a novel by

Stephen Kessler

Greenhouse Review Press

Acknowledgment is due to the editors of *Santa Cruz Magazine* and *Oxygen*, where excerpts from this work first appeared.

Lines from "Condition of the Working Classes: 1970" ("Anarchists Fainting") by Robert Bly are reprinted from *Sleepers Joining Hands*, HarperCollins, New York, 1973. Copyright 1973 by Robert Bly. Reprinted with his permission.

Cover photo by Solle Ayres

The author also wishes to thank Richard Brickner and Elizabeth Kadetsky for their early critical insights and encouragement, Dorothy Ruef for digital assistance, and Lynn Park for her sharp editorial eye. Gratitude is due as well to Stephen Pollard and Gary Young for book design.

This is a work of imagination. Any resemblance to actual persons, etc.

Greenhouse Review Press
3965 Bonny Doon Road
Santa Cruz, CA 95060

ISBN 978-0-9655239-7-4

Printed in the United States of America

for Rick

I travel'd thro' a Land of Men,
A Land of Men & Women too,
And heard & saw such dreadful things
As cold Earth wanderers never knew.

—*William Blake*

Your sons dream they have been lost in kinky hair,
no one can find them,
neighbors walk shoulder to shoulder for three days.
And your sons are lost in the immense forest.

—*Robert Bly*

The Mental Traveler

1

The Creature from Love Creek Lodge

That fall I was living in a cabin at Love Creek Lodge, a dormant resort and sometime nightclub nine miles north of Santa Cruz on Highway 9. The front of the lodge faced the highway, a winding road that ran through the mountains from Santa Cruz over the summit, shaded even on sunny days by the steep slopes of the San Lorenzo Valley and the density of second-growth redwoods. The back of the property, down an embankment, was bordered by the confluence of Love Creek and the San Lorenzo River, ordinarily a feeble stream that during winter months could build to a roaring torrent. In the rainy season the valley was said to be so dark and damp that you could get athlete's foot up to the knee. But the rains hadn't started and the cool autumn air was electric with expectation, streaming blue and lucid between the trees, charged with a strange urgency.

The lodge wasn't home but it was a good hideout. What was I hiding from? Everything. Julie. The fiasco of a bungled marriage. Graduate school. The pressures of respectability. History— I mean the pandemonium of the past couple of years, assassinations and insurgencies, a war supposedly overseas that had invaded us, violating our psyches with a shame and a rage too great to acknowledge, poisoning every thought. It was all just too confusing. I was a mess. I retreated to the woods in search of relief. Hiding. But it was a half-baked getaway. The other half was to play the role of the aspiring English professor, commuting to and from campus to attend my graduate seminars and earn my living as a TA. Imitation of a normal life, whatever that might be. From which at the same time I sought escape.

When Julie moved down the year before from Berkeley, leaving her apartment in what by then was already a war zone to join me in my cottage in the suburbs of Santa Cruz, she was sacrificing the independence she'd gained so painfully from her family. While I was back east being a sensitive poet and budding intellectual at Bard, Julie was struggling to break free from an alcoholic mother whom she hated, a gynecologist father with artistic pretensions who'd long since left the family and remarried, the ghost of a big brother who'd perished in a motorcycle wreck at seventeen, and a heroin addict older sister caught in a series of abusive relations with sub-bohemian men. With a little financial help from her father while working part-time as a restaurant hostess, she had done well academically, made a few friends, and established a tiny island of stability on which to construct her life. A good-looking, green-eyed, long-legged brunette, she had no shortage of admirers, but my return to California after two years away restored our bondage to each other in ways we didn't know how to untangle. The sexual revolution may have been fun for some people, an ongoing orgy of entwining limbs and freelance interpenetrations, but the popular expectation to make it with whoever happened to be there was more than I could cope with. When I was seventeen and she sixteen, Julie was the first one I was naked with. I couldn't believe my luck. She was voluptuous. At the touch of her skin I came. Eventually we learned how to do it, and we did it with others too, but Julie remained my muse, the one who could inspire me when other young women—even as I strove to be a liberated stud—would leave me shy and shriveled. I in turn was her emotional anchor, a relatively solid point of reference, a comrade and confidant. During the summer and fall of '68 I frequently found myself racing up Route 17 to her bed in Berkeley, or found her at my door for the same purpose. The more time we spent together, the more insecure we were about being apart. Finally, at the end of the quarter in December, I talked her into leaving school and giving up her place— the streets were getting more dangerous every day with student revolutionaries, Black Panther vigilantes, street people and hostile cops in constant confrontation—and moving in with me in Rio Del Mar, where she could hear the surf crashing peacefully beyond the eucalyptus and cypress trees and the sewage-treatment plant. At least she wouldn't have tear gas to contend with.

Tears, yes. Within weeks of her arrival she was panicking, insisting we get married. She'd given up everything. I owed it to her. She pleaded, she cried, she reasoned. A persuasive combination, especially as we breathed the same eternally smoky air, staying forever high, smoking the joints she was constantly rolling with her slender trembling fingers and sealing with her sweet wet tongue, applying that tongue to mine, melting my brain with the heat of her gorgeous body. The logic of eros and marijuana prevailed. I couldn't argue. I thought what the fuck and said okay already. In a matter of days we were standing before a justice of the peace in his room on the ninth floor of the Hotel Santa Teresa, a rundown retirement home downtown where all the tenants were about four times our age. The Reverend Smalley was ninety and didn't get around too well; if you wanted his services you had to come to him. We brought three witnesses—colleagues of mine from grad school—said two poems, took our vows, and went out for dinner at Javier's, our favorite Mexican restaurant. A painless enough procedure. The five of us went back to our place, drank champagne, got stoned, raved about the portentous prospects of the new year ("Sixty-nine is gonna blow everybody's mind," said Julie, and we all laughed nervously), the witnesses went home, and we went to bed, consummating our nuptials in a beautiful fuck whose climax practically took off the top of my head.

Next day I had a class to teach and Julie accompanied me to campus. After the session we were to meet and resume our antihoneymoon. I found her in one of the student lounges yakking with manic intensity to a group of undergraduates who apparently found her monologue compelling. It happened she was talking about me, portraying me, her husband, as a daring young bard and brain on fellowship in the doctoral program in literature but, more than that, a trippy wizard with awesome creative powers whose genius assured his imminent importance and, by association, hers. Inevitably we'd be famous, the Scott and Zelda of our generation, she to be known by her big floppy hats and high-heel boots and hysteria, and I for my brilliant as-yet-unwritten works. Of the half dozen students held captive by her rap, the most enthralled appeared to be a wiry little creature of ambiguous gender with short blond hair who couldn't take his or her eyes off Julie's face. When I appeared, interrupting the performance, everyone's attention turned to me, and as we excused ourselves I felt the focus of those androgynous eyes.

That was a Friday. The following Monday in the dining hall the skinny androgyne sat down across from me at lunch and introduced herself. Her name was April. "If you're a poet," she asked point-blank, "what are you doing in graduate school?"

Good question. I had to think. "Well, I'm avoiding the Army, for one thing."

"That's pretty smart. Anything else?"

"Trying to get a PhD, I guess."

"What for?"

I just looked back at her, incredulous. Her gray eyes were locked on mine, as if scrutinizing the inside of my head.

"So what makes you a poet?"

"I've, uh, published a few poems. I write poems."

"Where? Let's see some."

"Little magazines. I don't just carry them around."

"Maybe you could bring some. I'd like to read them."

"Okay. Sure. I'll bring some poems."

"Your wife's crazy, isn't she." It wasn't a question.

"She's . . . high-strung, is how I'd describe her."

"Does she always talk like that, like the other day?"

"I'm not sure; I didn't really hear her. Why? What did she say?"

April summarized Julie's hourlong monologue, a breathless account of our day-old marriage, our history, our future, all in the mode of mythic gossip crawling with obscure allusions and a certain manic romanticism that gained associative momentum as she spoke. "She was very entertaining," April concluded. "Why did you marry her?"

"What do you mean, why did I marry her? What is this? What's your trip?"

"Just wondering. You seem sort of low-key. She's so overamped. I was trying to figure it out."

Her directness disarmed, intrigued me. She was fresh. Within a week I was in her dorm room showing her my poems, which she didn't react to one way or the other. We might have gone to bed but the dorm made me nervous—all those young girls running through the halls shouting and giggling, playing their records, brimming with a wild nubility—I was distracted, intimidated. I wasn't lover enough.

By early spring, while Julie grew more frantic, unable to focus on anything but me and the fiction of our stability, April and I had seduced each other. I knew I was being a shit but what could I do? I was being yanked between two equally irresistible female forces. Besides, sexual freedom virtually demanded multiple lovers if you had the chance. Everybody was fucking everybody, at least in theory. What did marriage have to do with anything? Julie sensed what was going on. She was shaky enough in the first place, and when I confessed what she suspected it pushed her over the edge. She'd been seeing a shrink already, and at his suggestion she checked herself into the hospital. I'd visit her on the ward at Franciscan, where she was cooled out under the care of her doctor, Leo Hopkinds. Recently arrived from West LA, Hopkinds was the heaviest headshrinker in the county, a Freudian analyst turned chemical experimentalist whose favorite medication was a new psychotropic called Stelazine, which Julie, who loved pills anyway, was obediently ingesting. She did seem a little calmer when I saw her. We'd talk for half an hour, kiss goodbye, then I'd get in my Porsche and zoom up to campus in time for a class or a private meeting with April under the redwoods.

Like Julie, April was a painter. But where Julie dabbled in acrylics on prestretched canvases, April assured me that serious artists only worked in oils. De Kooning was her hero; she raved about his Women. She explained to me the importance of Abstract Expressionism. And she was studying philosophy, eager to discuss the finer points of Hegel's *Phenomenology of Mind* and Nietzsche's *Will to Power*, books I considered beyond me. It wasn't just that she was smart or flashy about her reading, she seemed to really care about what things meant, what human lives were for, and how to make the most of our creative potential. At nineteen she was a genuine intellectual, and on top of that she had imagination, and put those together with her boyish body and Botticelli face and I was hooked. Why the fuck had I married Julie? Why had Julie brought us together? If that wasn't Destiny, what was? April and I decided to run away together, we didn't know where, we'd just start driving. But I chickened out, leaving a note in her campus mailbox: "I want you, but I'm not ready for this kind of change." She wrote back: "Change, shmange, you've got to do something with yourself and it's a thing you'll probably never be ready for."

Julie's stay in the hospital was short. We spent the summer trying to repair the damage to our so-called marriage, with little success, neither of us mature enough to face the facts of our misplaced interdependence. April had meanwhile given up on me and gotten involved with a young physicist. When classes started again in September I was coming unhinged, a victim of my own contradictions, strung out between the pointlessness of my intellectual pretensions, the bureaucratic demands of my academic standing, the fearful desire to be a writer, a social conscience but no stomach for activism, the continuing but hopeless infatuation with April, and an increasingly impossible partnership with Julie. If I didn't have the guts to take off with April, maybe I could disappear on my own. One overcast late October afternoon I told Julie I was splitting and drove off into the mountains in our VW bus in hopes of finding refuge, a simple cabin under some trees, a monk's nest, an asylum. On a hunch I pulled into Love Creek Lodge.

Snooping around behind the main house, where I knew there were some cabins, I was greeted by the owner, a friendly red-headed lady in her early thirties at most. I told her I was seeking a place to rent and she explained that she was just beginning to renovate the premises, which were in disrepair, but I was welcome to have a look at one of the cottages. In its heyday the lodge had been a vacation paradise for summering San Franciscans, complete with swimming pool and gourmet kitchen, but it had been neglected for many years. The row of motel units in back looked scuzzy and desolate, and the pool was covered with a leafy scum. The cabins seemed more romantic but equally funky. My hostess, Nona Dolan, informed me that she and her husband, a corporate lawyer in Saratoga, just over the hill at the far end of Highway 9, had recently bought the property and it was her project to get the lodge going again, reopen the restaurant, bring in entertainment, rent out the units in back. I agreed it had great potential, sounded exciting.

We mounted the sagging porch of one of the cabins and crossed the threshold. "Please excuse everything," Nona said. "We've just begun fixing things up. We've been working on the lodge and the motel rooms. We haven't gotten to most of the cottages yet." The place was empty except for layers of forest mulch on the floor and a half-collapsed wooden table under one of the two windows. On the far wall was a huge brick fireplace, a feature I appreciated since it was obviously the only source of heat. The thin walls were papered with pale green painted cardboard—these were summer cabins—and in one corner was an unfinished mural whose central figure was a naked nymph, some kind of hippie goddess left in passing by a wandering artist. Cobwebs hung casually from the ceiling. I imagined rats scampering in the crawlspace under our feet. "There's no hot water yet," said Nona, "but we're working on it." The bathroom was, well, basic—a toilet, a basin and a clawfoot bathtub. There was a large brown spider in the tub, most likely a brown recluse, local challenger of the black widow for most-dangerous-spider honors. A brown recluse, like me. Nona apologized but I was pleased. The place felt perfect.

"When can I move in?"

She gave me a long look. "How about tomorrow? I can probably find some extra furniture upstairs in the lodge or in the other cottages."

"Beautiful." We agreed on the rent and I wrote a check. We shook hands. "I appreciate your being so open to me just wandering in off the street like this."

"You have the eyes of an honest man," she said. "Let me introduce you to Tanya; she'll help you get set up." We walked over to one of the motel units where a young woman was cleaning. She looked up from her bucket, her dull blond hair pulled back under a faded blue bandana. She and her old man, Jesse, lived in the unit two doors down from mine and were helping Nona with the renovation. Tanya gave me a warm and knowing look, as if to say, far out—another head—and welcomed me to their little community.

After classes, late the next afternoon, I pulled into the lodge and parked in front of my shack, prepared to do some heavy-duty housekeeping. A broom was leaning against the wall just outside the door. It was a cold day, getting dark, and I figured I'd gather some wood and build a fire. I opened the door to a totally different room from yesterday's. A kerosene heater stood in the center of a rug that covered most of the floor, a double bed was against the wall in the corner under the mural, a dresser stood against the opposite wall, and under the window a sturdy-looking chair and writing table. In front of the hearth was a funky old rocker. The place had been swept and dusted, the fireplace cleaned. There was a jar of flowers on the dresser. It was warm inside, the heater beaming away. Under the stark glare of the naked ceiling bulb, perfumed with the smell of flowers and kerosene, the room exuded welcome. Tears of gratitude welled up in me. Did I deserve such kindness?

It didn't take long to establish a pattern. I put my few pieces of clothing away, lined up my ten or fifteen books on the mantel, and placed my typewriter on the tabletop. The machine was a Smith-Corona portable that chopped out the "o" if you hit the key too hard. Lately I had lacked the clarity to write, lacked the patience even to sit still, but I hoped that left alone with the typer for a while I might be given the words to help me get a handle on what was going on. At night it was too cold to sleep on sheets so I unrolled my sleeping bag on the sagging bed under the benevolent gaze of the hippie goddess. She was hardly a de Kooning, much less a flesh-and-blood April, but I welcomed her company as a surrogate muse. Mornings I'd sit on the porch in the rocker, smoking hashish or a joint and admiring the light as it played in the turning leaves of two great maples that stood out among the valley's dominant oaks, madrones and redwoods, that cool autumn light coming over the river, waves of mist rising off the damp ground when the sun touched down, woodstoves perfuming the mountain sky with the sharp-sweet smell of smoke. Rocking and breathing, smoking and thinking, looking, drinking in the light, I absorbed the fullness of the fall air, the cleansing sound of Love Creek meeting the river, the birds' easy chatter. Even the passing traffic on Route 9 made its contribution, providing ironic commentary on my reverie, reminding me of my business in town, my daily duties on campus.

After classes and meetings I'd roam through the forest collecting deadfall firewood, filling the back of the bus with it, spiders and all, and returning to the lodge to stack it neatly at one end of my porch. When I remembered to eat I'd do it in one of the dining halls on campus, or grab a sandwich in town, or have breakfast at one of the local coffee shops down the road in Felton. Evenings I'd either hang out downtown, nursing a beer and taking notes in the Rodeo, or stay home playing the role of the studious monk. Coming or going I'd sometimes pause to exchange greetings with Nona or wave hello to my neighbors, but mostly I kept to myself, doing the necessary reading for school, keeping office hours on campus, attending classes, trying to stabilize the shaky days following the split from Julie. She would do better by herself, I was sure, would get it together as she had in Berkeley. And I would clarify my clouded awareness, rocking on the porch, listening to the birds, scribbling my spidery notes.

One day toward the end of November Tanya invited me to join her and Jesse and a few friends for a Thanksgiving get-together at their place. I was to bring a loaf of bread and they would provide dinner. When I arrived that evening Jesse was tending several chickens roasting on a grill in the fireplace. Tanya was in the kitchenette working up the rest of the fixings. Their friend Dirk, whom I had met once before, was sitting on the floor cleaning some grass and rolling joints. Another neighbor, Howdy, who also lived at the lodge and worked as a maintenance man for Nona, sat on the ratty sofa listening to the Doors on the stereo. Jesse handed me a beer as I found a seat on the footstool-stump next to the sofa.

The chicken smelled delicious. At last, a home-cooked meal. Dirk passed a joint. Howdy kept the records spinning—Dylan followed the Doors, and the Stones, Dylan—and the rest of the guests arrived: Spider, a wired little dude with a high-pitched laugh spilling over with enthusiasm; George, a burly mountain man who looked like a tired lion, whom I had seen before in the Rodeo; and Sparrow, a slender blonde with a downturned nose that kept her face from the kind of wholesome generic beauty found on billboards and the backs of magazines. Tanya had a thicker, earthier look, a compact natural power in her body. Both of them struck me as unbelievably beautiful. I needed the comfort of a woman. Was grateful they were here.

Jesse and Tanya served. The plates were passed. We all gave thanks. Chicken and rice, salad and bread, beer and wine. Tea and marijuana for dessert. And a savory pumpkin pie that Tanya had baked in the big house. After we ate, Jesse removed the grill and fed the fire with construction scraps. I went out and brought back some deadfall from my porch. Firelight and candlelight. Kerosene lamplight. Winelight. The light of well-fed brotherly-sisterly eyes together for a family meal. Lacking some other family. Dirk raised his beer, grinned from behind his droopy mustache, and shook out his long thick locks. "I'd like to toast all you fine freaks, you new and old friends, it's Thanksgiving and here we are, can you dig it? This is just beautiful, beautiful."

"Beautiful," we replied in chorus, laughing.

"And now for the main course!" Spider cackled. He drew from his pocket a small bottle and poured out on the low table nine small purple capsules.

"Whoa," said Howdy, "what could this be?"

"This could be the finest mescaline you ever tasted." Spider pronounced it mescaleen. "Comes with a factory guarantee: all the way there or double your hallucinations back. My treat."

Mutual survey of eyes. I'll do it if you will. George said, "Actually I'm just coming off a tripleheader. I'm going to pass." Is he saying he just dropped acid three days in a row? Jesus. The rest of us were game. We each picked up a cap and dropped together.

Howdy flipped the Stones album. *Beggars Banquet*. Not exactly easy listening. Maybe a comment on our dinner party. As designated deejay he lacked a certain sensitivity. The cat had a strange edge. Speed freak? No, not hostile or jumpy enough. Friendly but aggressive. Trying to take us on his bitter trip. Unconscious. Musical tyranny. Conversation could intervene.

"Did you hear the Indians invaded Alcatraz?" said Dirk, who looked like he might be part Indian. When I had my moccasins on I felt part Indian—how come now that I'd switched to boots for the winter I didn't feel part cowboy? Because the cowboys were the bad guys, and I was good. The Indians were good. "Yeah, they landed this morning and claimed the island as Indian territory. Too much."

Jesse asked, "What are they gonna do with all the prisoners?"

Spider let out a shriek. "Ain't no stinkin' prisoners, man. They shut the fucker down five years ago. Where you been?"

"Oakland," said Jesse. "Milpitas. San Jose. Then we lived in a cave up the river from here. I don't read the papers. It's lies."

"Who'd want to live on Alcatraz anyway?" asked Tanya. "It's so cold and foggy."

"Yeah, but it's got a cool view of the city," said Dirk.

George said, "The government should let 'em keep it. It's the least we can do for stealing their whole country."

"I think they should be given California, Oregon and Washington," I proposed. "Then there should be a process of repatriation, starting with Europeans—white folks back to the Old Country. Indians might do a better job with what's here."

"They should send 'em back to Africa with the spades," said Howdy. "No more race riots."

Dirk said, "Hear that?" The wind was rustling the trees outside. "Indians. They've got us surrounded," He shot a glance at Howdy. "And they're coming to scalp your ass, paleface."

"That's not funny," Sparrow said. "Ever see someone get scalped? It's not funny at all."

The walls were beginning to undulate.

"Can't we change the subject?" said Tanya. "This is getting a little weird."

"Wait a minute," said Spider. "I want to hear about scalping." He asked Sparrow, "What are you talking about?" As a newcomer to this group, I wasn't sure who knew whom, but maybe Sparrow was a stranger too.

"I was in LA for awhile," she said. "Living on a commune with some other runaways. A ranch in the Valley. Indian country, sort of. A place where they used to make Western movies. And we were living like Indians. You know, light. Off the fat of the land. At night we'd drive into town and scrounge in the dumpsters outside super-markets—you wouldn't believe how much stuff they throw away, perfectly good food. We ate really well. It was a beautiful trip. But there were some freaky people who'd come around, just to hang out, or there were some parties we'd go to sometimes that were sort of spooky. Witch people. Demon people. One night Charlie—he was the main guy, sort of like a father for some of us—said he was going to show us how Indian braves in the Old West earned their feathers. I couldn't tell if he was putting us on or not but he was, like, a teacher, you know? A powerful dude. There was this party in Topanga Canyon. A bunch of us went. I thought it was going to be a spiritual demonstration of some kind, you know, a ritual, eat some peyote or something. There was this kid who'd been hang-ing out at the ranch who Charlie said was on a power trip, bad en-ergy. This kid, who was maybe nineteen, was at the party. Charlie invited him to come down to the beach and get high. We were sitting around the fire playing mind games when Charlie got up, walked over to this kid, pulled out his Buck knife, picked him up by the hair, and started to scalp him. Actually he cut off the top of his hair and left the scalp, most of it anyway, the kid's head was sort of dribbling blood all down his face, it was horrible. That's when I de-cided that scene was too freaky for me. I got out of there, hitched back up north. People around here may be a little crazy sometimes, but LA . . . I don't know, maybe it's the smog or something."

"Shit," George said. "In Nam I saw guys actually take the scalp of gooks for a souvenir. But that was war."

Howdy said, "Man, I've seen worse than that—"

Jesse broke in. "Are the Stones responsible for this shit?" The side was just ending. "Maybe we can lighten it up."

"Play some Aretha, Howdy," Tanya said. Her face was radiating pink light. Pink and brown spots came pulsing off the walls. Blood of invisible Vietnamese dripped from the ceiling. We needed help.

Aretha to the rescue, the queen of soul, moving the room into a blue groove, gospel of sex and spirit, urban renewal, womanly wisdom, pain and betrayal, sweet salvation, gratified desire, Southern comfort, blacknight sunlight, waves of warm love, natural wet-womb earthquakesand, windows weeping amen, flames clapping in the fireplace, all eight faces transfixed for a few minutes, the music working a new mood.

Jesse—tall and sinewy-strong, stringy brown home-cut hair—took Tanya's hand. The bedroom was in back, behind the fireplace, and pretty soon we could hear them getting it on—hard breathing, giggles and low moans, bedsprings twanging in rhythm, the cottage shaking, it was their house. The guests were cool. Dirk took over the stereo, sonic camouflage and accompaniment, and the rest of us drifted off for a while into our individual trips, silenced by the sex in the next room. To hear their love, their groans, their brimming jism, was a torment, also a privilege, a share of their intimacy, including us in their orgasms, leaving us out, teasing, torturing, showing who had the true power of pleasure here. I kept the fire alive; it was something useful to do and it kept me grounded, steady. I'd never met people quite like these. Outlaws? It was a leap of trust to be tripping with them. Spider was right, the drug felt pure, a smooth rush, harmonic sensations flushing the nerves, fireplace bricks throwing off warm waves in rhythm with the flames and the fucking. Sparrow's story struck me with how much I didn't know. What kind of kids would live out of dumpsters and follow some maniac who scalped people? Runaways. She was a runaway. From what? Her parents? Well, weren't we all? My guess was that everyone here had parents they couldn't relate to, intolerant intolerable fathers, mothers who didn't get the picture, adults out of touch with the way the world was going. It had been months since I'd spoken with mine. I couldn't admit my failure, especially after they'd blown it over our so-called elopement. They suggested Julie was after my money, money I barely knew I had, and seldom thought about. Wasn't one reason for going to grad school to prove I could support myself? UCSC had given me their top fellowship, my obscure excursions into scholarship were paying off, literature could have something materially to do with living, I was getting paid for reading books. And here I was on the verge of dropping out. And dropping psychedelics with a bunch of renegades.

I felt the beer filling my bladder and stepped outside to have a leak. The stars were pulsing in the dark sky. The cold air purified my insides, passing through the lungs to the blood and bathing my brain and arms and legs in a smoky floating strength that was more than physical. The aroma of woodfires blended with the smells of food from hundreds of holiday dinners hovering in an air current over the river. A bobcat cried in the state park miles away. Coyotes yowling. Owls. Sounds of the mountains. Healing sensations. Breathing is being. You are what you breathe.

On the way back inside I stepped in shit. Fucking dogs. I wiped my boot on a patch of grass, scraped it on the dry dirt, doing the mashed potatoes. My sole is clean. The boots were new and are now inaugurated. Nothing can stop me.

Spider and Dirk were talking about the Stones and the free concert they'd be giving soon in the city. It was just a rumor but everybody agreed it would be monumental and they would be there. Tanya and Jesse had rejoined the group.

"Hey, Cord of Wood." She was talking to me. "We thought you'd split. Who was that masked man?"

"Nope, just getting some air. What did you call me?"

"Cord of Wood. That's you. Quiet, smoky. You know. Solid."

It was an honor to be called wood. Would any of my colleagues on campus have called me that? Tanya was a tough girl from the

East Bay. She was down-home real, she could be trusted. Cord of wood. Okay.

"Hey man," Howdy was addressing me. "You know your house burned down the other night?"

"Beg your pardon?"

"Your house. Your cabin. It burned down. You must've been out. The fire department pulled in and surrounded your house. Must've been five or six pickups, volunteers, plus the big pumper. I came out of my place and asked what's going on. They said, 'Can't you see? That house is on fire.' They went through the motions of putting it out. All but busting down the door. Then they packed up their gear and cut out again. Strange, huh. I guess it was a drill."

"You're trying to mess with my mind."

"No shit. I swear on my old man's grave—and he ain't even dead."

"Well, I'm glad I wasn't home. It's enough to make a person paranoid. I mean, can you see me surrounded by a bunch of rednecks with axes and firehoses? And me inside smoking a joint?"

A knock at the door. Dirk scooped the seeds and sticks into his jacket pocket, Tanya flipped the ashtray full of roaches into the fire. Be cool. Spider's little bottle was out of sight. Jesse went to the door.

It was Nona Dolan.

Nona was not your average landlord. Nor could Tanya, Jesse, and Howdy have considered her a typical employer. She took a personal interest in the welfare of the people living and working on her property, looking out for our comfort, letting us use old furniture from the lodge. From my first meeting with her I was touched by her trust, which I hadn't earned. She was one of those rare adults over thirty, apparently a citizen of straight society, who didn't act defensive or resentful toward the young. She was exceptionally open to what was happening. Still, there was something odd about her showing up alone in the middle of the night on

Thanksgiving. Her usual composure and meticulous grooming seemed slightly askew.

"I'm awfully sorry to bother you, but I came up to take care of a few things and I guess I've forgotten my keys. Do you think I could borrow yours? Forgive me for barging in like this but I just can't find them anywhere."

"No problem," said Jesse.

"Of course you can." Tanya fetched her set and handed them over. "Would you like to come in, have a cup of tea or something?" Can you smell the marijuana, sense the psychedelics? If so, then what? Have we blown it? Are we evicted?

"Oh, no thanks." She looked shyly around the room at the eight of us trying to appear relaxed and natural. Can she tell how loaded we are? She looks a little stoned herself. In some ways, I felt more connection with her than with these hippie outlaws. Despite the age gap—she was maybe ten or twelve years older—we shared a certain gentility, good middle-class manners. "I'll bring the keys right back."

"It's okay," said Tanya. "Just leave them inside the old washing machine on the service porch. I'll get them tomorrow."

"Thank you. Thanks. Good night, everyone." She looked at me. "Good night." A wave of agitation rose in my chest and lingered as she shut the door. What was in that look?

When she was gone the mood had changed. Suddenly it felt late. A mescaline hum still swam in my bones but the power of the drug had peaked. Pink and yellow halos hovered around the faces of my companions. Sparrow looked ravishing. Dirk was a wild Adonis. Tanya and Jesse, leaning on each other, had the love-gorged aura of the sexually sated. Spider's intensity had gentled but he was up, his energy unabated, his eyes darting happily among us in search of additional mischief. George was beginning to nod off, exhausted from his three-day odyssey. Only Howdy had a harsh edge—uneasy in his own skin, still struggling to untangle some inner snarl, his hurt dulled but jumbled by the drugs and drink.

"That's your landlord?" Spider said. "Man, she's something. Classy lady."

"She's really nice," said Tanya. "But something seemed funny about her tonight. She's usually so together."

"Maybe it was us. Maybe we're fucked up," said Dirk.

Jesse said, "At least we didn't lose our keys."

"Yeah," I volunteered, "just our minds." Good enough line to close on, I suppose. I needed to get some air. Sparrow's beauty was starting to pull me, awakening longings I didn't want. I hardly knew her, had who-knows-what in common, and yet I craved to get close to someone. Some woman. I didn't know what to do with that need. And this was no place for an overture. One-on-one I would have hung out for hours with Spider—he had the spark, was sharp and positive—but the psychic crosscurrents in the room were getting too hairy. Maybe some other time. Things inevitably got awkward in a group this size—too big to be intimate, too small to be anonymous—but there was a certain inertia. It took initiative to break away. "Well, thanks for everything," I said, getting up. "I need to take a little walk. Good meeting you all." I nodded to Sparrow, George and Spider. Betraying my upbringing. Too many words. Too courteous, formal. Somebody cooler would've just walked. Or stayed, just sharing the space. "Later."

The fresh cold was medicinal, dark green oxygen brightening the blood. No moon. The river whispering. Cat vision coming on. I could go left toward the creek and my cottage or right toward the road and the lodge. Not thinking, I went right, possibly pulled by the beam of a streetlamp arced over Highway 9. *Dark is a way and light is a place.* Where was I going? I saw lights in the lodge kitchen. I wondered how Nona was, why she was here so late. Did I dare knock at the back door? Was it any business of mine? Nerve was walking me in that direction. I knocked.

Nona opened the door a crack. "Hope I didn't scare you," I apologized.

"Not at all. Come in." A ledger book was open on the kitchen table. A bottle of red wine and a glass.

"I was just wondering," I said, looking for the right spot to put myself. "Is everything all right? Are you okay?"

"Oh. Sure. Yes." She seemed slightly embarrassed, smiling weakly, looking off into the unlit end of the cavernous kitchen. "Here, sit down. Would you like some wine?"

"Water is fine." I got myself a glass, filled it from the tap, and sat down across from her at the table. "I just . . . It seemed . . . you looked a little . . . different, tonight. I was sort of . . . surprised to see you." Hope I'm not acting too strange, too stoned.

"It's very kind of you to ask. Very sweet. I know it's unusual for me to be up here at night. But, well, this place—we've only owned it for a few months, you know—it's very special to me, kind of a personal domain, a private sanctuary." She paused to assess my reaction. I was focused on her face. She looked more at ease than I'd seen her. There was a fire going in the woodstove. You could feel the hugeness of the house around us, empty dark and cold, but the kitchen was cozy. "Actually, I had a little trouble this evening. A . . . misunderstanding with my husband. I needed to get out of the house for a while. It's such a beautiful night. I started driving"—her BMW was parked in front—"and I ended up here. I like it so much. And I knew there'd be other people here, some of you anyway, so I wouldn't be afraid. But I forgot my keys." She took a sip of wine. "I was just writing in my journal."

"That's a nice notebook." I admired the quality of the bound book, black cloth trimmed with red leather. Classy lady. "I used to keep a journal. Until I started graduate school. Now I just write papers. And a poem every so often, with any luck."

"A scholar and a poet. You are lucky."

"I'm not really doing so well as either. I'm thinking of leaving the university. I want to travel awhile. See if I can get the writing back. I don't think I'm cut out for professorhood."

"I know what you mean. I was an English major at San Jose State. I taught high school for five years. But it wasn't satisfying, or too satisfying, I don't know, I got too involved with my students, it was exhausting. So I got a real estate license. Sold houses for a while.

It was exciting, I was making a lot of money, but then so what, it seemed stupid pretty soon. Then I wrote copy for an ad agency. 'Creative writing' quote unquote. Then I met my husband."

"Working on this place must keep you busy." I don't want to hear about your husband.

"It does. It's wonderful. There's so much to do. Sometimes it's overwhelming, but I love it. I want the lodge to be the cultural center of the valley. Fine food, music, art exhibits."

"Poetry readings."

"Poetry readings, of course. A meeting place."

"Sounds great. Maybe I could be your literary director."

"Marvelous!" She was loosening up. The wine. She raised her glass. "To the new Love Creek Lodge."

"To the lodge." I clinked my water glass lightly against her wine glass. I wanted to stay pure, feel the clarity of the trip, not get clouded with alcohol. The water kept me calm. What a lovely woman. I was smitten by her sincerity and her beauty. The agitation—half fear, half thrill—rose in my chest again. I drank more water, trying to stay cool. She was old enough to be my . . . landlord. Aunt. Big sister. Teacher. Too young, thank god, to be my mother. Too old to be my lover? "Nona," I said to her, "you're great." I had to say something or I'd explode.

"Not really." She flushed, smiled, looked at her glass, looked up at me. "But if I am, I guess it takes one to know one. You know, I used to want to be a writer but I didn't have the courage. It makes you so vulnerable."

"Maybe you just weren't vain enough, not enough ego. You have to be kind of presumptuous, I think."

"Perhaps," her left hand swept back a lock of red hair from her face. "But you have to have something to say." She got up and placed another log in the stove. Her tailored slacks hung snugly on her butt.

"What do you write in your journal?"

"Oh, letters to myself, ideas for stories. Dreams. Recipes, lists. Meditations, reflections. It's just a way of thinking about things."

"Been thinking about anything interesting lately?"

She laughed. "Sure. Everything."

"You've been thinking about everything, or everything you think about is interesting?"

"Everything I've been thinking about everything is interesting."

"Oh, yeah. Everything is everything. Sounds like you're on drugs. You're not a plainclothes hippie, are you?"

"You know, that's one of the things I've been thinking and writing about. Hippies. The youth culture. The counterculture. How kids seem so much freer than when I was young. So many taboos are gone. You can experiment. It's exciting, isn't it?"

"Yeah. More fun than a disaster in progress. As far as I'm concerned, when everybody expects you to be so wild and free, when it's mandatory, it's just as oppressive as being told Thou shalt not. I don't mean to say the prevailing free-for-all and all-for-free and all-for-all ethic is bad or anything—I mean it is interesting—just that all this so-called freedom is existential: it makes you responsible for your choices, accountable for your conduct, no excuses. Not that everybody thinks about like this—unless they happen to be philosophers—but it's more complicated than it looks. More difficult. At least for me. But maybe I'm not so typical."

"Certainly not."

"Anyway, we lost our illusions earlier. I bet when you were coming up you never suspected the country was run by gangsters. Never had your hopes assassinated. Never hated your parents as much as we do. Sorry. I'm getting a little heavy. Must be the acid in the drinking water." In fact, the mescaline was mellowing. A smooth descent.

"Every generation has its difficulties," she said. "I was expected—girls like me were expected—to find a man and get married, and that was happiness. Everything would be taken care of. Ozzie and Harriet happily ever after. I didn't do that. I was looking for something more . . . challenging. More fulfilling than that formula. When I finally met a man I felt understood me as a person, and married him, it turned out he had a lot of those same expectations. The old assumptions about a TV wife." She refilled her glass. Thought about what she was saying. Shifted gears. "Barry's a fine person, a good husband." She was trying to convince herself. "It's just that sometimes he has a hard time seeing me as an individual, someone with my own needs, my own desires, ideas. I've got to make the lodge work. It's my big project, my poetry."

"I'm sure it's going to be terrific, Nona. And if not, so what? You can start another project. As Dylan says, there's no success like failure." Hope I'm not being too wise. Nothing worse than a precocious wise guy.

"That's good. I like that. But this would be an expensive mistake."

"Sounds like you're into something much more daring than drugs and rock'n'roll and sexual liberation." Why did I have to say sexual? My guts fluttered.

"Hmm. That's an interesting way of looking at it. Daring."

I was hearing double. Ambiguous language. Undercurrents of implications. Half-hidden meanings. Her own desires. Expensive mistake. Daring. What did she mean? What did I mean? Don't be paranoid. Don't assume anything. Relax and take things literally. I got up, went to the sink, refilled my glass, sat down, took a long sip, looked at Nona, she looked at me, we both looked at the table. I asked her, "Have you ever smoked hashish?" What am I doing?

She didn't flinch. "I can't say that I have."

"Would you like to?"

"I don't know." She wasn't being coy. She really wasn't sure.

"Not that I'm trying to corrupt you or anything. It just seemed you were curious. You're not driving home tonight anyway, are you? It must be pretty late."

She looked at her watch. "Ten past three." Looked at the woodstove, rippling flames behind the mica window. Thinking. "I could stay over. There's a bed upstairs." A bed. "It won't make me anxious, will it?"

"You'll probably just feel more of whatever you're feeling." More. "Are you anxious?" I am. But pleasantly.

"A little tipsy perhaps. But not nervous."

"Mind if I use the bathroom for a minute?" My bowels were in motion. "Excuse me. Think it over. I'll be right back." I left my jacket on the back of the chair, walked quickly to the john at the far end of the kitchen, flipped on the light, shut the door, pulled down my pants, sat on the crapper, and had a beautiful psychedelic dump. A thoroughly happy evacuation. Catharsis. I'd scared the shit out of myself. Move over, Sophocles. I wiped, flushed, washed, and was back at the table in no time. Enlightened, loose. "Well?"

"Okay. I'll give it a try." She was smiling. Confident. She could handle it.

Outside, a car started. Another. The party at Jesse and Tanya's was ending. Had Howdy finally flipped out, broken down? Had anyone seduced or been seduced by Sparrow? Had the hosts given another sexual exhibition? Had there been an all-around orgy? Had everyone crashed out? I'd never know and it didn't matter. I was turning Nona on.

Out of my jacket pocket I pulled matches, penknife, the slender wooden pipe with the small screened bowl and a slab of hash wrapped in tinfoil inside a matchbox. The ritual was essential, the tools and materials sensuous. I unwrapped the black-green chunk of fragrant resin. "Smell this." I handed it to her. "Rub it between your fingers."

"Mmm. Like flowers." She handed it back.

I opened the knife and sliced off tiny slivers, dropping them in the bowl. My left index finger over the end of the pipe, I struck a match under my chair with the other hand and put the flame to the hash, taking a hit, just enough to get it lit, a ribbon of dense sweet smoke rising from the bowl. I handed her the pipe. "Put your finger over the hole and draw."

She closed her eyes and took her first toke. Smoke rose. The pipe stayed lit. She coughed, opening her eyes. "That's strong. Am I supposed to feel something?"

"Take your time." The pipe had gone out. I gave her another light. "Inhale slowly. Open the hole to mix in some air. Hold it in your lungs."

After a few passes back and forth, she had the technique. She felt the drug in her brain. "Oh. Well. Yes. I think I'm getting high." She giggled.

"See? It's no big deal. Just further and deeper. More of what's going on. This is Vietnamese hash. The best. See how gummy it is? Smell how rich? Too bad you don't have a stereo here. Music would make it complete." The smoke was giving the fading mescaline a boost. Nona's face looked handsome, serene. She was at ease, with only an occasional flicker of disquiet shadowing her brow. The fire gave the room a sense of security. We watched the flames, bathed in the stove's radiance, luxuriated in the smells, the soft light. The rustling silence outside had dimension, richness, shades of the subtlest music, punctuated by the firewood's crackling percussion.

"I scored this hash last July in the Haight-Ashbury. The day they landed on the moon. It was sunny outside. I went with my friend Misha to a dealer's pad on Clayton Street. Various hairy hippies hanging out in the dark with the shades drawn. The TV was on in the back room, and while this transaction was happening, the moon landing was being broadcast—live, like a ballgame. A giant trip for mankind. The people watching the show weren't convinced it was real. Consensus was that the whole thing was staged in a vast television studio under the Astrodome. A government conspiracy to distract the public from what was going on in Vietnam. The moon would be declared the fifty-first state. Strip-mined for precious metals. Used as a garbage dump. If it was a hoax, the people were bamboozled into believing the US had accomplished something. America had conquered the universe. A red-white-and-blue herring. Showbiz in space beats reality on earth. If it was for real, they were violating mythology, defiling the purest sphere of the human imagination. Leaving their trash up there. What would Keats say? Let alone Yeats."

Nona just looked at me, appreciative but puzzled, as if to say, I don't quite follow you.

"So," I concluded, "this is lunar hash."

She laughed. I laughed. We were happy and goofy, tired but excited, like little kids up late, getting away with something. She trusted me—whether to keep my distance or seduce her, I wasn't sure. I wanted to affirm my tenderness for her, acknowledge the singularity of this night, complete or consummate our special friendship. But I didn't know whether the way to do it was to play it cool or come on. Had sex always been the standard, as it was now, for measuring everything? Was Norman Mailer right about a man's life being only as good as his orgasms? I could imagine kissing her but didn't have the courage. Fortunately the table was between us. But I didn't want to keep raving either; I was sure to say something stupid. For a long time we let the silence play with our minds. Phantoms and angels dancing in the synapses. Laughter and grief in a game of cosmic leapfrog. Reverence and mockery spinning in spirals of dialectical euphoria.

Finally I asked, "Do you want to smoke some more?"

"I don't think so. I feel fine."

You look fine. I couldn't say it out loud. I turned my gaze to the stove, a neutral zone. The flames were copulating. The smell of the burning oak was wholesome. That's how her hair would smell. I looked at the tabletop, studying the grain. It rippled in waves like the muscles of a woman's back as she removes her shirt.

Very deliberately, focusing on the act, I rewrapped the hashish. Returned pipe, matches, knife and hash to their pocket. Then I went over to the stove and warmed my hands. "I don't mean to keep you up," I said. "I can go now if you need to get some sleep."

"That might be a good idea," she said, rising. "It's almost five. This has been wonderful. Very interesting for me. It's so unusual just to be able to sit quietly with someone. And it's nice getting to know you a little. Really. I know that sounds so . . . polite, or something. But I mean it. You're such an interesting young man." Young.

I pulled on my jacket and she followed me to the door. I placed my hand on the knob, half-turned to face her. An awkward pause. "Well . . . I hope I haven't been too bad an influence."

"Not at all. I appreciate the experience."

I opened the door, stepped onto the service porch. The cold air broke the spell, I couldn't touch her. She couldn't or wouldn't move toward me. A married woman. Reserved. Discreet. Surely that was part of her appeal. I didn't know how to approach her. Not man enough. Maybe that's what appealed to her about me. Her tenant. I wasn't tough. A gentleman hippie. No threat. What's wrong with me? How can I be so harmless? Maybe she wanted me. If I had made the move. Too late now. "Good night, Nona." You know where I live.

"Good night." She stood in the doorway, outlined by the light. I turned and entered the dark.

2

Altamont Nation

The Rolling Stones were coming to California for an extemporaneous West Coast answer to Woodstock. An apocalyptic aura surrounded word of their imminent arrival. Those who were tuned in knew that a rock'n'roll nation was being founded and a wave of revolutionary psychedelic awareness would rise in an irresistible tide to lift the congregation, and by extension the country, into a newly enlightened and redemptive state of being. Surely some revelation was at hand.

Or so it seemed to me that first week of December as I monitored the latest radio reports on when to expect the Stones. They would be playing in Golden Gate Park in the city. No. Anticipating an avalanche of stoned humanity, logistical chaos and a parking crisis, the promoters and the local authorities had ruled out San Francisco. Next it was Sears Point Raceway in Sonoma. But for some reason that plan also fell through. The counterculture was beside itself, every freak in the region poised to receive the latest bulletin like the old RCA Victor dog. Finally another racetrack, at Altamont Pass near Livermore, east of Oakland, was settled on as the site. Altamont, Thomas Wolfe's fictional town. Mythic echoes for a mythic moment. And I would be there in my new Frye boots, worn brown cords that hugged my skinny butt, white wool turtleneck purchased in London on my big trip in '66, and funkily stylish fringed split-cowhide jacket, its ample pockets packed with survival gear: car keys, notebook, ballpoint, penknife, hash pipe, Chapstick, harmonica, kitchen matches, a stash of smoke, rolling papers, and one large tab of mescaline scored from a stranger in the Rodeo, Santa Cruz's cavernous coffeehouse/saloon that hosted the local collective unconscious. Water? Food? Way too mundane. Angelic spirits didn't need to eat. Or, as Abbie Hoffman said, *This revolution runs on electricity*. The gathering at Altamont was set for Saturday. Friday evening I rolled up my sleeping bag, threw it in the back of my Volkswagen bus, and headed up Highway 9.

The bus was gutless. A few months earlier, when we were still together, Julie and I had bought it off a used-car lot in Sunnyvale, trading in our '63 Chevy Impala convertible (a gift from my parents on my sixteenth birthday) for something less bourgeois, more soulful and nomadic, less suburban, less flashy, more functional. I'd sold her the Impala when I'd bought my Porsche, and now as we were married and our cars consolidated I could turn the Porsche over to her and assume the downward mobility I desired with this boxlike high-center-of-gravity cool-looking suitably hip vehicle that we could sleep in if we had to. We took out the back seat and I installed, with minimal carpentry skills, a plywood platform and a mattress. And when in October I could no longer stand the strain of our intimate melodrama, I chose the bus to make my getaway, packing up one box of books and a bag of clothes and driving off into the unknown. When we'd test-driven the bus on the flat streets of Sunnyvale, true, it lacked the power of the Impala but it did seem to have a certain character that distinguished it from the spoiled-brat image of my first automobile, a relic of the upbringing I was trying to unload. But once the deal was done and we drove back into the hills toward Santa Cruz, I had the pedal to the floor and we were barely chugging up the snaky grade of Highway

17, the same road the Chevy had climbed with ease. Such was the price of abandoning the luxuries of an overprivileged adolescence and joining the shaggy ranks of road rats high on rebellion. Now I was creeping up Route 9, alone, slowly negotiating the curves as night deepened and who knows how many other pilgrims were making their way toward Livermore. Alert, ready for whatever, I steered the bus carefully through the steep dark, envisioning an experience I couldn't quite imagine but sensed as a kind of collective apotheosis. Ordinarily crowds made me claustrophobic, but this would be no ordinary crowd.

My plan was to spend the night at the speedway, avoiding Saturday's massive traffic, and stake out a decent spot next morning to catch the afternoon's music. On the road I smoked and felt the desolation of the stark landscape of the East Bay. The drive seemed longer than it actually was, as usual when you don't know where you're going. After traversing what felt like a wilderness, stopping several times to ask directions, I managed to find Altamont Pass Road and turned north toward the raceway. Flares lit the approach to the parking area; flashlights signaled me in. I found a spot, climbed down, and wandered around among the cars and vans and buses parked in the darkness. Little campfires were focal points for circles of hairy faces. Radios were playing, the thumping basses and sexual guitars and incendiary lyrics invoking tomorrow's live performances. Out of sight, on the far side of the racetrack, construction crews were at work erecting the scaffolding for the sound system. Portable toilets were arriving on trucks. Instant civilization. As I walked past one huddle I was waved in, friendly nods and warm eyes all around, I squatted, was handed something to smoke, a jug of wine, ceremonial intoxicants to pass on, no names, no introductions, we were anyone, gathering to share in a rite of innocence, reaching for the primitive, something real, our eyes reflecting the fire.

Headlights kept arriving, sliding into place, then the gate was shut, guys with flares and flashlights directing new arrivals to park on the approach road, full cooperation, people pulled over, parked, collected their stuff, and hiked in to set up camp. After a while in one of the circles, engaged in eager yet understated specula- tion on the next day's unplanned program, I made my way back to the bus—my mind was swimming—and climbed in to cop some sleep.

By midmorning, streams of people were pouring over the hills into the barren expanse of meadow adjacent to the racetrack where the day's festivities were taking shape. Spread out before the make- shift stage and gigantic towers of the sound system were thousands and thousands of arriving rock fans gathered in the natural waste- land that was fast becoming an amphitheater. Though it was well before noon when I got there, the December sun just starting its low arc into a hazy sky, the closest I could get to the stage was a spot a couple of hundred yards away. The figures down front were barely visible beyond the swarms of vibrating colors cover- ing the dry slopes. A couple of custom-painted schoolbuses and a circus-style tent were the sole structural interruptions of the hu- man landscape's oceanic sprawl. As I claimed my square yard of bristly ground amid the patchwork of blankets and sleeping bags marking the multitude of little colonies camped for the afternoon, it dawned on me that the music that occasioned this convocation would be dwarfed by the vastness of the crowd itself. From where I sat you could see, on the far side of the stage, an endless proces- sion of spectators filling the meadow, spilling over the surround- ing hills, rivers of color flooding the beige terrain, a scene all the more surreal for the fact that apart from the meager structures of the concert facilities and racetrack grandstands there was no civi- lization in sight, just miles and miles of humans come for what must be a cosmic occurrence, a get-together the likes of which I'd never even imagined much less seen. It could have been out of Ex- odus (were there this many Israelites?). Multitudes gathered in the wilderness—for what? A rock concert, or a revelation? Entertain- ment, or deliverance? A celebration, or a crucifixion? By the time the Jefferson Airplane fired up their instruments in the distance, warped electric sounds looping weirdly through the charged air as if in sonic slow motion, cool sun blazing away in rippling blue, the smell of dry grass mingled with drifting marijuana smoke, a certain nervous murmur circulating through the crowd, I felt I had entered some other realm and was floating through an awesome zone of vital danger and discovery.

The big brown tab of mescaline, which I had swallowed like a morning vitamin as soon as I found my spot, was beginning to kick in. By chance I'd chosen to sit in front of a group of folks from Santa Cruz, friendly strangers who adopted me into their circle as the music started. Two women and three guys were passing joints and apple juice and fruit and a bag of granola from hand to hand, sharing a little picnic—a congenial clan, if a little jittery as a small cloud crossed the sun. One of the women assumed the role of nature-nurture mama, a common enough Santa Cruz Mountains archetype. Though nobody said much, her ample form and warm demeanor, her movements and the way she managed the flow of food and drink and smoke suggested a sense of order and control, of responsibility for her friends' well-being, while individually they seemed a bit spaced, gazing off toward the stage or tripping out on the spectacle unfolding around us. In the interest of getting as high as possible I declined to eat more than a couple of bites of apple, but as Sharon, our lady of sustenance, leaned forward to offer me a toke of homegrown, her breasts swaying loosely under her dress, I sucked at the joint as if it were mother's milk—and immediately felt queasy for assuming, even for a second, an infant's posture in this situation. I couldn't afford to relinquish autonomy. As the drug came on I realized this was no picnic at all. The wild colors and serpentine motion of the surrounding throng evoked kaleidoscopic hallucinations, pulsating abstract patterns and liquefied visions that in safer circumstances would have been welcome, a synesthetic swim in visual nirvana, incredibly trippy, but here and now they only served to increase an already mounting sense of disorientation. I had to pull it together, get my senses under control, focus on staying conscious of where I stood in these surroundings. As if to confirm this apprehensive instinct, the Airplane stopped playing in the middle of a song. It was impossible to see what was happening. Grace Slick, her voice trembling with fear, admonished the audience, "We've got to quit fucking up!" Terrific. Just what the herd needs, a panicky chick with a microphone and umpteen zillion watts of amplification. There was trouble of some kind in front of the stage, nobody this far back knew what. I turned around: swarms of human bodies as far as the eye could see in every direction. I was dead in the middle of a mass of hippies tripped out on every imaginable drug and bummed by the bad energy of an unidentified fuckup. Scanning the landscape I took strength from the understanding that the day was going to require mindfulness, the sharpest possible sense of reality. Hallucinations were out. The psychedelic I'd ingested now served to focus my attention on purposeful conduct, survival strategies. A long afternoon was ahead. There was no telling what might happen. I nodded so-long to my adopted family and made for the outskirts.

Fitfully the Airplane resumed their set, with ominous interruptions. During the silences waves of dismay flowed out from the stage like shadows over the captive audience. Rumors of violence, fighting, Hells Angels out of control. *We are forces of chaos and anarchy.* I made my way outward, seeking a clearing, fearing a stampede, an assassination, stepping over and around huddled and puzzled people, their beautiful long hair looking ragged, visionary eyes clouded with creeping dread, bewildered citizens of a wasteland turning to one another for solace and reassurance, taking off their clothes, exchanging substances. *Everything they say we are we are.* As I stumbled among them I saw faces I recognized only to realize they were unfamiliar. A woman turned around and clasped my hand in a comforting gesture only to recoil when our eyes met— my fear was a mirror. I called out excitedly when I saw an old high school acquaintance, Robbie Rosen! He jumped as if zapped by a thousand volts, reminding me how uncool it was to yell, so I just waved meekly and wandered on, uphill, toward the fringes of the crowd.

Miles from the music, where the listeners thinned and I roamed to ease my angst, feeling relieved at not being boxed in, hunger caught up with me. A guy about my age, seated on the ground, was eating an orange from a crumpled paper bag. Our eyes met and his expression invited me over. He looked as messed up as I was. I sat down beside him, gratefully accepting the few wedges of fruit. Silently we ate, surveying the terrain from its outer reaches, a vast undulating rock'n'roll ocean, Santana's percussive rhythms arriving on rippling breezes over enormous distance, the music audible but abstract, as if from another dimension, another century.

"Pretty weird scene," I ventured.

"Freaky."

"I wonder when the Stones are gonna play."

"I wonder if they're gonna play."

"They've got to. If not, there'd be a riot."

"There already was, sort of. Hells Angels with pool cues, people getting creamed. I couldn't handle it. I was down there."

I shook my head. "Too strange."

His name was Norm. I had no idea whether or not he was tripping. By midafternoon my own high had leveled into the streaming phase, the bones in my face vibrating in the breeze, muscles humming, body light and relaxed but wired for endurance, consciousness clear now that I was outside the claustrophobic mass. We sat there for hours, or a timeless interval that felt like hours, listening to sounds traveling out to us warped by the remoteness of the loudspeakers, watching the light change as the sun swept west, helicopters circling overhead—Highway Patrol and TV news crews voyeurizing the show—December air cooling, darkening, electric guitar licks noodling through the sky. I felt more secure now, comforted by the presence of a partner, warm in my boots and turtleneck sweater and jacket with the fringes dangling, fingers actively fondling the few key items I carried with me. No need at this point to smoke the hash but the smooth wooden cylinder of the pipe felt good, as did the handle of the penknife. Around us wandered the lost, the spaced, refugees from the prevailing mood of turmoil, their faces disfigured by the ravages of acid, warped visages their mothers wouldn't recognize, foreheads melting in waves of psychic distress, eyes that in lucid moments were windows of serene enlightenment now oozing impure anguish, mouths losing their shape, cheekbones drooping waxlike in the sun, but it wasn't warm, maybe my vision was deforming theirs, no, they were distorted, stoned, blasted, twisted, definitely ripped, so many wine jugs making the rounds laced with god-knows-what that people had no idea what they were ingesting and at this point it didn't matter, if you couldn't handle it you shouldn't be here and now that you were here it was pointless to play it straight, drugs were as central as music to what was happening.

The Stones took the stage as the sun went down. This is what everyone had come for. They opened with "Under My Thumb," but they hadn't been into it for more than a minute when the music abruptly stopped. God, what's going on—my worst apprehensions of earlier in the day—has Mick Jagger been murdered? Jagger's voice, speaking not singing, boomed out spookily through the silence. "Brothers and sisters," he implored in his British English, "why are we fighting? Please. Let's be cool now." Actually he was cool, so much more in command than Slick had been. Whatever was happening down by the stage, out on the edge where we were Jagger's voice inspired some sort of confidence.

Norm and I looked at each other, shrugged and hunkered down hoping the mood would mellow. The music resumed, with the timewarped rhythm imposed by distance and the natural contours of the land. The stage was nowhere in sight. Twilight. People were starting fires with whatever they could find, mostly fence slats and the scrap tires that lined the racetrack. In the cool darkening air the stench of burning rubber and painted wood made for a fittingly nasty incense.

Both of us rose to move at the same time. It was getting too cold to sit still. Maybe we could find some wood and make a fire.

Maybe we could scrounge something to eat. We were both hungry. The land was raw: stubbly dry grass, hard dirt, the litter of the afternoon. Scattered bands of demoralized revelers scavenging for something to burn. In front of us on the ground, in the deepening dusk, I spied a potato. A potato! I picked it up. We gathered a few sticks and bits of brush and grass, some scraps of paper, a few dried cow chips, and built a small fire, crouching over it to nurse it to life, stare into its twisting flames. I tended the blaze while Norm went off in search of more fuel, returning soon with a little bundle of twigs, sticks, and fence slats. It was a tiny fire but comforting, and when it was hot enough we placed the potato carefully in the coals, warming our hands while it cooked, feeling the fatigue of the long day but satisfied with our luck, pleased with our primitive ingenuity, content with the silence of companionship. We removed the potato, cut it in half and scooped out the steaming pulp with our pocketknives, feasting.

People approached. "Mind if we share your fire?"

"It's god's fire," I said. In a few minutes there were eight or ten people clustered around the flames, bringing more fuel, passing bottles and joints. We'd founded a settlement. Words were useless. Everyone seemed reflective, turned inward by the day's strangeness, music way in the background, and the wilderness harshness bringing everyone down to an elemental gravity even as we kept getting high. I sliced a few pieces of hash into my pipe and passed it, took a swig off a passing jug, a toke of grass, and fixed my eyes on the fire. As the flames died down Norm and I once more felt the simultaneous urge to move. We excused ourselves—"See you later. Keep the pipe"—and walked, collecting any scraps of fuel we saw. The pattern repeated itself: we kindled a fire, a circle of people gathered, we stood or crouched smoking and drinking, the fire faded, and we moved on.

Once the concert ended and the hundreds of thousands gradually dispersed, day trippers trudging back to their cars parked who knows how many miles away, hard-core settlers hanging on for the night, we made the rounds of the remaining meadow dwellers, collecting news and rumors of the day. Word was that the Angels had blown it: somebody had been stabbed to death in front of the stage as the Stones were playing, witnesses had been unbelievably bummed. One scraggly-haired hippie with fringe like mine told us that the victim had been running toward the stage with a pistol drawn when he got knifed—confirming my vision of a crucifixion in progress, with Jagger in the role of Jesus. But the assassin had been intercepted. Maybe the Angels should have been Bobby Kennedy's bodyguards. The smell of smoke from the burning tires and trash and painted scrap wood blended with whiffs of passing pot smoke to create an atmosphere of putrid ruin, but somehow sweetly peaceful too, as after a battle, the vast field strewn with beer cans, wine jugs, ragged blankets, rolls of toilet paper, plastic wrappings, T-shirts, lone shoes, magazines, fruit rinds, chicken bones, hats, bandanas. Survivors meandered, befuddled by the day's mayhem. Yet amid all this I felt exhilarated, amazed to have made it through as well as we had, still accompanied by this quiet partner with whom I was so attuned that we moved in the same rhythms, felt the same needs, wordlessly supporting each other. Eventually we made our way back to my bus, unrolled my sleeping bag under the stars, and bedded down on our jackets on the bare ground with the bag spread out on top of us. We were about the same size and build, small and wiry, and it was cold, so we pressed close to each other, our bodies finding a comfortable fit. He had an erection.

"Doesn't this turn you on?" he said.

"Not really."

"Strange." His tone was curious, puzzled, patient.

When I was little, in second or third grade, my buddy Gary Book and I would sometimes wrestle shirtless after school. There was something thrilling, I didn't know what, in the skin-to-skin contact of our young torsos. That was the closest I'd come to a homosexual experience, and now this other penis was pressing against me. It felt good, a little confusing, a little disgusting, further evidence of the intimacy we'd built in the course of our daylong ordeal. Without one another it would have been a far more difficult afternoon. Our connection had transformed a nightmare into a triumph, a peak experience, a blessing. I was still sailing on the pure energy of our union—Whitman would have called it the dear love of comrades—as we lay there together under a writhing sky.

Sunday broke brilliant, the clear sky tingling with the nip of imminent winter as we cruised west on the freeway back toward the bay. Norm was headed for Oakland, and I was giving him a lift. The bus was humming along when a sickening *thunk* in the engine lit the oil-pressure light and we lost all power. I coasted us onto the shoulder, breathing the smell of burning oil. The car was dead but it didn't faze me, just another challenging twist to be negotiated with grace. Norm caught another ride west and I hitched into Livermore to phone for a tow. We parted, with a handshake and a long look in the eyes.

"Well, take it easy."

"You too, man."

I never saw him again.

The tow-truck driver informed me that yesterday had been the craziest his business had ever seen. "Shoot, you never saw such a mess. People was parkin' their cars right on the highway. There was breakdowns everywhere, flats, dead batteries, fanbelts, lost keys, you name it. We was workin' these roads all night. And boy, did they wreck the raceway—tore down fences, trash all over the place—who's gonna clean it all up? Don't these people have any respect for property?" I, his passenger, was one of *them*, hair too long for Disneyland, Pancho Villa mustache, LSD-laced see-in-the-dark eyes. He was a working man, skilled with his hands, young but over thirty, Marlboro smoker, country music, none of this marijuana rock'n'roll shit.

I left the bus at a Livermore garage, everything closed on Sunday, I'd deal with it later. I walked along Route 84 till I found a fruit stand, bought a crisp apple, savoring it as I waited for a ride. Not much traffic but I was elated to be standing on this road close to nowhere I knew, bathing in the gorgeous morning light. Cool sun. Light wind. A hawk in the high air. What the fuck am I doing, will I do? It doesn't matter. The present is a present, a glorious gift. Infinite possibilities. Life is a miracle. People are beautiful. And I am a poet.

Within minutes a purple bread van, converted for living mobility, pulled up, its bearded driver and his long-haired lady grinning at me through the windshield. The side doors swung open, two more smiling faces, and Dylan's "Mr. Tambourine Man" ringing with brilliant clarity through the speakers. Our national anthem.

I tossed my bag in the back and climbed on in.

3

Revolution Number Five

My last ride back to the lodge from Livermore was in a pink VW bug with a wholesome blue-eyed nineteen-year-old blonde named Pam. Standing on Highway 17 south of San Jose, I was amazed to see her pull over—she looked so straight, like somebody's little sister studying to be a bank teller. As it turned out, she was a student nurse who lived up the road in Campbell. She was headed for Felton via Bear Creek Road, which meant she'd be able to leave me at my door. Everything falling perfectly into place. With hitching luck like this, who needs a car. A beautiful afternoon, a cute and friendly driver, and the evergreen wildness of the mountains more glorious than ever, layer upon layer of brilliant and shady greens, dozens of tones, bathing the eye in luxurious waves of cool fall early afternoon light, the bright sky conspiring with the trees to welcome my return. I was still loaded on survival euphoria and whatever residual juice remained from the previous day's drugs. After a brief exchange of pleasantries Pam observed that I seemed to be glowing, emitting some sort of radiant light. I told her I was coming back from the Stones' free concert at Altamont and that I was sure there were thousands of other freaks all over the Bay Area today wandering around in similarly illuminated states. Every time we passed some long-haired person walking or standing by the roadside I'd say, "See? I bet he's coming back from the Stones," and she would laugh, but I wasn't kidding.

As the bug climbed the switchbacks above Bear Creek, redtail hawks circling overhead, sunlight glinting on the windshield, I told her this weekend was a watershed, a turning point in the times, I wasn't sure how, exactly, but some major change was in the air, I knew. Focusing on the road, she said she thought she knew what I meant, she felt it too, it was a special time, the atmosphere carried an electric charge. Maybe she was more hip than she looked. Maybe you didn't need the help of drugs to sense what was going on. *You don't need a weatherman to know which way the wind blows.* In some circles of the underground, rumors had Yippie commandos spiking the reservoirs with LSD in order to speed up the revolution; unsuspecting civilians drinking from the tap would be instantly psychedelicized, would see the light of love and peace and cosmic oneness and spiritual freedom and would convert these revelations into a new harmonious social order. No more war. No more oppression, liberty and justice for all. More paranoid scenarios had the FBI or CIA using acid as a mind-control experiment on masses of involuntary trippers, also by way of the water supply. High as I was, it seemed to me that everybody else was tripping anyway, so drugs or no drugs in the drinking water, the air itself carried invisible streams of hallucinogenic potential: all you had to do was breathe.

We pulled up in front of my cabin and I invited Pam in for a smoke. She declined politely, wishing me best of luck and proceeding down the road. How many other well-scrubbed drugless girls and boys were secretly sympathetic to the movement of which I was a freelance ambassador—of which all hip spirits of goodwill were ambassadors, improvisational acting diplomats, agents of psychic change. Pam and her kind, which included the likes of mature adults such as Nona, were fellow travelers, invisible allies threaded through the fabric of the status quo who, once the new consciousness was fully fledged, would give the revolution—a magic carpet—flight. There was no other hope but to overthrow, by acts of angelic sabotage, the crushingly oppressive machinery of evil that ruled the world by force. Given the choice, the people would opt for peace over war, music over news, liberation over enslavement. The movement was shapeless, transpolitical, aimless and ecstatic. Transformation was our only chance.

I rushed to the lodge to look for Nona, eager to share my stories of Altamont—ignoring for the moment that the concert had been essentially a disaster—and to convey my growing realization that the revolution was at hand. It had been more than a week since our encounter in the kitchen, during which time we'd scarcely seen each other. I wanted to run up and give her a hug and rave the news. Although it was Sunday, her car was parked in front, along with a pick-up I didn't recognize. I knocked and walked in the front door. Nona was in the entry hall conferring with two middle-aged workmen. I excused myself, didn't know what to do, I couldn't talk to her in front of them, they were hostile, suspicious, I sensed their disapproval of my existence. "Sorry, I'll speak with you later," I said, and split.

My cottage couldn't contain me. I was bouncing off the walls, had to be outdoors or I might break something. In the interest of burning off some energy, I hiked up the road into downtown Ben Lomond, a row of shops mostly closed for the day, and bought a Sunday *Examiner*. There on the front page, four columns wide, was a photo of a section of the crowd at Altamont, dozens of hairy revelers writhing in the foreground, fringes bell-bottoms beards and sideburns flying, faces warped by the strains of the day on drugs yet mimicking a party mood, and in the background a human landscape filling out the frame. The accompanying story reported that though there had been three deaths—a knifing, a heart attack, and someone run over by a vehicle—there had also been two births, and despite some difficult moments the crowd of close to a quarter million had generally enjoyed a festive day, free of the chaos and mayhem predicted by some alarmist conservatives. Right. A wonderful time was had by all, a pleasant day in the country, an idyllic romp in the meadows of rock'n'roll. Only trouble was, a look at the expressions on the faces of the freaks in the photo revealed a different story: around their eyes were the hollow shadows of anguish, a desperate effort to be having fun poisoned by an aura of pure horror. The paper was putting a happy face on an unsettling situation, presumably in the interest of reassuring its readers that kids will be kids and hippies will be trippy but there's really nothing to worry about, the Stones have flown, the frenzy has passed and things will be back to normal any minute. Sure. As if Altamont were the finale of the cultural revolution, dropping the curtain on the changes of the last decade. As if thousands of little satellites like me had not been launched to beam our anarchic impulses into the population at large. I returned to my room, ripped out the picture, and stuck it on the wall above the dresser. I wanted to study it for signs, remind myself of its hidden terrors, use its bum energy as an inoculation, a homeopathic antidote, a tonic. If I could face the reality of the photo, scrutinize its most minute disturbances, see in the demeanor of the foreground figures my own most noxious fears, confront them, acknowledge their power, then I could carry a visionary awareness forward without illusion. In order to be an avatar of compassionate magic, I had to be able to brave these twisted faces.

Footsteps on the porch. A knock at the door. "Anybody home?" It was Nona. "I didn't see your car. I thought perhaps you'd left."

"My car's in Livermore. It died on the way back from the Stones concert."

"I'm sorry I was busy earlier. You seemed rather upset. Is anything wrong?"

"No, everything's right. It's all coming together. The concert was just the start, I think it was some kind of test, a radical experiment, not everybody could handle it, lots of people freaked out, it was about survival, how to stay clear in chaos, some of us made it. I get the sense I've been chosen for something important, some special role. I'm not sure what but I've got to keep on this course, trusting my intuition, watching, listening, reading the signs, *acting*, you understand?"

She looked at me intently, curious.

I told her about Saturday, the music, the violence, my wilderness adventure with Norm, the crowd, the edge of panic in the atmosphere, the beauty of getting through it, the illumination of understanding that this was much bigger than rock'n'roll, the whole culture was on the brink of a breakthrough. The lodge would be an important part of it, a model, our little community a living example of possible transformations, turning the setting and ourselves into beams of revolutionary light, a contagious radiance that could stop the war, turn the country around, unite humanity.

"Stephen," she said, "did you take any drugs?"

"Of course. Everybody did. Didn't you?"

"No. What do you mean?"

"Don't you feel different? Haven't you noticed how different everything is?" We were standing in the cabin and the sun was sinking. The warped floor floated on a sea of deepening shadows.

"Well, I don't know. I mean, yes, things have been different. A lot has been happening. There is a strange feeling of something, I'm not sure. It's a confusing time for everyone, I think. It's hard to say exactly."

"Exactly. That's what I'm saying. It's happening to everyone. There may be acid in the water supply."

"What? What are you talking about?"

"The Rolling Stones were messengers. It was time to turn everyone on. I've heard that guerrillas dumped LSD in the reservoirs. There's something going around, people are getting more disoriented—look at this picture." I pointed to the photo on the wall. "Do these people look enlightened?"

"Are you sure you've had enough sleep?" She seemed worried. "You should try to get some rest. I understand you're excited. I feel the excitement too. But you shouldn't push yourself too far. Have you eaten anything? You need to replenish your strength."

"I can't eat. I'm not hungry." Suddenly I felt exhausted. "Maybe I can lie down for a while."

"Yes, why don't you lie down. I'll sit with you for a few minutes. I have to get home, it's almost dinnertime. My husband's waiting." Her husband.

I unrolled my sleeping bag, unzipped it flat, lay on the bed, and pulled it over me. I still had my boots on.

"Let me help you off with your boots." She pulled them off, set them carefully on the floor, and sat beside me on the sagging bed. With her right hand, gently, she stroked my forehead, swept my hair away from my face. Her touch was soothing, calming. When I shut my eyes my mind careened in vivid electric patterns, blood-vessels inside the eyelids dancing, pulsing galaxies of light and color, but I couldn't bear to look at her either, she was too beautiful, too kind, I lacked the strength to embrace her, I was weak and sexless, a child, a kitty cat getting its chin tickled. Eyes closed, I tried to let her cool hand erase the hallucinations. Slowly the patterns softened. When my breathing had regulated she said, "I have to go," and kissed me on the right temple. "I'm sure you'll feel better after you've slept." And she was out the door.

I lay there a long time, unable to sleep, letting the images and visions of the last forty-eight hours percolate through my consciousness, reexperiencing the storm of conflicting impressions, impulses, intuitions, prophecies. As twilight deepened outside, indoors it grew dark, too cold to get up now and build a fire. I had no transportation, nowhere to go. I burrowed deeper under the warm bag and let the night take over. Tomorrow I had things to do on campus.

The University of California at Santa Cruz, which had been open only since '65, was spread on a hillside above the city, affording spectacular views of the town and Monterey Bay beyond. Covering two thousand acres of the old Cowell Ranch, its expansive meadows and soaring redwoods gave the campus an otherworldly air, not exactly of an ivory tower but of a naturally enchanted zone of lofty thought. This ethereal quality was grounded by the presence of grazing cattle in the fields and the forest's humbling heights. During my first year in the doctoral program I spent more time in the woods than in my seminars, awed by the power of the trees, filled with the rich pure smells of the land as I padded along the soft ground in my moccasins. Some afternoons I would walk from some particularly lifeless class, a contest of neurotic intellectual egos over the fine points of critical theory or erudite abstraction ("In general I think the absurd can be referred to as a subcategory of nothingness," as one of my professors, Leon Blowfish, put it), into the purplish vibrating light of the redwood cathedrals, supple trunks subtly bending in the breeze or, absolutely still, shooting skyward like ancient missiles launched eons ago from deep within the earth. The contrast was too much for my saturated brain to bear. There was no question where my loyalties lay. I pledged allegiance to the trees.

The campus was divided into five colleges, each with its academic emphasis: Cowell (humanities), Stevenson (social sciences), Merrill (Third World studies), Crown (natural sciences), and the newest, for now called simply College Five, whose focus was the arts. Cowell was named for Henry Cowell, the California composer whose family's land had been given to the university; Stevenson for Adlai Stevenson, the statesman; Merrill for brokerage titans Merrill Lynch; and Crown for the Crown Zellerbach paper empire. Speculation was that, depending on the source of the gift, Five might soon be dubbed Disney or Sinatra.

Beyond my instinctive affiliation with the trees, the cows, the hawks, the redwing blackbirds, the redwood mulch of the forest floor, the smells, the views, and the other sensory pleasures of the terrain—all enhanced by the recurrent rolling and smoking of superb grass—I had trouble conforming to the expectations of the program and my professors. One typical encounter occurred in a seminar in the spring of '69, when I broke into Blowfish's discourse on the formal harmonies of *Madame Bovary* to ask him and my fellow scholars what we were doing engaging in such a discussion while people were being *shot* in the streets of Berkeley. Such questions didn't exactly endear me to the graduate faculty, and at the end of the academic year in June I was informed that the fall would find me working as a teaching assistant in College Five, a setting presumably more congenial to my artistic temperament.

That was my destination Monday morning. After catching a ride into Felton where, starving, I stopped for breakfast—scanning the front page of the *Chronicle* for personal messages hidden in the headlines to prove my sense that something more immense and amazing than the news was afoot—I hitched into town with another head from the valley, and up to campus from town. I was expected at the workshop section of the class I was TAing for Morgan Hurst, a.k.a. Dr. Scraps, a visiting artist from Berkeley whose educational specialty was an art form—an "activity," as he called it—known as woodscrap sculpture. I worked with the students on their reading and writing skills, complementing both the hands-on studio time they spent with Morgan and the larger lectures on esthetics by the distinguished art historian and philosopher A. J. Hergesheimer that rounded out the "core" requirement for all freshmen at College Five.

Morgan stood about six-five, big-boned, with a florid face and a heavily waxed handlebar mustache. He must have been blond in his younger days, a Swede or Norwegian from Wisconsin, but now his hair and whiskers were a vivid silver. After working for years as a high school teacher, he'd developed woodscrap sculpture as an alternative both to standard teaching techniques and to established notions of "the arts." Collecting scrap wood from Los Angeles area furniture factories and pattern shops, he'd truck tons of this raw material up to San Francisco and organize giant "glue-ins" in public places like Ghirardelli Square. He'd spread out piles of woodscraps and plastic bottles of glue on tables and invite the passersby, children and adults, to create their own freestyle art.

"You know," he would say to me in one of his frequent diatribes, "the whole academic establishment, and the arts establishment too, don't know shit about art *or* education!" Morgan always yelled when he spoke. "They think that children need to learn all the rules, observe all the formal laws, in order to know what art is about—in order not only to do it properly but to know what to hang on the walls! It's the cultural equivalent of Law and Order! Leonardo and Michelangelo and Rubens and Rembrandt are the goddamn police force—the secret fucking police!—looking over people's shoulders when they paint! And the art professors and gallery owners and museum directors and bourgeois collectors all see the artist as some divinely inspired genius put on earth to supply the market and enhance their status as the real gods of the art world! It makes me sick. Sick! The only hope for this society, for the spiritual misery and loss of meaning, is for people to discover their own genius, their unique personal vision, their individuality. Art is dead. It's dead! It's become a spectator thing, completely passive, consumer recreation for the elite! Art means nothing if the individual has no sense of his own creativity."

That summer, just before school had started and we were to begin working together, I contacted Morgan to get some idea of what his class would be about. He insisted that I accompany him on a three-day trip to Los Angeles to collect materials for the fall quarter and thus attain an understanding of the entire process that would culminate in the student workshop. One Tuesday morning I met him in Berkeley, where he had rented the U-Haul truck that we were to take to LA empty and bring back north with a groaning load of woodscraps. After a stop in San Leandro, where we picked up a dozen five-gallon plastic barrels of Elmer's glue, we rolled off into the San Joaquin Valley, a curious couple of truckers. Morgan raved at me the whole way down about the corruption of the arts by capitalism, the insidious influence of masterpieces, his disillusion with painting as a path to salvation. "In the fifties," he yelled over the sounds of the engine and the wind pummeling the massive surfaces of the truck, road vibration shaking the cab, parched central California landscape whizzing past the windows, "we thought painting could change the world. Abstract Expressionism was like the hydrogen bomb, nothing could be the same again after. Inside every artist was atomic power! The artist was a liberator, a revolutionary! But look what happened! The Abstract Expressionists became art objects! Not just the paintings, the artists themselves! They were turned by the market into just another commodity. They got rich! They killed themselves! The paintings hung on the walls and nothing changed! You don't know what a tragedy this is. I mean, they painted themselves into a corner, they lost all power to change consciousness, they became pets of the art establishment! Interior decorators! People have to understand that art is not out there, it's in here!" He pounded his chest with his right hand while steering with his left. "Andy Warhol is absolutely right, art is nothing but a goddamn product—brand names, supermarket discount crap—canned soup and celebrities!" He was spraying the dashboard with spit. "Warhol is a true genius of our time because he understands that art in this culture is marketing. Marketing!" And so on, over the Grapevine into the LA basin.

We spent the next two days zigzagging across the industrial district south and east of downtown, going from one furniture manufacturer and pattern shop to another, collecting woodscraps. My reading hadn't prepared me for this work, nor for Morgan Hurst, but the physical exertion involved in loading the huge cardboard boxes we'd brought with tons of wood—my tender hands protected by heavy gloves—was an antidote to academic ennui. The sawdust smell of the factories, the lung-burning eye-stinging smog, the sooty grime of industrial LA—a side of the city I hadn't known in my youth on the West Side—were toxic and tonic at the same time, sickening me with their unbreathable oppressiveness and refreshing me with exposure to the actual working texture of my town, the grinding machinery beyond the facades of Hollywood and the manicured lawns of Beverly Hills. We'd back the truck into one warehouse, one loading dock or another, and Morgan would jump out and exclaim exultantly, handling the scraps like precious artifacts, that these were priceless and irreplaceable shapes. "Look at this! Isn't this marvelous," he'd beam, turning in his hands a piece with a particular curve or unusual angle to its cut. "Do you realize that if we weren't here to save it, all this precious material would be ground into sawdust or incinerated! There's so much waste! All this material should be saved and distributed to schools throughout the city, throughout the state, the country. These pieces of wood, this waste, could save kids' lives!" We'd pick through enormous bins and mounds of wood, sometimes scooping armloads indiscriminately into our boxes, sometimes selecting pieces with special character, distributing the shapes variously in the boxes so that each box contained a mix of diverse forms. "The reason this country is going down the toilet," Morgan lectured as he maneuvered the truck through traffic from one establishment to the next, "is that we waste everything, we throw it away, when so much can be reclaimed, reused, turned into something else! That's what art is, that's the essence of imagination, recognizing and recombining what everyone else ignores. You've been to Watts Towers, haven't you."

I was embarrassed to admit that I hadn't. Watts was another world from where I grew up, terra incognita, and since the riots of '65 it felt off limits to white boys like me who didn't think much about homemade monuments or folksy local landmarks. I couldn't just drive my Porsche into Watts to be a voyeur at this primitive tourist attraction.

"Well, Stephen,"—he pronounced it Steffen—"before we leave LA you're going to see them."

The next day, following a morning and afternoon of woodscrap reclamation, our truck loaded five feet deep with cardboard cartons full of magic shapes, we made our way south down Alameda Street to Watts. The towers stood on a triangular lot adjacent to the railroad tracks, rising from the street to a height of a hundred feet. Into the structure's intricate framework of steel rails, pipes and iron bars were inlaid shards of broken bottles, pottery, seashells, bits of tile secured with cement and chicken wire, assembled in patterns of staggering detail, complex and simple at the same time, alive with color and mosaic juxtapositions, the whole construction artlessly masterful in its spontaneous design, its wild yet careful execution. "You see," said Morgan as we walked around the towers gasping at the street-level details and gawking upward at their soaring forms while the sun dipped orange into the noxious ozone, "Sam Rodia, who built this thing, was a tile setter; he didn't see himself as an artist but a collector and assembler, a simple craftsman. It took him thirty years to build these towers, and you know what he did when he was finished? He walked away. That's art. That's an artist. He couldn't stand to see his creation turned into something the culture mosquitoes would feed on. He didn't want to be a star. He disappeared!"

College Five was still under construction when classes started. The unfinished concrete buildings, the gashed ground littered with scraps of wood and rebar and cement, the dust and dirt and mud, the dumptrucks and cranes and bulldozers growling and belching around the site, the stark unlandscaped rawness of the architecture, made for a suitably fluid setting in which to study the arts. Numerologists say that five is the number of change, of tricks and transformations, creativity, a mercurial figure. The number name fit the college's character.

When I arrived Monday for Morgan's workshop, the students were already working on their sculptures. Extraordinary forms were rising from the tables, elaborate abstractions that suggested birds and animals and skyscrapers and dancers or whatever fanciful shapes their creators could improvise. I walked unnoticed into the group and approached the instructor. "Morgan, can I talk to you for a second?"

We stepped outside and walked around the building where we could look out on the rolling meadow slated for the construction of dozens of units of married student housing. Outraged by this imminent violation of the natural landscape, Morgan had organized student opposition to the project, had written letters of protest and pledged to block the bulldozers with his body. Accordingly his contract would not be renewed. He'd have to take his woodscraps and his politics elsewhere. Beyond the meadow was Empire Grade Road, then woods and more meadows sloping down to the coast. A crisp day, sunny, the Pacific tossing in the windy distance. Morgan, who was never exactly calm, picked up the charge that I was putting out, which automatically raised his level of natural agitation. The tops of a nearby grove of redwoods thrashed in a sudden gust. "Yes," he said to me, "yes! What is it?"

I told him where I had been during the weekend and tried to give some idea of the momentous forces working on me, moving me to pursue some plan of action whose implicit instructions were being laid out as I went along. As at Altamont, which had become my model for survival, I had to follow an instinctive internal compass, reading whatever signs I was given that would lead to my destination. I figured Morgan would understand me if anyone would, would be able to read the underlying meaning of my rap. He was a revolutionary, wasn't he? "I can't stay in the workshop today," I explained. "There are people I have to speak to." Just which people I wasn't sure. I thought Morgan was one of them, but he seemed confused, disturbed, by what I was telling him.

"Sure, of course!" he yelled. "But are you all right? Can I do anything for you? Tell me what's going on!"

Oh, no, he's so uncool, there's something wrong here. "I can't say anything else right now, I've got to go across campus, somebody's waiting for me." Who? Possibly April—she had the psychic smarts to tune right in to my condition, my predicament, my mission. Or Randy Chatsworth, my fellow graduate student and pothead, witness at my wedding, aspiring novelist and intellectual rebel—

we were parallel spirits in some ways, different personalities but similar torments, maybe he was on the same trip. Then there was Herb Frankfurter—some of us called him Hot Dog Herb—head of the literature program, my academic nemesis, Shakespeare special-ist, high-intensity dialectician. If Blake was right, that opposition is true friendship, Frankfurter might be the person to steer me in the direction I needed to go, tell me what I needed to know to carry out my assignment. Whoever I was to meet, I had to keep moving, could not stay here. Morgan didn't have a clue as to what I was up to.

"Fine, okay!" he said, unable to argue with my lack of explana-tion. "I'll be in my office this afternoon. Please! Come talk to me about this. I want to help!"

I hiked across campus to Merrill, taking the footpath through the upper woods, pausing to breathe and hallucinate on the webs of sunlight streaking through the trees. I hadn't touched drugs since Saturday but I was still tripping. The earth hummed under me. Tiny psychedelic insects swarmed overhead in buzzing clus-ters, wings glinting, scattering the light. Merrill was April's college. I hoped to find her, but no such luck. A friend of hers informed me that she wasn't living in the dorms anymore, had rented a stu-dio in town over a garage on Riverside Street. I couldn't go down there, it was too far. Maybe I could catch Frankfurter in his office just down the hill at Cowell. I knew that Herb was an unlikely ally. He hated me. But I was also the only student who openly questioned his authority, and for all I knew he admired my nerve. I was a nuisance but a presence to be addressed. I didn't just sit there soaking up his instruction—I engaged him, I argued, I chal-lenged, I wisecracked, I kept things interesting if disruptive. I had no class with him this quarter but whenever our paths would cross I'd try to strike up a conversation. He'd try to hide when he saw me coming, obviously didn't want to deal with me. But I liked to see him squirm, the sonofabitch. At least I wasn't one of those punk student revolutionaries who, in a guerrilla action last year, had sent selected faculty members razorblades through campus mail with anonymous notes enclosed that said to kill themselves, their lives were wasted anyway. (The same people, probably, who set fire to the administration building.) I wasn't that kind of mindfucker. But who knows, the culprits had never been caught, and maybe Frankfurter suspected me. I had insinuated in a seminar that he'd wasted twenty years developing a critical theory that no longer applied to literature under current circumstances. He had his own insecurities, no doubt about it, though he masked them with an aggressive don't-mess-with-my-superior-intellect style. Well, fuck your intellect, Hot Dog. You can't just terrorize your students into submission. Maybe that's what they do at Yale—where you and half your asshole colleagues came from—but this is California.

His office door was open. I stood and knocked, looking at him across his desk surrounded by walls full of books, his back to the window. He looked nervous, as always, and lashed out with a typically hostile greeting. "Yeah. What is it?"

"Hi, Herb. Just thought I'd stop by and say hello. Got a minute?" Casual. I'm fucking with his head. My thick mustache and three-day beard, under the piercing acidic eyes and homegrown outlaw hair, must have made me look a little menacing. LIT PROF FOUND WITH THROAT CUT.

"Maybe a minute." His eyes ricocheted around the room, anything to avoid meeting mine. He's freaked. I've got him cornered. This must be what I'm doing here. Changing the rules of the game. Turning the tables. "Have a seat," he said. "What's on your mind?"

I remained standing in the open doorway, leaning against the frame. "That was pretty cute the way you and your colleagues exiled me to College Five this year. A clever way to get me out of your face. I like it, I really do. Some great people over there. Hergesheimer, quite the esthetician. Morgan Hurst—you know who he is, the guy I'm working with, the woodscrap man? Julius Trailerman." Julius! He was the one I should be looking for.

Obviously. But I continued. "I'm taking a leave of absence after this quarter, though. I'm not sure this is what I want to be doing."

"Sounds like a good idea. Get some perspective. Maybe this academic stuff isn't for you. Too tame. Sometimes I feel that way myself."

"I heard you used to be a poet. That you won some writing prize as an undergraduate. How come you switched directions?"

"Yeah. I wrote lots of poetry. Stories too. Then I read Dostoyevsky. I realized I could never be that great. What was the point? Poetry's sort of self-indulgent, don't you think?" Hot Dog on the offensive. "Scholarship takes so much more discipline." Twisting his little knife.

You decided against writing literature because you couldn't be Dostoyevsky. Because writing literature is self-indulgent. So instead you became a professor of literature. He's trying to be ironic. No, he's serious. Unbelievable. The man's more fucked-up than I thought. "I guess I like indulging myself," I said. "Anyway, I'm not quite that ambitious. I'd settle for García Lorca." Keep it light. No need to rub it in. Whatever it is. The poor motherfucker's in pain.

"Exile's not exactly what I'd call it. I mean your reassignment to College Five. We thought you'd be happier in a more creative-oriented environment, that's all. They needed writing instructors over there. We were just trying to keep you in the program. You're a pretty smart guy. If you ever decide to apply it. A couple of your papers were first rate. You could still make it here if you wanted to."

"I guess we'll see." I shifted my weight, prepared to split. We'd scored our respective points. I had discovered what I'd come for. He'd squirmed enough. "Listen. In case we don't see each other." Ever. Again. "You've definitely opened my eyes to some things." Like what I hate about this institution. "You've helped me clarify my direction." Out of here. "You know, I heard about that razor-blade business." His face went white. "And just in case you were wondering, I had nothing to do with it. Way too chickenshit a gesture—violent—not my style at all. Anyway, no hard feelings." He looked as if I'd pulled a knife. Then I was gone, savoring the image of that speechless face.

Now all I had to do was find Julius Trailerman.

4

All My Fathers

Finding Julius might not be so easy. For one thing, though he kept an apartment in one of the unfinished dorms at College Five and stayed there two or three nights a week, his home was in San Francisco. For another, he'd informed us last week at the regular Monday night meeting of his advanced poetry workshop that he was going to Arizona and would not be on campus tonight for our scheduled session. Come to think of it, in his absence I was supposed to host a reading to be given this evening by several students in the class—a commitment I remembered as I was leaving Frankfurter's office. Julius had asked me to cover for him, which meant he trusted me to act as his personal stand-in, his understudy. When I had approached him last September to ask if I could join his workshop, he'd said how pleased he'd be to have me participate. Then, just weeks ago, he'd asked me to work with him next quarter as his teaching assistant in improvisational acting—an offer that took me totally by surprise as I had no experience at all in theater. I was honored by the confidence this eminent editor, publisher, poet, playwright, actor, director and teacher placed in me, especially since my many submissions to his magazine had been consistently rejected. Julius's one-man vehicle, *semi*, was one of the country's outstanding poetry journals, an off-beat quarterly known for its independent spirit, its surrealist personality, its bizarre and humorous graphics—mostly collages assembled by Julius himself—and especially for the quality of its writing. In just five years of publication *semi* had established itself as an important force in contemporary poetry, publishing most of the bigger names in American verse while also introducing numerous unknowns. I had been sending Julius my poems since I was an undergraduate back east, hoping to break into the bardic big leagues and make a name for myself, but thus far all I'd received were prompt and often comically illustrated printed rejections, with an occasional handwritten note from the editor saying "Sorry, not these" or something equally terse. The invitation to be his TA was both encouraging and tempting, but it was clear I couldn't endure even one more quarter in grad school. Regretfully, I had to decline the offer.

Nevertheless I had to seek him out. Julius, of all the teachers I'd met since Crazy Jake Hertzberg at UCLA, had the most flexible imagination. Maybe his trip to "Arizona" was really code for another kind of trip. Maybe his asking me to host the reading, in effect a request to be him for an evening, was an inside-out suggestion that I follow him, find him, find myself in him, find out from him (and thereby from myself) what I needed to be doing in light of my recent revelations. Like Morgan only less excitable, Julius was a cultural revolutionary, steering his rebellious *semi* against the flow of current literary traffic, awakening readers and writers to the fact that poetry needn't be either the dull pale utterances of formalist esthetes or the often sloppy extravagances of the Beats, but could create for itself a sharp-edged irreverent and vital place in the changing national landscape. Julius was a maverick, and thus in the current climate also a leader, a teacher by example. Finding myself in his sphere of creative influence was inspirational.

With luck and perseverance I could be like him, and enough of us with poetry in our hearts could make a difference, like roving bands of rock'n'rollers, but operating in more intimate zones. We could help change the world. Lots of big-name literary writers—like Mailer, Allen Ginsberg, Denise Levertov, LeRoi Jones, Robert Duncan, Robert Bly, James Baldwin—were applying their skills and visions to current history, addressing issues like the war and racism in profoundly penetrating ways, and numerous new journalists were writing a kind of literature charged with style and personal perspective rarely seen before in the news media. Combine these poetical and journalistic movements with the powers of pop music, spontaneous street theater, documentary film, and public art like murals and woodscrap sculpture, and culture as we'd known it would never recover. College Five was a laboratory for experimental subversion. Now was the time to take these experiments further afield—to "Arizona," for instance. Wasn't the *Arizona* one of the battleships sunk by the Japanese at Pearl Harbor twenty-eight years ago practically to the day? Arizona could be code for a new benevolent offensive, an antiviolent invasion from within to conquer the country with love and imagination. It was an awesome prospect, with few clear guidelines, no identifiable chain of command and limitless possibilities. Julius could help me get a grip on what it all meant, where I fit, how to apply my energies. I needed a mentor, a coach, a father—my own old man was hopelessly out of touch with me and everything else—and Julius was the outstanding candidate.

Not that he ever gave any such signals or even invited followers, unlike so many other would-be gurus of the moment. Julius was cool, a bit gruff and unapproachable—he even struck me as depressed sometimes, subdued, privately moody. Like Morgan, he was a big man, at least six-three, with a shaggy mane of silver-gray hair. He often walked with a cane—one couldn't be sure whether it was functional or just a dramatic prop—and wore silk scarves or rakish hats in the vaguely Edwardian style of an English dandy.

Though he was in his fifties, his female companionship often consisted of several young drama majors apparently basking in his eccentricity and the wisdom of his theatrical experience. He wasn't truly great at anything, with the possible exception of editing, but his versatility set him apart from his professorial colleagues. In his poetry workshop he rarely said much, preferring to let the students critique one another's efforts. One got the feeling it wasn't because he didn't have strong opinions or poetic principles but because of a laissez-faire approach to verse and its instruction: the best way for young writers to learn to write is simply to write—the serious ones will keep on and improve, and the dilettantes will fade out soon enough. Of the eleven students in our group, it wasn't yet clear who might have the long-distance calling, but to be a poet was my sole ambition. Maybe that's what Julius saw in me.

And that's what Mom and Dad just didn't understand. My father, whose business genius was in sales, and a designer partner toward the end of the forties had launched a line of ladies' underwear that made them instant stars in the garment industry. By the time I was three we were living in Beverly Hills. Now, less than twenty years later, my parents watched in helpless dismay as their youngest child, a well-groomed conservative lad with a smart tongue who might successfully have gone into law or advertising, grew the mustache of a Mexican insurgent, let his hair hang loose, married a girl they disapproved of without so much as notifying them, and had decided on a literary career. What, they must have wondered, had happened to their happy Little Leaguer, the social-climbing high school politician, the car-conscious clothes pony who had pledged a nice Jewish fraternity during his freshman year at UCLA? Just because he depledged almost immediately it didn't mean he couldn't still be a regular mainstream guy. But then he started reading books in earnest, and writing verses in his room, and arguing with them about the war and patriotism and communism, and brooding over ultimate questions they couldn't hope to answer. How could this have happened? They'd been good par ents, liberal, supportive. Excellent providers. He had everything—including the slack from them to chart his own course. And that's what he'd gone and done.

I didn't blame them for not digging my trip. I didn't expect them to. Even though my mother had been an English major, she knew as well as anyone else that poems had nothing to do with making a living. And my father, an avid reader of the daily papers and the *Racing Form*, was a grade school dropout who rarely if ever opened a book. When I started to publish as an undergraduate I sent them a copy of everything, but beyond that there was nothing I could do to prove that this was a profession. Poetry and wherever it led was all that mattered to me, was the only discipline or skill or craft that yielded any meaning or satisfaction. In another life I might have been a musician, but I'd given up piano at the age of eight, choosing to play baseball after school rather than sit on a bench beside my grandma's friend Marina Klimov pounding out the chords to "The Volga Boatman." Going to graduate school had been a way of keeping one foot in the respectable world. My parents could tell their friends that their son might still wind up a doctor of philosophy, an English professor smoking his pipe in some prestigious university. I wanted to please them, sort of—show them something to be proud of, impress them with my intellectual status, whatever it might mean to them. But respectability was now beside the point. There was far more important business to take care of, even if I couldn't be sure exactly what it was. Poetry, or some similar force entangled with the time's riptides, was pulling me deeper into serious mysteries. I was getting lost.

One Monday night that fall in Trailerman's workshop a student brought the news that Jack Kerouac was dead. (Jack K, my father's name.) Found on a bathroom floor somewhere in Florida. At first, no one knew what to say. Kerouac, not yet fifty, the original Beat writer, the hipster than whom there was no hipper, reluctant illegitimate granddaddy of the counterculture still on a roll with momentum gathering since *On the Road* in 1957, desolate angelic rapper of rhapsodies never before heard in literary America, had in recent years grown increasingly reactionary, increasingly drunk and belligerent, according to all accounts, increasingly divorced from the social movement his books had played a part in generating. He'd advocated a US victory in Vietnam, maintained the war was a plot by the Vietnamese "to get jeeps into the country," disowned the flower children who tried to claim him as a progenitor, and withdrawn deeper and deeper into the clutches of his private demons. Kerouac, self-made legend, unbound adventurer, promethean slinger of souped-up flaming prose, woeful singer of ecstatic stories, nemesis of constipated critics, scholarship jock star, proto-pothead, speed freak, chronicler of living history, immortally out-of-control passenger riding beltless in the suicide seat, had taken himself out on an alcohol overdose. Heart attack, stroke, whatever. A famous corpse. In far-out California a chorus of young poets mused aloud:

"Jesus, how old was he? He couldn't have been much more than forty, could he?"

"Forty-seven. But he was over the hill. He never really improved on *On the Road*. He lost the spark, the innocence."

"The cat turned into a right-winger, man. Like Steinbeck. He was a hawk."

"That doesn't mean he deserved to die."

"He did it to himself. Everybody knows he was drunk the last few years."

"Wasn't he Catholic? I wonder if he went to hell."

"His life was hell. Look how he died. Maybe he's better off."

"It's so sad."

"It's disgusting."

"It's pathetic."

"No, it's tragic. He was major. Nobody took him seriously enough. Like Melville."

"It sort of feels like the end of an era."

"Why not the beginning? Time to go beyond this beatnik bullshit."

"What do you mean bullshit? The Beats are the most important movement since Surrealism. They blew everything wide open. Kerouac was a leader."

"The Fidel Castro of fiction."

"I'd definitely trade Yvor Winters and I. A. Richards for Kerouac and a couple of future draft choices."

"Kerouac's no great innovator. He didn't do anything Thomas Wolfe and Henry Miller and Bellow in *Augie March* hadn't done before and better. He had heart but no understanding. No wisdom."

"As a person he was notoriously obnoxious, a horrible human being."

"Yeah, he could have been improved upon."

"How can you deny that Kerouac was great? So what if he was a shit? Lots of great artists you wouldn't want as friends."

It went on like that for half an hour. Finally everybody'd had their say, shoveled their dirt on the coffin. Thrown their flowers. Paid their respects. Silence. Followed by a round of pedestrian poems. Nobody coming close to the power of the stiff's sound. He had us beat. Even dead, he was more alive than we were.

What would Jack do in my boots? (Kerouac, not my father.) Would he have made it to the reading Monday night? Or would he have followed the unrolling road and the subterranean word I was certain Julius was harboring. I had to pick up Trailerman's trail and track him down. Kerouac was hardly a hero to me but I needed more of his adventurous nerve, his daring. Even my father said, "You gotta dare to do." The sense of risk was giving me a lift, urging me along, assuring me the trip I was on was sound as I strode away from Herb the Hot Dog's office, across the Cowell courtyard with its vast view of the bay, into my favorite campus bathroom. The restrooms up here were truly restful—clean, well-lighted places where you could unload in peace with confidence there'd be plenty of toilet paper, hot water, soap and paper towels to perform a thoroughly civilized ablution. The facilities were so much nicer than those of my funky cabin that I took advantage whenever I could and did my business on campus. This particular comfort station, adjacent to the coffeehouse at Cowell, was especially dear to me both for its spaciousness and hygiene and for its association with a crucial encounter I'd had when I first arrived the previous year. As I entered the stall, slipped my pants over my boot tops and sat, I flashed on that afternoon in October of '68 when, standing before a urinal in this very room, I glimpsed at my side the unmistakable form of Misha Krazovich.

Three years earlier Misha and I had met at UCLA, both of us English majors taking the survey. The following spring we'd been together in Jacob (Crazy Jake) Hertzberg's famous Introduction to Poetry course, a class known all over campus for its impromptu readings, its outdoor meetings, its desktop-drumming snakedancing transliterary and otherwise unusual goings-on, not least of which were the professor's lectures. Hertzberg, a gifted Bronx-born lyric poet of the LA Beat scene, was a brilliant scholar and inspired teacher whose freely associative chainsmoking monologues sent us out of the classroom reeling from the contact high of his visionary intelligence. Misha and I would often sit by the Gypsy Wagon snack bar next to Humanities, munching hamburgers and discussing ideas from Crazy Jake's rambling orations. Hertzberg had since left UCLA to write in Europe; I had gone east to Bard to get my Bachelor's as far from home as possible; and Misha had transferred to the newly opened Santa Cruz campus, dropped out, hitchhiked with his girlfriend through Central America, joined the merchant marine in Panama, sailed to Thailand and back, and now had returned to complete his undergraduate career. It was splendid to see him and oddly comical to find ourselves pissing side by side like characters in a Kerouac book. We laughed, pissing and talking, picking up where we left off. That was his final quarter at Santa Cruz, and we spent much of it getting stoned together, listening to music, discussing books, testing out philosophies, remarking on current events. Now Misha was attending law school in San Francisco. He and his girlfriend, Gloria, had an apartment on Dolores Street just a few blocks up from the Mission. I tried to get by and see them whenever I was in the city. Though he was only a couple of years my senior, I considered Misha more worldly wise than I was, far more exposed and seasoned, and thus a trusted psychedelic guide and trip companion. His lanky physique, his balding dome, bad skin, black beard, piercing gaze and demented grin gave him a most distinctive look. And his predisposition toward the absurd, the weird and the surreal, combined with his philosophical streak and a sense of ironic mockery made him one of my favorite people. I savored the thought of Misha and our talks, our friendship, as I dumped my load. The vacuum-breaker sucked away the shit. I washed my hands and face, relieved to recognize myself in the mirror. I looked clear. Pure. Almost as if I knew what I was doing.

Coming out of the john, I ran into Randy Chatsworth, who insisted I join him in the coffee shop next door. He looked even jumpier than I was, it gave me the jitters just being around him, but he said he needed to talk and I couldn't just ditch him. He ordered coffee, but caffeine was the last thing I needed so I had a hot cider. Sitting there sipping our drinks, watching students and faculty come and go, groups at other tables engaged in urgent conversation, I got the feeling that everyone was tripping, they seemed unusually wound up, almost frantic, expressions on their faces reflecting more than the usual college tensions. The supercharged atmosphere somehow calmed me, relaxed my own sense of urgency. Randy told me he'd gone to see the Stones, had dropped acid, and "it wasn't entirely pleasant." He wanted to know what I'd heard about the concert.

"I was there, man," I said. "Didn't you see me? I was the one with the long hair."

He was in no mood for jokes. "It feels like something strange is happening. Does it look to you like everybody's tripping?" He nodded toward a girl across the room with her face in her hands, then at another rapping nonstop to a companion, then at a table of disheveled faculty and students staring spacily at anything but each other—out the window, at their coffee cups, at the walls. "I can't concentrate on anything," said Randy. "I haven't been able to sleep. I can't write. I can't read. I don't know if I can talk. My mouth muscles aren't coordinating. I don't even know what I'm doing on campus. I don't have anything to do up here but I couldn't stay home, the walls were throbbing."

"Maybe you should lay off the coffee."

"I can't. It's the only thing that keeps me coherent. What did you think of the concert?"

"I can't say I really got off on the music, I was too far back to hear anything but the echoes. But I don't think the music was the point. It was more like, let's get a million people into the wilderness together and see what happens. I was lucky. You know how sometimes when you drop, it's like a test of systems, the drug checks out how everything is working? That's what it was for me, and I came through. I feel good. Like my psyche's been rinsed out with a fire hose." I wanted to bring up the larger issues, the revolution and everything, but Randy wasn't ready to deal with that. He was barely keeping it together at a personal level. He wasn't on the front lines of social subversion. No help for my own uncertainties—though compared to him I had things under control. I had to get across campus and look for Julius. "Listen," I said. "Why don't you have something to eat? I ate this morning and it helped a lot. I've got to get over to College Five. After you eat, go home and try to sleep." Chicken-soup wisdom. What else could I offer? If I'd hung around Randy he'd have brought me down. I couldn't risk it. I left him sitting there looking as fucked up as everyone else. Altamont was following me around.

Maybe as a way of faking out my phantoms, my boots turned left into the dining hall instead of setting out directly across campus. I might meet someone I needed to see, a comrade in consciousness—like Norm (day before yesterday, it seemed like years)—

though I had no idea who. The hall was crowded and roaring with lunchtime noises, voices, plates and utensils clattering and clanging, institutional food smells—generic sauces, gravies, grease and sweets—floating nauseatingly through the huge room, December light stabbing through the big windows shaping sharp edges on every face. Sterling Davis, a young history professor I'd met a couple of months ago at a party, was taking a seat near the center of the hall, setting down his tray at a table half-filled with students. As one of the few black faculty, Sterling was cool; he exuded the self-assurance of one acutely aware of his rising status, casually radical, admired—envied—in this nursery of liberalism. I made my way to his table, took a seat beside him. "Hey, Sterling."

"Hey, what's happening." Friendly, nonchalant.

"Everything, right? Everything's happening at once." Give me a clue, Sterling my man, tell me what I need to know. The other students at the table looked on anxiously, as before an oracle. As a renegade grad student, I had status too. Either of us might utter something heavy.

Nodding, Sterling twirled his spaghetti and took a mouthful. No problem with his appetite. "You bet," he said.

I bet. Take a gamble. My old man's a gambler. Go for broke. Is that it? Dare to do. Simple clear steps. No stops. Everything at once. Fuck—here comes Randy, following my advice, coming this way with a tray. I said to Sterling, "Thanks, man. Just checking in," and got up, turning to Randy. "Here, take my place. I'm gone. See you." Keep the poem in motion. You bet. Get going.

Passing the water fountain as I left I took a good long drink. Tanking up on vitamin L.

In the full light of midafternoon College Five looked more desolate than ever, even though there were plenty of people around. The unfinished architecture had a sinister quality of decay, as if the buildings were coming apart instead of going up. The barren concrete walls of the dorm where Julius had his apartment were prisonlike in their forbidding uniformity. The whole place felt like that. It was creepy. I climbed the stairs to his second-floor door and knocked. Nobody home. I crossed the courtyard to the other unfinished dorm, where I shared a faculty office with Morgan Hurst. Morgan was in there writing.

"Hi, Morgan."

"Stephen!" Steffen. "I was worried about you. I'm so glad you came back. Sit down."

"I'm looking for Julius Trailerman. Have you seen him?"

"No. Is he on campus today?"

"He usually is, Mondays, but he said he was going to Arizona. But I think he might be here anyway. I've got to talk to him. Can you give me a ride to San Francisco?" Morgan had a classic 1955 Jaguar XK-140 coupe, a ruby red. Fenders with lines that rhymed with his mustache. "Are you driving back to Berkeley this afternoon?"

"Not until later. I have office hours. What do you need? Maybe I can help you."

"I need a ride to the city." I don't know what convinced me of that, but I wasn't getting anywhere here. I knew Julius's address from having sent all those poems to *semi*. I could go camp on his doorstep till he showed up. Or who knows, he might be expecting me. "I can't wait till later."

"Why? What's the matter? What's your hurry? Talk to me! I'm willing to help if you'll just tell me what's wrong!"

For godsake, Morgan, be cool, will you? His big red face was shaking, pitched toward mine. A pained expression. I could see his pores, anxious sweat beading his cheeks and forehead with a greasy sheen. Why was everyone so freaky today? How could I explain what I didn't understand myself? "I'm sorry, Morgan. See you in Arizona."

Walking down the hallway I bumped into Willard Slate, philosophy professor and senior faculty member. We'd never been formally introduced but like most of the college's staff, we knew each other by sight. He was a big man—another one—why was everybody so tall? Or was I shrinking? Unlike his more casual colleagues, Slate wore dark suits, which served to accentuate his stern demeanor. As we passed within inches of each other we paused as if to acknowledge or trade greetings, but his bearing suggested extreme unease—something in his posture, his face, his walk—possibly fear, or anger, I wasn't sure. I stopped abruptly, turned. "Have you seen Julius Trailerman today?"

"Why, no, I haven't." Trailerman was the kind of person Slate would forever avoid. Julius was too irregular, noninstitutional, bohemian. I suddenly had the horrible thought that Slate was the state, a CIA snoop in this nest of anarcho-artists. He scrutinized me suspiciously from under his thick dark eyebrows. "What do you need him for? He's not in his office?"

I moved on past him. "Thanks." No way could I carry on that conversation. How many more like him were prowling these corridors? Trying to scope out what we were up to. No wonder Julius had disappeared. The heat was on. As the pressures of this occult offensive built, the authorities were reacting. Or maybe they were trying to surrender, recognizing the inevitable. Slate and his fellow agents were only attempting to join up, in their clumsy authoritarian way. They'd tasted the drugs in the water and were coming on. They needed the guidance of little guerrillas like me. Were there any sides in this whole overthrow? Morgan, overwrought as he was acting, may have been urging me to strike out on my own, find the key to my course of action without his influence. Julius could have been prompting me precisely to get lost, jump in the deep end, not look to him for direction of any kind. To improvise. Improvisational acting. Yes, I could be his TA anyway. An extracurricular course of conduct. Improvise the script, inventing the new culture in your every move, each speech brimming with revolutionary images, rhythms of a new measure, every encounter a dramatic one, every look and gesture a cue to your fellow performers. Theater of the real. This is what Julius meant. But I needed more—just a few points of reference, hints, like Davis's "You bet." I'd never played in such a production, acted in such an uprising before.

It must be almost four o'clock. Time to get off campus. The construction crews were shutting down for the day. I climbed into the passenger seat of a pickup parked in the loading zone and waited for its driver to arrive. Here he comes, eyeing me curiously. Rugged-looking dude at day's end; painter's overalls, spattered hat. An artist. Gets in his truck.

"Take me to San Francisco?"

"Sorry." He started the engine. "You'll have to get out."

Of course. That would be too easy. "Sure. Thanks anyway." I nodded knowingly, opened the door, hopped down, walked to the exit road, stuck out my thumb. Waiting. A test of patience. Perseverance. People weren't stopping. Was I invisible, so pure, so clear, they could see right through me? Transparency, the peak of genetic evolution. Or were they deliberately ignoring me? All these cars, these people, going somewhere without me. What was I missing? I started to walk, turning, looking back over my left shoulder, right thumb extended. A blue Comet pulled over and stopped. I opened the door. It was Larry Bagley, a fellow poet from Julius's workshop.

"Going to San Francisco?" I asked him.

"Huh? No—just downtown. You want a lift?"

"Sure." And I hopped in.

On the way down the hill toward town I tried to cajole Larry into taking me to the city. I had important business with Julius and had to see him as soon as possible.

"But I thought Julius was in Arizona. Aren't you supposed to be running the reading tonight?"

"Yeah, but I'm doing it by remote control. You know, like Orpheus? Cocteau-radio waves. Muses are universal. They're everywhere at once. Tune in and take down the lines. Say a flock of blackbirds, redwings, sweeps up near you in a meadow and settles again—you copy the notes. Sheet music without the sheet. Ever see those signs on campus, 'Watch for Animals'? That's that they mean." Pick it up, Larry, it's poetry time. I leaned toward the radio. "Mind if I turn it on?"

Marvin Gaye was singing "I Heard It Through the Grapevine."

As I was saying.

And I'm just about to lose my mind.

Larry concentrated on the traffic. Mission Street eastbound just before sunset. A worried look on his face. A corner-of-the-eye glance at me. "Are you on LSD?"

"I sure am." Not that I knew of, really, but I couldn't prove I wasn't. Any more than he could. "You look pretty tripped-out yourself." Maybe it was true—acid was the new gasoline—whoever can handle it drives. Larry was driving but he couldn't handle it.

"I'm gonna have to drop you off up here."

"Okay. No sweat."

He let me out at River Street. Bottom of Highway 9. "Sorry. Good luck." The Comet disappeared down River. What the fuck. I could walk to San Francisco. Or I could hitch to the lodge—it was on the way. But that would be irresponsible. Escapist. Going to my cottage would accomplish nothing. Highways 1 and 17 were more direct routes to the city, either of which I could take from here, but something was pulling me into the mountains, the trajectory had been set, it was as plain as placing one boot in front of the other. I crossed the highway with the green light, fringes streaming in the breeze. Crossed again to the northbound side of 9. I turned, extended my thumb. No ride in the first five cars and I take a hike. Five cars went by, one after another, not even slowing down. Some redneck leaned out a window and yelled, "Get a haircut!" I smiled and flashed him the peace sign. Take it in stride, as my dad would say, one of his favorite teachings from the streets. Even he, out of it as he was, had something to contribute to this trip. This journey. Maybe I'd meet him on the road, who knows, anything can happen. I'll find my father. I set out north, on foot. Take it in stride. The sun was setting.

5

The Long March

Highway 9 revisited at twilight. Commuters tooling north into the hills. Not a lot of traffic, no steady stream, just spurts of two or three cars at a time at average speeds. Walking, I read their license plates for signs, clues, encouragement. Each was a vehicle of information directed at me in code as they blew past. Alphabet soup of nutritious units of occult significance. Kabbalistic algebra of mythic logic guiding my wired steps. Practically gliding on the power of the mysterious force propelling me, I moved with pure assurance into the valley's deepening green, filled with the understanding I could do no wrong, watched over by invisible guardians, signaled to by birds—a hawk circling high on my right above the river, an omen worthy of Odysseus—instructed by the postures and choreography of the trees, reading the texture of the road for meaning. An elaborate system of sustenance was being erected around me as I went along. Success—at what, it wasn't yet clear—was inevitable. I was entering another realm. My destination was San Francisco but the route was equally vital. Destiny had a plan.

As I approached Paradise Park, the railroad trestle on my left and the redwoods thickening ahead, a light blue Dodge van pulled over onto the shoulder beyond me and stopped. A woman's head, long dark hair, leaned out the passenger window and called back to me with an inviting smile, "Need a ride?" Walking to the city would not be necessary.

I climbed in back and sat on the bed beside a giant husky-shepherd whose name was Che. A formidable beast, but calm, poised on the mattress, wagging his tail as I got settled. After introducing me to the dog, the driver, a blondish Brit a few years my senior, presented himself as Keith. His navigator, Clara, was one of those olive-skinned dark-eyed people of ambiguous origin, like me, who might be Greek, Italian, Jewish, Latin American, whatever. A convenient attribute for the coming denationalization of the planet. We pulled back onto the road and settled into a comfortable silence. They didn't ask where I was going. We were simply here, in motion and on the way, peering out the windshield into the darkening woods, tape player serenading us with The Band. *When you awake you will remember everything* . . .

Che was the mellowest dog I'd ever met. A credit to his species. Ordinarily I found his kind obnoxious, always begging for affection or approval, jumping on you with their filthy paws, nuzzling your crotch with their wet noses, shitting in public, whining for sympathy, lacking all self-respect. Cats were so much more subtle, dignified, indifferent to human validation and therefore more worthy of esteem. Most dogs imposed themselves in such a way that unless you whacked them on the nose or did something equally forceful to repel them, they never left you alone. Che was different, an impressively solid hunk of animal, serenely self-contained. His agreeable demeanor spoke highly of his humans, though they themselves said little. Had Che been lapping the acidified water and thereby transcended his doggishness? Or was he a naturally revolutionary creature, living up (or down) to his name as people so often do? If a dog could achieve such equanimity, there was hope for humans. I scratched the fur of his enormous head, impressed. He looked at me as if to say, What did you expect, a poodle?

Past Felton, within a mile or two of the lodge, Clara turned around in the passenger seat. Night had fallen. "Where would you like to go?"

"I'm headed for the city. How far are you folks going?"

"All the way over the top," Keith replied, the phrase resounding with ambiguity. "You want to come with us into San Jose?"

"You can just let me off at Skyline, thanks." Skyline Boulevard ran the ridge the length of the peninsula almost to the city. I'd driven it in the Porsche, the scenic route, with intermittent vistas of the bay on one side and views to the Pacific on the other. A suitably epic path for tonight's odyssey—top of the world, the geophysical and spiritual heights, well above workaday sea-level civilization. It was pointless to take the mountain road at all if not to continue along the crest, breathing the wild air, taking in the sweep of the signs, absorbing the expansive perspective. Staying high. The constellations could watch me. "You coming from Santa Cruz?"

"We started from Big Sur this afternoon," said Keith. "We're on the road. Coming down from the Stones. It was a consciousness-wrenching concert, out there in the countryside, you know? Rather heavy, I'd say. Wouldn't you, love?"

Clara said, "Absolutely. Nothing like it. Once in a lifetime." She turned to me. "I'm not sure we've come down."

"I'm hip," I said. "I was there." The event was still in progress. Keith and Clara were part of the continuing conspiracy unfolding anew minute by minute. That's why they'd picked me up.

"We knew there was something about you—"

"Even from the back," she caught his thought and carried it, "the way you were moving, springing along, your energy—"

"It's catching," I said. "Spreading. We're everywhere. Some kind of psychic epidemic." Don't say too much. They know it or they don't.

As we approached the lodge a hundred yards or so ahead, a silver BMW pulled onto the road. Nona. Going home. Joining our caravan over the mountain. Leading us. Confirming this was the way. Did she know I was in this van? Had she picked up my presence on the telepath and chosen just this moment subconsciously to coordinate our journeys? Saying yes, follow me. For an instant I had the urge to overtake her, get in beside her, let her drive me where I was going. But there were other drivers to come, each one special and irreplaceable yet equally qualified to play St. Christopher, Charon, Cassady. Thousands of drivers and passengers ready to trade roles at a moment's necessity, adopting different identities, acting out the changes as they happen. Shape shifters improvising the required forms. Che might be more than a mere dog. That could account for his character. Wasn't all life inherently related, immanently entwined, all beings part of the same continuum? On acid, people could trade faces. In sex, individual bodies lost their boundaries. Variations on ecstasy. Transformative powers could be directed, channeled, harnessed for the new evolution. The more highly evolved one's psychic skills, the more forms one might assume. Shamanic practice. Alchemy of being. Poetry made flesh. Technicians of the sacred. Was this the order I was being asked to join—inducted into so mysteriously? Were the ranks of such mastery expanding so fast under the demands of the moment that novices like me were being recruited before we fully knew what we were doing?

We reached the summit. Nona's car continued across, down Highway 9 toward Saratoga. Keith pulled over at the intersection of 9 and Skyline, Highway 35. I thanked them, opened the side doors, placed my feet on the packed dirt of the turnout.

"Good trip," said Keith.

"Stay high," said Clara.

Che looked me in the eye attentively. Whoever he was.

"Maybe we'll meet again," I said. In these or other forms.

It was early evening but night to the eyes, and so quiet at the summit. Two arc lamps and a flashing yellow lit the intersection. A good place to hitch. I'd wait here a while and see what came along.

Conserving energy. I could have a long walk ahead. I crossed the highway, boot heels echoing sharply in the dark, then the textured crunch of my soles on the shoulder, the surrounding silence spreading and settling. Soon I could hear the arc lights humming. An owl, close by, conferring with a colleague farther off. Crickets' consistent lyricism. Bobcats and cougars roamed these slopes. Wild boars and coyotes. Deer in abundance. Foxes. The bears were gone, driven out by development. But thousands of other creatures made their home here. Eagles and tree rats. Skunks and hawks. You heard about them. Saw them, with luck, while walking in the woods. Your headlights caught them crossing the roads. A year ago I couldn't have stood in this spot without fear of something, animal or human or supernatural, doing me harm. I was from LA. Now I felt I belonged here, if only passing through; was welcome as part of the pattern. I wanted the animals' blessings. Wanted to feel their presence and approval. They could be anyone. I could be one of them.

Headlights approached from 9, Big Basin Road. Stopped at the top. A generic compact, American made. It proceeded on over to Saratoga. After a while, another car, then another, all going over the summit, nobody turning north on 35. Cold night, temperature dropping, eighth of December. The last few days of an amazing decade. A decade that coincided—coincidentally?—with my coming of age. I'd graduated from grade school in 1960, Kennedy elected president that fall as I was elected president of my freshman class at Beverly. JFK killed in my senior year, his brother and King in my senior year of college. Violent milestones. K's picked off at the peak of leadership. No leaders left. A lonesome darkness in the outside world. But I was alive, adult and without heroes. This was essential to the new reality. Self-reliance. Emersonian versatility. Responsible individuals lead themselves. Be your own hero. Live your legend. A chill breeze stirred the evergreens. Good thing I had on my turtleneck. White wool, visible and warm. Jacket pockets packed with the basics: Chapstick, matches, notebook, penknife, pen. No keys, no car. Nothing to smoke, but who needed that? As Dalí said, I do not take drugs, I am drugs. No sleeping bag this trip. I'd sleep in a bed, no bed, or not at all. No traffic whatsoever on Skyline. I must have stood there an hour. Every so often a car would come up 9 and go on across. I decided to try the opposite corner; if someone stopped, I could go either way. Maybe a ride along the ridge was too much to ask. Whatever was in the cards. The cars. You bet. I'd wait here a while longer, a few more cars, then set out walking. Take it in stride.

A Jaguar just like Morgan's, only white, pulled up and stopped. Morgan? It could be his car, bleached with LSD—magic ingredient of transformations. The passenger door opened. The driver was a big man with a pale round face, light hair, high voice. "Where you going?" Morgan, is that you? No, but maybe. Yes. He'd shifted shapes. As in a dream, when someone is more than who they appear to be—composite people. Morgan in another form. The Jaguar gave him away. Morgan, the trickster, coming through in the clutch.

"San Francisco," I said.

"I can take you into Santa Clara." Clara. "Come on, get in."

It was the only ride around. Morgan as someone else, or maybe someone else as Morgan. And who was I? I couldn't see myself. Was I an impersonation? Versatility. How many beings encoded in each of us, waiting to be released? Liberated. The car, Clara—codes, and I was the key to their translation. I got in, pulled the door shut with a satisfying thump, and over the top we drove. Leather seat close to the floor, deep wells for the legs, the car slung low to the road, long hood out in front, and those elegant leaping-feline fenders. Morgan wasn't copping to who he was. Were we undercover? The driver was wound up, just like Morgan, and his voice was loud, only higher-pitched, like Morgan at 45rpm. The Jaguar cruised down the curving road, taking the corners gracefully.

"Been standing out there long? Not much traffic, I guess." His voice was a hoarse whistle, dry air strained forcibly through a tight windpipe.

"I don't know. An hour or so." What is time?

"Nice night," he squealed. "A little cold, though. You wouldn't want to be out here all that long. Could be dangerous, you know. There's all kinds of things in these mountains. Strange people living up here."

"Yeah." Like me. I didn't know how to engage this guy. Who was he? Was he testing me? I had to trust him, didn't I? Luck of the draw. Flow with it all the way.

We drove through Saratoga and on into Santa Clara. He said, "I'm going just a few blocks from the Bayshore. I can take you to the freeway if you like."

"That's okay, I'll just go with you."

A quizzical look, but no other reaction. Two or three turns and we were on a quiet suburban residential street. Santa Clara Valley contemporary. Tacky ranch-style tract homes. He pulled up in front of one. Would he invite me in? I wasn't sure what to do. Was he taking me to Clara and Keith? I didn't see their van, or anything else familiar. Was this just a stop en route to the city? He might be testing my trust. "Well, this is it. Good luck getting to San Francisco. A right at the corner, a left two blocks up and a right, and you'll find the onramp."

I didn't budge. Waiting for something. "Mind if I just sit here a minute?"

"Matter of fact, I do. I need to lock the car."

All right. I get the message. I got out. He locked the car and went into the house. I waited there, pacing the sidewalk. Something would happen. Someone would come. Finally I went to the front door and rang the bell. He opened it. "Aren't we going to San Francisco?"

"Listen, friend," he said. "You'd better get going. I don't want to call the cops." He shut the door.

I walked back out to the sidewalk. Something was wrong.

Get going where? The neighborhood was stark. Anonymous. No signs for me. This was much scarier than the mountains. Who was watching through these barren windows? Enemy territory.

Walking out would mean traversing a minefield of hidden psychic explosives. The sterility was terrifying. I stood there, pondering my options.

Soon a police car pulled up. The squealer came out and talked to the cop. The cop came over to me. "Need a ride to the freeway?"

"Sure, that would be fine," I said. A cop? Was this a joke? Another trick? He seemed sincere. He opened the passenger door, front seat. Shotgun. He trusted me.

"How are you doing?" he said. "You all right? Any problems?"

"I'm just trying to get to San Francisco."

We crossed over the Bayshore, Highway 101. He stopped by the northbound onramp. "Here you go." Just what I needed. A lift out of the anxiety zone. I felt much better. Even the police were looking after me.

"Thanks a lot, officer." Who are you, really?

"Stay on the onramp, hitching. This side of the sign. You're on the freeway and the CHP will cite you." Okay. Sure. I slammed the door shut and he pulled away. Nice guy. The cops were tripping too, offering free instruction. This is turning into one weird night.

Within half an hour I was cruising north on the Bayshore in a clean but comfortably funky old Ford pickup driven by a guy who said his name was Mitch. Sandy short hair, clean shaved, straight-looking, definitely not Jewish, no acne scars yet tall and thin, low-key, familiar, with an ironic glint that reminded me of Misha. Another assumed identity, a guardian, to ferry me safely to the city? Misha, Mitch. The landscape along the Bayshore was the usual hideous mix of factories, warehouses, motels and tract developments lit by the glare of industrial fluorescence and neon. The dirigible hangar at Moffett Field looked more ominous than ever, looming on the right like a swollen tomb. It reminded me of driving by Camp Pendleton as a kid, on the way to the track at Del Mar with my dad, and seeing the mines or whatever they were stacked up like black tomatoes in a grocery store display. At ten years old, with Khrushchev shaking his shoe in our faces, knowing the Marines were well stocked with explosives made me feel secure, I suppose, however spooky those pyramids looked, but now, a dozen years later, here on the same highway five hundred miles north, the Navy's enormous hangar, so much more massive than anything else in sight, gave me the creeps. The military was killing everything. Evil was being done inside that cavernous monstrosity.

We sped along toward San Francisco. If Mitch was Misha, maybe it was him I should be looking for. If so, I'd found him, or he'd found me. Everything embraced by the grand plan. I knew him much better than I knew Julius. Had tripped with Misha and was acquainted with his mischievous twists of thought, his pranks, his aphorisms. Misha on good intentions: Those intentions are best that never existed. On psychogeography: Your head can't be too far from where your feet are. On the mind/body question: If you lose your mind you've still got your body, but if you lose your body you lose everything. He too was a teacher. He'd introduced me to Nietzsche's *Zarathustra*, to Bartok's *Concerto for Orchestra*, to the joys of paranoia, the understanding that a fine edge of fear sharpens one's attention, gets the adrenaline pumping, awakens survival instincts. He seemed old for his age, emitted a shaggy rabbinical vibration that suggested he knew more than he knew he knew. This occult wisdom was evident in his grin, which seemed to reach back several generations to his ancestors in Eastern Europe. Land where our fathers died. In our more laconic and cryptic exchanges—Misha's and mine, but also mine and Mitch's as we drove—we tried to out-nonsequitur each other, spout spontaneous poetic truths, as if to speak a complete or coherent or comprehensible sentence would be to overstate the case. Like, I'd say: "When King Kong returns, the natives will get no rest." And he (Mitch/Misha) would reply: "The jungle's a hairy place to hang your hammock." Or I'd say, "The moon is a meatball in god's spaghetti." And he'd say, "Which cloud are you on?" Misha's ancient grin was visible through Mitch's, giving him away, I thought. But I kept the thought to myself. He'd take me to where I needed to go, initiate me into the necessary mysteries.

Into the city. He took the freeway to the Fell Street exit, down the ramp to the signal, across the intersection, and parked by the corner—Laguna Street—in front of a liquor store. "End of the line, my boy." His boy. He killed the engine and got out. Walked around back of the truck. Yelled at me, still sitting in the cab, "That's it, pal. See ya later." And disappeared into the store. I couldn't believe it. He wasn't serious. He was going to take me all the way. Wherever I was meant to be going. I was getting a little tired of these tests. Hadn't I proved myself yet? I got out and hopped in the bed of the truck. When Mitch came out of the store he saw me sitting there, walked over, set down his sixpack, and said, "This is as far as we go." He grabbed me with both hands by the shoulders of my jacket and in one motion lifted me out of the truck and threw me onto the sidewalk—I felt myself flying in slow motion toward the street corner, bouncing once on the concrete and springing to my feet like a gymnast. Light. In balance. Indestructible. Mitch gave me one last ambiguous look, got in his truck, started the engine, and drove off, his taillights disappearing down Fell.

Julius lived on Laguna, twenty or thirty blocks up, in the Marina. I could walk and I'd be there in . . . an hour? Time and space had melted. What's time in eternity? I was Odysseus making my way, with detours, to my inevitable destination. Penelope, Julie, would be there to receive me. Julie, the one woman, even now, two months apart, whose bed I belonged in. During that time I'd gone to see her at Rio Del Mar once a week or so. We'd smoke, talk, fuck, and I'd be gone, never staying the night. The phantom lover, visiting husband, horny disappearing prick. This might be the path to our reunion, circuitous route to reconciliation. Julie. Julius. I took off walking up Laguna.

Within a block or two I felt the eyes. People on the street, all black, were checking me out. Lone hippie, the only white person in sight, boogieing through the Fillmore on a Monday night, nine or ten or eleven o'clock, looking a little confused, as if he'd fallen out of a cloud. I had no clear idea, nor did these folks, what I was doing in the neighborhood. But why else would Mitch have dropped me, actually tossed me, at Fell and Laguna if not to set me off in this direction. An ageless woman standing in a doorway as I passed said to me, drawing out the words with a conspiratorial tone, "Hi, Zodiac." The Zodiac Killer was San Francisco's most legendary criminal at large, an astrologically inclined psychopath who had the police outfoxed. The woman must be joking. I was angelic, the furthest thing from homicidal. Or was she saying that only a madman would be out here as I was? At Turk Street, opposite a darkened playground, her words still echoing in my head, I turned around. Spooked. Retraced my steps toward Fell, passing the same woman, who said, "Mmhm," as if she understood my change of course, had been placed there to suggest it, was confirming the correction. If I hitched down Fell as far as Golden Gate Park I could find my way to Misha's by remembering the route we'd taken back to his place from the antiwar rally we'd attended with Gloria and Julie and some other friends last summer. A hundred thousand people in the meadow listening to speeches and music, dancing, sailing frisbees, smoking grass, laughing, weeping, looking for some relief from the grief of so much slaughter overseas—a bloated reflection of the homicides at home—trying to turn it over, end it, change it. Buffy St. Marie had sung a piercing chilling version of "The Universal Soldier." We'd walked home, quiet, under a cloudy sky. If I found our point of departure I could reconstruct the way. At Fell I turned right, walked a block and turned around to hitch. A clunky sedan came lumbering to a stop. Hippie girl at the wheel. I opened the door and smelled a strong blend of marijuana smoke and patchouli.

"Going as far as the park?" I asked.

"Sure am," she said, handing me the joint as I got in. "Just let me know where." The inside of the car was filthy, littered with clothes and newspapers and empty cardboard Chinese food containers. The Rolling Stones were on the radio singing "You Can't Always Get What You Want."

"Stanyan, I think. That'd be cool."

"Groovy."

But if you try sometimes you just might find you get what you need.

We passed the reefer back and forth rolling westward down the Panhandle, not much to say, windows up, letting the smoke envelope us in its richness, so sweet and bitter, healing and toxic, calming and stimulating at the same time, heartbeat up, anxiety down, layers of nutritious translucence enclosing us like an onion. She took a left on Stanyan, then right at Lincoln, past Kezar Stadium.

"This is good," I said, and she pulled over. "Thanks a lot."

"Sure, whatever. Stay loose."

I strode back across Stanyan, revitalized by the smoke, and headed east on Frederick into the Haight. Liberated territory. If I turned south on Clayton—where Misha and I had scored the hash I'd smoked with Nona the other night before giving the rest of it and the pipe away at Altamont (all of which seemed like centuries ago)—and east on 17th, I'd wind up in the Mission. It was a lengthy hike, almost as far as from Fell to Julius's, but this turf was more familiar. Late as it may have been, on these streets a freak like me wouldn't attract so much attention. No Zodiac vibes. No eyeballs peering out of African faces. People I passed appeared to accept my presence. Our eyes glanced off each other in understated greeting. Longhairs. Gay men. Stray dogs. Cats. I nodded hello to each in turn, establishing that I belonged. Was almost home. Misha. Julie. Someone would welcome me in. Surprise me with a meal, a bed. My legs were getting tired. It had been an endless day. Rich with myth. But I was ready for a break. It must be close to midnight.

Trudging up Clayton toward Twin Peaks and down the hill toward the Castro I lost all sense of context, absorbed in the immediacy of each acidic sensation, here is everywhere and now eternity, the houses shimmering with immanence, streetlights bathing the parked cars in a dreamy liquid amber through which I also swam, or floated, surrounded by intense presence. The street names were unfamiliar—Uranus, Mars—as if I had strolled into space. Lost in the cosmos. Someone was changing the signs. The streets had been shuffled in an act of sabotage as part of the larger plot to remap minds. Seventeenth Street went on forever. Temple. Ord. Douglass. Eureka. Diamond. Each cross street seemed to resonate with meanings addressed directly to me, faceted with loaded associations. At Market Street I turned south into the Castro. The bars were open, the street was alive with guys in tight jeans and leather jackets, stylish omnisexuals, queens and loveboys swishing down the sidewalks eyeing everything that moved, including me. I picked up the pace, avoiding eye contact now, as out of place as earlier in the Fillmore. Everything here was exaggerated, the sizes of the guys' mouths, the suggestiveness of their gestures, the self-conscious swagger of the way they carried themselves. It was too theatrical for me, a parody, perspective twisted through a fisheye lens, funny and scary at the same time, a house of eerie mirrors in a menacing amusement park.

I took a left at 18th Street, had to escape that scene. Dolores couldn't be far. And Misha's, what a relief. Sure enough, there was the park. But which way now? I couldn't remember the address, the cross street, the signs had been switched, my circuits were fried, memory vaporized in the heat of the here and now. Must be fatigue. I'll feel my way, let radar do it. Navigate by force field, magnetic waves, some psychic homing device. Misha's place was above the park. I turned right on Dolores. The park was still, its grassy slopes and foliage reflecting a restful light onto the surrounding buildings, pastel colored, the houses softly secure, families inside asleep, peaceful, shielded against the chaos of the streets. My legs ached. When had I eaten last? I wanted to lie down. Arrival at Misha's house was the payoff. Surprise. They'd be waiting for me. Misha and Gloria. Julie. Maybe Julius. Nona. Morgan. Keith and

Clara. All the players at the curtain call. Who knows what other friends might be there? April. Randy Chatsworth. Sterling Davis. I'd made it. They'd congratulate me. Welcome to the new world. You've proved yourself. We love you. You're a poet.

It looked like Misha's building. Above the park. A duplex. Pastel pink. The porch light shone. I climbed the concrete stairs, nearly delirious with gratitude, summoning all my strength, as if crawling over a sand dune to an oasis. I rang the doorbell. Voices. They were home. The door inched open, held by a chain. The face of a young Mexican man peered out. "Who is it? What do you want?"

Come on, Misha. Enough's enough. No more masquerades, okay? "It's me. Is Misha home?"

"Is who?"

"Misha. Misha Krazovich. He lives here. I know he does."

"Sorry, wrong place. Good night." He shut the door. The light on the porch went out. Inside I heard laughter. They were dragging this out to the limit now that I was safely here. A big joke on the initiate.

Come on, people. I rang again. Rapped the knocker. Waited. The light came on. The door opened a crack. The same young man looked out. "Let me in, will you? I'm tired. Where's Misha? Is Julie here?"

"Sorry. You better go. You made a mistake." He closed the door again. The light went off. More laughter. I can't believe this is happening. Where am I? Try to stay calm. Step back and look at the situation. It's funny, sort of. A practical joke. Another test of your composure. Grace under pressure. But I was losing it. Was on the verge of crying.

I sat on the top step. No place to go. I'll wait. They'll let me in. Sure enough, after a while the light came on. I got up, stood by the door, but no one came. Then a car pulled up in front. SFPD. Two uniformed cops got out, slowly mounted the stairs. Okay. So these guys will take me to Misha's. Just like the officer in Santa Clara.

"Good evening," said the thinner one.

"Hi," I replied wearily. I surrender.

"Just come with us." They took me gently by either elbow, ushered me down the steps.

"Are you guys taking me to Misha's?"

"Sure." He opened the back door of the cruiser. I got in. The seat was comfortable. Clean.

We drove a few blocks, took a few turns. I gave myself over to my protectors, assuming that's what they were. I had no choice. Was grateful to relinquish volition.

The car pulled into a garage. They helped me out, led me through a door. Blue-black uniforms. Bright lights. Typewriters clattering. A secret poetry clubhouse? Mission Precinct. ID. Fingerprints. I was being booked.

6

Bard Behind Bars

Something was wrong with this scenario. They couldn't really
be arresting me—I hadn't done anything. I was not Franz K or
Josef K but Stephen K, and this was not Prague or Budapest or any
other nightmare police-state capital but San Francisco, most liberal of cities. The social torments of the 1960s were giving way to
a new improved decade of drug-induced understanding, musical
union and peaceful harmonization of diversity. I was a composer
of this cultural future, the furthest thing from a criminal. And yet
these uniforms surrounding me, the institutional indifference of
the men inside them, the naked harshness of the room's hard surfaces under the glare of unforgiving lights told me I could be mis-
taken. Maybe I'd wandered into an alternate universe where poets,
like Shelley's unacknowledged legislators, were cops. Or this
could be an elaborate charade, a skillfully improvised masque of
poet-actors whose purpose was to induct me into their ranks. My
brief career as a fraternity boy, or for that matter as a graduate
student, had taught me that in order to enter any exclusive group
you had to be hazed, subjected to absurd rituals, a process of

humiliation that bonded you to your colleagues. The guys behind these typewriters—desk sergeants or whatever—might actually be banging out celebratory verses to welcome me into their club. I was getting tired of the aggravation of not knowing what was going on, but if this was the price I had to pay, okay.

Seated alone on a wooden bench, instructed by one of my keepers to wait there, I surveyed the room, observing that but for the uniforms this was pretty much like any generic office, an English department message center, insurance agency, or other administrative command post. An infinite number of interchangeable bureaucratic monkeys—or in this case pigs—running the overpaperworked engines of civilization. Enough of them sooner or later might compose the works of Shakespeare, or Bacon, or whomever. Ghost writers. They had to keep at it. Replacements had to be recruited constantly to boost their numbers and improve the odds of coming up with a masterpiece. That's why they needed me. Shakespeare of course was a figure of speech. Saber rattling for dramatic effect. Innovative peers could shake free swords or lances into spades, digging up traditions to overturn them, planting new seeds, dealing new hands, cultivating creative gambles. This was the world I wanted to help invent. Even a place like this, whatever it was, could yield and be redeemed by imagination.

An officer came over and escorted me to the door, same one I'd come in, opening on the garage. I was given a hand into the back of a paddy wagon, took a seat on one of the benches and soon was joined by another guest prisoner poet, a middle-aged gentleman, evidently drunk, who didn't fit any visionary profile or remotely heroic image I might have hoped to see across from me as the doors thumped shut. He was surly, dirty, and he stank, cheap booze on his breath and body, mumbling unintelligible protests in the dimness of the van as we pulled out into the street. This wasn't the kind of companionship I was seeking. I had no desire to team up with anyone who couldn't maintain. I might have been stoned or tripped out or otherwise high, on precisely what substances

I wasn't sure, but at least I wasn't a stumbling, blubbering slob. I wanted to conserve some dignity, some poise, to prove I was worthy of release from this deepening abduction. I wanted out—into what, I didn't know—but facing my fellow passenger I had serious misgivings about where we were being taken and what would happen when we got there. After a painfully protracted ride we entered another underground garage. The doors of the van were opened. Our escorts hustled us into an elevator. We rode up six or seven floors and stepped out into another administrative staging area, more stark and secure than the previous one, pale yellowish-white walls, no windows, larger, doors leading off in different directions, different dimensions maybe, as in a Borges story or an Escher print, I envisioned Möbius staircases and labyrinthine corridors twisting through the building and back again, going nowhere. I felt like a cat being taken to the vet for an unknown operation. The fluorescent lighting was relentless, the walls and counters cruelly linear, rigid. Only the irregular clackety-clack of typewriters varied the sterile rhythm of straight lines and slamming doors. One of the cops at one of these machines, a corpulent fellow with curly dark hair and ruddy cheeks, resembled Dylan Thomas. Maybe I'd died and gone to poetry hell. Maybe my partner in the paddy wagon, now standing just down the counter, was a poorly reconstituted Kerouac. Could I already be joining the immortals? Was this the deeper meaning of being booked?

An officer ordered me to empty my pockets on the countertop. My stuff was scooped into an envelope and taken away. I was led through a door, down a corridor, around a corner, another corridor, another corner, it *was* an Escher print, a Borges story—or possibly Poe—mazes of steel bars, locked doors, dungeons, echoing surfaces, musical keys opening and closing bolts and latches. Off in the distance, typewriters. Indistinguishable voices. An odd smell of stale paint and belched air, sweat and metal. We stopped in front of a large cell. Benches around the periphery. Eight or ten men inside, some seated on the benches, some curled on the floor asleep or trying to sleep. Mostly older guys, winos I guess, and one young longhair. And over in the corner, crouching, a Mexican-looking dude—resembling a mixture of my brother Hank, Bob Dylan and Cantínflas—who seemed to be trying to disappear, become invisible. Rattling his keys my escort unlocked the door and motioned me into the cell. I stepped over a puddle of vomit near the face of one of the drunks unconscious on the floor and took a seat beside the other hippie, hoping to form an alliance. He seemed at least relatively sober compared to most of our other cellmates. Shyly, subtly, we nodded, the slightest acknowledging glance. Sort of like meeting Norm at Altamont. How the hell did I get here from there?

"What is this?" I asked him. Almost whispering. "Where are we?"

"Hall of Justice. City Prison. What are you in for?"

"I don't know. Are you sure this isn't staged? Are you a poet?"

"Huh? Staged?" He looked at me as if to ask, What are you on? Then he reflected for a few seconds. "Yeah, well, I write songs sometimes. So what?"

One of the drunks on the floor woke up and started groaning loudly. Struggling to set himself half-upright, his elbow propped against the bench, he let loose a torrent of profanity directed at no one in particular but loud enough to dominate the scene. The old fart was fucked up, knew it and wanted everyone else to know he didn't appreciate how he was being treated. "Motherfucking shithole cocksuckers! I want some respect, goddammit! How the goddamn fuck am I ever gonna get home if you don't let me outta here! Asshole prickface cuntlickers! Little copshits! Give you pukeheads keys and you think you're god. Jesus fuck."

Little as I liked his style, I had to agree. The pukeheads with the keys were in control. I turned back to my benchmate. "Well, maybe it's poets' theater. Initiation night. Everyone has to go through this ordeal. If you can take it, you've made it. You're in."

"Listen, man." He shrugged, a spooked look flickering in his eyes. "You're too far out for me."

"No, it makes sense. Like that old fuck over there." I nodded toward the loudmouth. "He could be Charles Bukowski or Robert Bly on a bad night. Having to go through hazing over and over. That's why he's so pissed off. It's the price they pay for inspiration. This is all a dream, but it's everybody's. Maybe we're all home asleep having a nightmare, how do I know?" Didn't Borges say that when you dream you're awake in another dimension, the waking world and the dream world are just complementary sides of the same reality? What's so far out about that?

"Don't fuck with my head, man. This place is freaky enough already. This is jail. Get hip."

But what would I be doing in jail? There had to be some other explanation. I mean, yes, on one level it seemed like jail. Totally authentic. But something else must be happening as well. Maybe the Hall of Justice had been captured by acid commandos and converted into a psychic research facility, testing the advanced for endurance to extreme situations. Boot camp for shock troops. The snake-pit treatment. How much can you stand? All right. I'm game. If these guys can take it, I can too. Unless it gets too much worse.

I edged over toward Hank/Cantínflas/Dylan, still in a crouch in the corner trying to stay unseen. I squatted beside him. Murmured, "Hey." He glanced at me but beyond that, no response. If he was who I thought and hoped he was, in any combination, I was safe. Hank, my older brother—eight years my senior, three years older than our sister Gena and three years younger than Don, the firstborn—was the ultimate level-headed practical man of balance, my father's protégé, managing his investments and the rest of the family business at thirty, hero and guardian of my childhood, model for so many moves and gestures of mine. So what if he'd gotten married at twenty-one and settled with his wife in the suburbs and had four kids, a life so straight I could scarcely conceive it, he was still Mr. Reliable, always available for consultation, unconditionally trusting no matter how radical a pose I struck. If Hank was in on this, going through this for my sake, even in some dream or nightmare he'd never remember, everything would be fine, no harm could befall me. Cantínflas, master comedian-actor-singer-dancer, reflected my Mexican side—my brother Don used to call me Pancho for my brown complexion—the LA native kid with a Spanish subconscious due to the place and street names soaked up for eighteen years in the city of angels, *nuestra señora reina de los ángeles*, a Latin American capital in love with the movies. His role in this performance was to keep me loose and humble, joky, light and ironic for my own good, versatile, raceless and multilingual. And Dylan, well, he was poet laureate, a bard to end all bards, author of countless deathless songs and still going strong wherever he was hiding. The crouching recluse in the cell with me, uneasy as he seemed in the situation, silent, withdrawn, could be all three of these guiding lights combined, all asleep someplace else, as maybe I was, but here with me in this collective unconscious drunk tank someplace in eternity. I was riding the line between fear and euphoria, thrilled to be hunkering down beside this mystery mentor. Even if he wouldn't talk to me. What would he say, anyway? *Something is happening and you don't know what it is, do you . . .*

Mister who? Who was I anymore? They'd taken away my ID. Well, who needed it? I was becoming another than the person I'd been impersonating going on twenty-three years. That boy was dead. Buried in the rubble of his childhood home demolished after his parents had sold it and moved. A big white wooden colonial house where everybody's friends came in through the back door, made themselves comfy, swam in the pool, ran around the yard to the gardener's distress, raided the fridge at whim, hung out with the help, played hide and seek—idyllic setting for secure memories of marshmallow pillowfight pancake happiness that may or may not have happened in the past, what past, the house was flattened now, a pile of dusty debris to be bulldozed out of the way for some ostentatious monstrosity. Yes, he was dead and buried there. I needed a new name.

The belligerent drunk who I imagined might be Bly or Bukowski was at it again, coming out of a stupor with a streak of obscenities

to notify his keepers he was still indignant, outraged to be subjected to this bullshit. It was an insult, a degradation, unconstitu-
tional and rude. He demanded to be released. Most of the others
were trying to sleep and stirred a little, grumbling at the noise. But
one old wino, seated slumped on the bench, was awake whether
he wanted to be or not. His face was grizzled with a few days'
growth; he looked unspeakably sad, ashamed, humiliated, holding his mangy overcoat tightly to his torso, half for warmth and
half in an effort to erase himself. His frayed humility reminded me
of my father—not his looks exactly but his bearing: this is how
Jack would hold himself if he were here. He'd be appalled to find
himself in this cell, not just because it was filthy and a horrible
smear on his fastidiousness, but because it was so undignified, such
a wretched place to be found. Whatever my father's other problems, ego was not one of them. If anything he was too meek, yielding to his wife and children in family discussions, effacing himself,
rarely asserting authority. He was too busy with other matters, the
business, to be involved in the small-scale squabbles of domesticity. Mother knows best. So it wasn't that he was proud, this father
figure, but rather disgraced to be stuck with these other drunks,
possibly brought back to a deep past he had escaped—not his personal past, he scarcely drank, but his father's, who'd abandoned the
family and ended up homeless on Skid Row—a past he was reliv-
ing for his father's sake, unearthing the old man's mortification in
a drunken dream of his own. Or was it mine? In the mythic mind-
warp of this otherworldly night had my father joined me here,
unconsciously chosen while asleep at home to share in this weird
experience? I left my Mexican brother still squatting mute in his
corner and sat beside my dad, heartbroken, humbled by his sacrifice. How terrible it must be for him to be here. I placed my arm
around his shoulder to comfort him. He tried to shrug me off but
I held on. "It's okay, Pop." It didn't matter anymore how badly we
misunderstood each other, my lack of aptitude for business, his for
poetry, our political and philosophical differences. He needn't be

ashamed of his situation. It was heroic of him to enter this crummy underworld, such a generous act of solidarity, proof of his love. I was crying. Jesus, what was going on? It was and it wasn't him, and who was I if, as I'd sensed, I'd shed my former self? Whose father was he, then?

"Get off me," he grunted. "Leave a man in peace."

I backed away. "Sure, Pop." Don't embarrass the old guy. Give him the space to suffer in privacy. At least I'd acknowledged who he was. Made the association. Maybe that's what I was here for. To meet my father, forgive each other. Maybe they'd let me out now. Open the doors and let us all go home. It must be almost dawn.

I stepped across the bodies and the puddle of puke to the cell door, pressed my face between the bars, felt the steel's coldness in my cheekbones. "Hey!" I yelled. "It's all right now! The war's over! Let us out of here!" Metallic echoes gave way to a deepening silence. Blykowski grumbled, "Sonsofbitches," snorting and slobbering. Everyone else was now deep in some private retreat from their imprisonment, curled up sleeping on the floor or the benches, leaning against the bars, the walls. I staked out an unoccupied stretch of bench, took off my jacket, folded it under my head and lay down, knees against my chest. Maybe I could doze off. Asleep, there might be a chance of breaking back into the other world.

Good luck. My blood was electric, surging through the brain in bolts of consciousness. Pulses thundered through the silence of the building, scrambled voices argued their cases and recited verses in my inner galleries. Eyes shut, I saw the intricate colorful networks throbbing in the eyelids. The sour smells of the cell and its inmates invaded me. The walls' drones resounded in my humming bones. Every lost sensation sought me out. I prayed for daylight.

Two guards coming with keys meant it must be morning. We were all herded through gray corridors into a large room, not a cell but a central holding area where other men also milled, waiting for something. Natural daylight filtered through the opaque glass of one wall, giving at least a suggestion of a world outside. The long windowless night of dim electric lights and gloomy hallways dissolved. It was like coming up for air from the sea floor.

An officer handed me a slip of paper. "Receipt for your personal property." Right. As if property, much less personal property, at this point were anything to claim. Hadn't I last night acknowledged the death of whoever I'd been till then? Was this yet another test to determine whether I'd truly given up ego, or was I still clinging to some useless notion of self in this sea of transformations? Personal property, my ass. My ass itself had ceased to be personal, my "my"—that most presumptuous of pronouns—was disappearing as a point of possessive reference. Nothing belongs to anyone. Property is just a capitalist scam to trick people into believing in law and order. All such deceits were up for exposure, delusions to be debunked. The items I'd carried with me and given up were "mine" no longer. I crumpled the paper and dropped it on the floor.

A big cop was hassling my father. Or maybe the old man was hassling him. I didn't see how it started but they were in each other's faces and I wanted to protect each one from the other. I stepped between them like a referee, telling them both as calmly as I could to cool down, back off, lighten up. Incredulous, the cop stepped back for a second, the old man grumbling his annoyance, with me or the officer it wasn't clear. Then the policeman said to me, "Boy, you're stepping way out of line. If you don't get your ass out of this, I'm gonna have you thrown in the hole."

"Hey, man," I answered, addressing him as a peer, oblivious to the power of his uniform, "why do you have to pick on him? He's harmless." I was assuming, since the cop was black, that he was more human, more approachable than his honky colleagues; he could be reasoned with. Blacks were the vanguard of the new culture, spiritual and revolutionary leaders. Their historic suffering symbolized most vividly the urgent need for change. The fact that this man was in uniform, unlike the typical redneck piggy, could not negate his humanity.

The old man said, "Stand back. It's not your business." Business.

The cop said, "You're on very thin ice." Just then the door in the corner swung open, and we all started shuffling through. My peaceful intervention had succeeded; the tension eased. The cop backed away as the couple of dozen detainees filed into the courtroom next door. The room was almost empty, the judge nowhere in sight, but seated in the front row of the spectator section, all by herself and visibly distraught, was my mother—or was it my sister—or a woman who resembled them—one or the other—or both.

"Oh, no," I groaned aloud. This is too humiliating. Why do they have to bring her into this? It's just too fucking much. They've gone too far. Haven't we all been through enough?

Immediately a bailiff pulled me out of line and led me back through the holding room, where another cop took over, leading me through a series of echoing corridors back into the bowels of last night's underworld. This time, though, I was taken to a block of smaller cells, four on either side of a little vestibule, a window at the far end, eight cells altogether, one or two prisoners to a cell. The bars of one—third down on the left—slid open with a slam and I was shoved in, alone, the steel clanging shut behind me. The cell was four or five feet wide by eight or nine feet deep. Bolted to one wall, two metal doubledecker bunks, no mattresses. Along the back wall were a sink and a seatless toilet, both stainless steel. The other wall was blank, dividing this cell from the adjacent one. The bars across the front faced the opposite set of cells. Sunlight strained through the barred wire-mesh window. A triumph of functional design.

At first I wasn't sure which was worse, last night's collective incarceration, crowded with smelly drunks in a pen like pigs, or this more personalized facility, not exactly private but at least set apart, with a rack on which to lay one's bones if need be. And this little wing's inhabitants were different: instead of old winos and surly bums, my fellow inmates were flaming queens and strung-out junkies, most of them pressing their faces to the bars to see who had joined their ranks. My arrival was greeted by whistles and appreciative murmurs, and I was flattered to be thought so attractive. But the space was tighter, the reality of being trapped here more intense, and the prospect of release apparently more remote.

A pattern was emerging. Each time it seemed my ordeal was about to end, something went wrong and my fix would take another horrible twist. Like floating and drowning in a dream, or more like falling, only instead of waking up you just keep falling and the thought of hitting bottom becomes more dreadful than continuing to plunge. In order to endure this deepening feeling of doom I still had to see myself as caught in the drama of heroic adventure, a trial by fire, the survival of which would season me for greater deeds. My physical and mental stamina were under pressure. The reality of the revolution I envisioned was far more demanding than simpleminded proclamations of peace and flower power. The world was tougher than I'd anticipated from the privileged perch of my intellectual outlook. The powers that be would not give way so easily. It would take toughness as well as grace, nerve as well as gentleness, to make the world come around. Victory had to be earned, liberation won. Imprisonment was training. Part of the process. A difficult privilege. An honor.

But I had to get out of there.

I might rest a while here, take advantage of the bare bunk, restore my strength. But I was already strong, I didn't feel tired despite not sleeping, and how could I stay still? To rest at this point, lie down and withdraw into an inner world as some of my cellmates across the way were doing—smack addicts, I presumed—would be to concede defeat, a crushed spirit. There was too much going on in here, or nearby, I could hear it—keyrings jangling, typewriters rattling, layers of voices talking, steel doors clanging open and shut, silverware and plates as in a cafeteria ringing with rumors of food, coded messages echoing through the pipes, footsteps sounding up and down the halls—the place was so much livelier than last night, so much less gloomy and subdued, cooking with activity. Surely

I ought to take part however I could. But how? I was locked in. I tested the bars, tried yanking them aside, focusing my powers of psychic light on the act of springing the latches. Nothing budged. "Hey!" I yelled. "Let me out of here! I'm locked in!"

Some of my fellow inmates found this funny. "Hey, he's locked in," one of them mocked, and laughter echoed through the cell block. From that point on, I felt myself the center of more attention than I wanted, but if that's what it took to get me out of here, okay, I'd keep them entertained. The fags and addicts, the cops, the thugs, the trustees, hippies, drunks and bums, criminals and initiates, blacks and Mexicans, revolutionaries and undercover creeps, whatever friends of mine may be in on this, whatever relatives, poets masquerading as police or prisoners, actors improvising outlaw roles, the whole acidified Boschian audience excited to some kind of rolling boil in the steady cacophony beyond my sight would be treated to an irresistible performance, a solo concert of poems and jokes, extemporaneous orations, dramatic monologues, dialogues done in different voices, dialects, accents, invented languages, double- and triple-talk, songs and dances, no turn of phrase unstoned, no move unmade as I raved for my life, my freedom, my release.

I started out with an acceptance speech.

"As long as we're held overboard I'd like the floor. I am the floor, the dance floor, van Gogh's palette, Gene Krupa brushing his skins in rhythm, let's smush these colorfuckers, what do you say? Do I hear a second? Okay, I second myself. And I accept. Mr. Chairman! Members of the faculty! Friends, Romans, cowboys and Indians! Butchers, bakers, burglars and murderers! My fellow delinquents. It is indeed a shot in the arm to be here facing your collective needles. Within sound of our voice are hundreds of people standing in line to receive lunch, a meal they could live without if they'd just rewire. Electricity is the key, naked raw organic electricity. Our future relies on our blind speed traveling through the dark with our lights on 'off,' seeing by vision, and I don't mean television. Whose magic show do you remember first? Go back to that, rewire your understanding, you'll understand. This coven of buzzards hovering over the bones of dead men yet to come is more than crow magnetism, nevermore those ravenoid illustrious pictures of exhibitionism, we're above all that, higher than Hells Angels, doves and hawks put together! We're cleanup hitters, jug band bass players, jugglers, acrobats, troubadours and troubleshooters. Our deeds fly with the speed of drivers on leave or absent without. This is why we're missing. The devout sisters of our womanhood glide on lakes too clear to mirror the faces we'd be pleased to depend on coming off slime in a trench too deep to defend. So violently have our one-nation-indivisibles and our civil wars collided that the very air is a showerhouse, slathering us with the scumbag fallout of sick government. Our cars, black and white and packed like iced patriarchs in postmortem concrete parking structures, are not our own. They don't move even as we drive but we dive in anyway and swim them home like Johnny Wiseass and his mulled appleseed cider high octane ichor, a few sips and you're safer than Curt Flood stealing third. Curt Flood, get it? A quick deluge, a downpour that sweeps you into the sewer like Alice down the rabid hole into the maws of big dogs baring their teeth. Wonder rhymes with under, the way up is the way down. So it's time to get down, brothers—you too, sisters, if you're out there—get down and get up and get lost, shred those old documents, become somebody else. You can sleep like rats, you can soak your sore arms in giant coffee cans of bacon fat, you can go up and down in smoke like a holocoaster and hire real ghosts to ghostwrite your burnt Norton, ashes to ashes, dawn to dusk, graveyard shifts on automatic transmission, the stiffs singing through you, or at least me, which must be why I'm here. I'd like to thank our keepers for the concentrated accommodations, and my family who couldn't be here for the perishables. In closing, keep up the mood music, it's an honorary enigma to be your soloist."

Applause. Catcalls. Dog howls demanding an encore. The walls and steel bars murmured their approval, voices came up through the crapper and I talked back, broadcasting to the entire building and probably beyond, the pipes were a PA system for waves of irrational nonstop eloquence sent out against the tides of babble swooshing shitlike through the vacuum-breakers, the plumbing roared like crowds in football grandstands coming unglued at a bowl game, and I roared back like a sportscaster calling plays and doing color at the same time, quicker on the commentary than Chick Hearn, voice of the Lakers, up to now the fastest mouth in the West but not anymore, I was supplanting the sucker and without the assistance of a basketball game, I could call them as I envisioned them, spinning them out of air, mixing Elgin Baylor antigravity jumpshot metaphors with Dylan Thomas dyed-in-the-ocean tropes, tossing in Rosemary Clooney riffs or Roberto Clemente one-hop on-the-dot throws from deep right-center to home plate nailing the runner and Yeats or Auden stanzas reeled off verbatim or blended with Smokey Robinson lyrics on a song-and-dance option rollout, swiveling my linguistic hips like Jaguar Jon Arnett on a kickoff return, faking one way, pivoting the other, leaving the tacklers baffled and collapsing, turning unassisted triple plays, run-on lines and runaround lawsuits sweeter than Dion and the Belmont Stakes, Triple Crowns crashing as records tumbled and my name went down in the books like Swaps and Nashua, more than mere human heroics, animals too and Willie the Shoe to boot, invoking all crafty masters and handlers of excessive horsepower, Artaud Andretti at the wheel, a Juan Fangio in every pothead, zoos letting loose their beasts and wild poodles running in packs through the suburbs, all unleashed by an oral tradition unraveling out of nowhere, I was the medium, strenuous tongue cut loose with Keats's cherry, Shelley's cloud pouring storms of ro-mantic locusts over the illusion mongers soon to be swamped in torrents of truth and beauty, I was unstoppable, turned on, coming into my own as a dummy for some ventriloquist, saying whatever came, leaping logical chasms, pirouetting on my own pinhead, evoking hoots and groans of awe and approval from my captive audience—"Tell it, brother"—"Can you dig this shit?"—"Let 'em have it, sweetheart"—"Rave, baby"—but nobody came to open the doors, the cell stayed locked. What did they want from me anyway? What would it take to spring these latches, what magic words? Did I have to be an infinite number of Monks composing on penal pianos a philharmonic cure for celibacy? I saw Thelonious nodding at the keyboard that night last summer after the demonstration, stoned at the Both/And club on Divisadero, was he among these legions of listeners I pictured recording my every syllable at this once-in-a-lifetime recital to celebrate my release, my coming out? Would the sordid and gorgeous queers and weirdos welcome me into their underground order once I smashed the record for consecutive non sequiturs, ripping off their masks at last to reveal the faces of the bardic varsity, the all-star poetry squad, the revolutionary word wizards come to power? Where was the climax? How could this rap be brought to resolution? Just when I thought I'd pulled out all the stops, kicked out all the jambs, twisted every oxymoronic mantradiction to its manic maximum, more jambs and stops would kick me, demand more jamming, more scatterbrained scat, like Ella Fitzgerald on an EEG or Jonathan Winters reading Joyce aloud to a nuthouse crowd gone lucid with literary hysteria or Little Richard doing the bob-bop-a-looma-balop-bam-boom on Pat Boone's bones at some revival meeting in Mississippi, an endless reservoir of excess nonsense with sense mixed into it just kept streaming out of me like one long strand of everlasting linguine, a signifying muckrake of a myth-making filibuster that wouldn't say die until these doors, these bars, these walls gave way like Samson's luggage dropped from a plane and I flew free of this joint. Wasn't this epic mouthing off enough? What else could I do to prove my worth as a freelance earthshaker and spearhead? You need to see me naked? Okay, it's not that cold. The clothes were my last layers of separateness, the last line of definition between me and everything else. To abandon completely the old identity, the pretense of a self, the ex-"I" I needed to shuck, meant removing these last shreds of insulation, standing stripped in public in December to declare my independence from the past, walk pure into a new future clothed only in the creative freedom alive in my mind and body. No disguises. Naked powers of vulnerability. Transmutation. Metamorphosis in motion. I took off the jacket, the turtleneck, and T-shirt underneath with BARD embroidered over the heart for my alma mater, then sat on the bunk and removed the boots and socks, wiggled out of my cords and undershorts, and stood there nude behind bars while the inmates around me cheered and whistled, egging me on—toward what? Could I turn myself any more inside out? Trustees from other sections came around to have a look at the naked freak. I thought maybe one of them would spring me. One reached through the bars and gently fondled my scrotum, saying, "Come see me when you get out, honey." Another lit a match and tried to set fire to my hair. A third came over with a glass of water and tossed it in my face. I stood there unfazed, shaking it off—rolling with the punches, as my pop would say—as if this were simply required of anyone doing what I was doing, whatever it was, rising to whatever heights of realization, joining whatever secret society of Homers or home run hitters. It was as far as I could go, it had to work, yet for all the attention I was getting the bars never parted, no Moses-at-the-Red-Sea miracles, I was still stuck and went on wailing as the day darkened, night fell, lights went out, and trustees returned to their cells. Somewhere in there I'd been fed some bread and a cup of lukewarm soup—no doubt spiked with a psychedelic mickey—that might account for my mood, this wired vitality streaked with panic and dashes of hallucinogenesis. Somewhere I'd seen or heard a hint of comic relief for my incarceration, yet nary a squeak or clank of locks uncoupling, not a trace of the keepers who carried the keys or threw the switches of my liberation. I had to keep talking, singing, reciting, chanting, ranting and raving till I got a response beyond the impotent comments and passing pranks of the afternoon. A few voices shouted "Shut up!" but that wouldn't stop me, this was an epic undertaking, muses on the loose with legends to tell, a test of endurance for all of us. We were breaking through into a new form.

Then came the man with the keys. At last. The bars slid back. He took me by the arm, leaving my clothes behind, and walked me naked through the Borges-Escher memorial hallways as if to reverse the course of these last eighteen or twenty hours and have me come out again where I came in. We stopped outside a door of heavy steel with a little shuttered window for a peephole. He inserted a large key, pulled the door slowly open. "In here," he said, pushing me through. Into isolation. The hole.

The cell was smaller and squarer than the one I had just come from; the ceiling was higher, with a single light glaring in the center. No bars, no fixtures, no windows save for the peephole sealed from outside. Dull white walls with a tinge of jaundice streaking their creamy surface. A strange smell, clean and stale at the same time, institutionally putrid, as if layers of fresh paint had absorbed and entombed the odors of years. Cold painted concrete floor with a drainhole in the middle. A naked room for a naked person. Sounds from the rest of the prison—footsteps, jangling keyrings, typewriter tappings, telephones, voices, vibrations droning in the walls—echoed with piercing intensity. Likewise I understood that whatever I said would resound out there and be recorded by the authorities. My disbelief at being here soon turned to claustrophobia, faintly tempered by the expectation it couldn't possibly last, the cruelty must be reaching its climax, the performance approaching its curtain, with some reward for me at the far side of my suffering—a commemorative edition of my collected works capped by this afternoon's magnum opus monologue now being furiously transcribed by a poet-cop whose fingers I could hear on the keys so teasingly close to my confinement, background music for the final phase of this phantasmagoric persecution show. Anything I said could be held against me, but it could also be applied to my poetic credit, included in the text of the historic typescript coming into being as I spoke. But what was left to say? In the midnight chill of my imprisonment, bare-assed, facing the bare walls, talked out all day in hopes of being sprung, my reservoir of inspiration was spent, exhausted, shot. What more could I offer?

I could read the walls.

True, at first glance they looked totally blank. At most the average eye might discern a random pattern of murky swirls tracing the path of the brush that smeared the yellowish-white paint over the lumpy plaster, a texture of careless strokes revealing nothing but the indifference of the painter. But the visionary eye, the Homeric eye, the blind lyric eye of the universal "I" seeking the song of itself—the Whitmanic eye—beamed in on the patterns with lysergic clarity to detect their interior colors, their shivering pinks and vibrating purples and undulating greens and shooting blues moving musically under the surface, and saw the hidden hieroglyphs spelling out stories that lay there awaiting the voice to spring them into the world. This must be why they had put me here, to give the tales on the walls a public sound, to act as interpreter, one final test of my skills as a medium for the muses. I studied the runic figures a while, looking for a way in. The walls' ambiguous textures gradually took on dimension, a relief map or musical score depicting the history of everything, starting with me. If I could articulate this cryptic script, narrate this mural of subliminal signs, my freedom would be forthcoming. Friends and family would greet me outside with wreaths and garlands of congratulation, the police would publish my complete poetry and, most utopian of all, my temporary retreat at Love Creek Lodge would be converted to a permanent community, a true home where all the players in my personal odyssey would gather to live a collective life of shared skills and resources balanced by absolute individuality, our respective uniquenesses perfectly harmonized and complementary in love and work. For all I knew the lodge was right outside—this formidable door was all that stood between me and my revolution come true—this isolation cell was a space- and timewarp transport vehicle, a decriminalization chamber, the hieroglyphic mural proved it, illustrated my journey in the vaster context of universal mythologies, biblical prophecy, panegyric medicine, trans-Zen-dental tabloid journalism, early-fifties radio programs listened to as I drifted into dreamland, *Lucky Lager Dance Time*, baseball broadcasts, television comedies, *The Twilight Zone*, Hollywood movies and their real-life local fallout, English poesy, Motown love songs, rhythms of traffic on the LA freeways, eternal curves of breaking waves where I bodysurfed supple as a dolphin, sports car crashes fatal and otherwise, absent soldiers stranded overseas never to return from nowhere, protest marches and political speeches, aimless roamings and heroic homecomings all were visible in the swirls and bumps and streaks of moving pictures peopling these walls that it was my role to interpret, the naked truth and nothing but, and before I knew what I was doing I was telling the whole story out loud for my keepers to record and the world to witness, oblivious in my naked butt to the fact that I should have been freezing but was instead somehow generating heat by the grace of some inner furnace, saved by my faith in the greater purpose of absurdity where I floundered, swamped but swimming for the sake of something I didn't understand, seeing my fate spelled out by what I could make of my hallucinations, my battered ability to improvise under impossible pressures credible testimony of uncrushed passionate imagination spilling its guts in a gift of trust as typewriters took down everything, the key accompaniment that kept me going as I cast my net for every conceivable meaning I could find in the barren sea of my cell, reaching for the courage to drown despair, find solid ground for myself, find some form of relief, some rest, release. I carried on the narration as long as I could, I don't know how many hours, eventually running out of steam or gas or heat or whatever kept me going in the early morning chill of the hole. *No worst, there is none.* This is what Hopkins must have meant. Comfort, deliverance endlessly receding. *More pangs will, schooled at forepangs, wilder wring.* Like Fay Wray's predicament in *King Kong*: just when she thinks things can't get worse, they do. The bottom keeps dropping away. *Comforter, where, where is your comforting?* Exhaustion was setting in without a hint that I'd succeeded, passed whatever test it was I'd taken, made the necessary impression, said the right words, drawn from my darkness the correct unconscious testimony. *My cries heave, herds long; huddle in a man.* Finally I lay on the floor, curled in a ball like the unborn, clutching myself for whatever warmth my electric blood might be able to radiate, shut my eyes and hoped for the freedom of sleep.

I felt my intestines stirring. My first instinct was to pound on the door and ask to use a bathroom, but something told me that was pointless. I was to have my catharsis here. I squatted over the hole and let loose a frothy flop that came out quick and clean, as if my system understood there was nothing to wipe with and provided for its own hygiene, the body intelligently attending to its needs.

Then keys were coming. *In the jingle jangle morning I'll come following you.* The peephole opened. Eyes looked in. The lock rattled, turned. The door was pulled back. An officer stood there, holding a folded set of green fatigues. He handed them to me. I put them on, pants first, then the shirt, U.S. ARMY over the left breast pocket, where BARD had been on my abandoned T-shirt, just above the heart. So this was my new uniform. The universal unknown soldier. There was no welcoming party, no joyful gathering of family and friends, no cameras to capture my triumphant liberation, no typesetting sergeants to present me with immortal volumes of my works. Two cops walked me past the front desk where I'd checked in night before last. My so-called belongings were gone, my clothes nowhere in sight. My very self was being left behind as we entered the elevator. *Pero yo no soy yo,* wrote Lorca. But I am not I. Or Rimbaud: *"I" is someone else.*

Down half a dozen circles of hell to the basement garage. Into the back of a paddy wagon. Up and out into the gray light of a San Francisco morning. Another long, disorienting ride. At least we were in the world. Eventually we pulled up somewhere, stopped. One cop opened the doors and let me out. I stood on the sidewalk facing a complex of large brick buildings on the hill above me, it seemed to cover several blocks, ringed by a low stone wall topped with a black wrought-iron fence. A school? A hospital? A housing project? Another penal colony for poets?

The officer pointed toward the building in front of us. "There you go." He got back into the van. They pulled away. I stood there barefoot in the green fatigues. Nobody else around.

7

The Healer

San Francisco General Hospital. So I'd graduated from City Prison boot camp, had been issued a uniform, and now I was a general. A general practitioner. Guerrilla healer. Warrior rabbi medicine man. These buildings housed a secret command center for psychomilitary operations. Of course. A natural connection for chemical warfare—medicinal doses of LSD administered to the confused along with the spiritual counsel of those like me who'd mastered the déjà vu in the drinking water, everyone witnessing once again what they thought they'd seen already in a dream. I was a decorated veteran, fatigued by my ordeal but seasoned and stronger for having endured it. It was my duty to assist others in coming to terms with the times. I followed the concrete walkway up to the entrance.

Inside I found a pleasant sense of low-key anarchy. Nurses, technicians, doctors and patients strolled the hallways with no clear distinction as to who was which. I wandered at random through various wards, shoeless, friendly, pausing to chat with whoever needed the companionship. An old woman on a gurney took my

107

hand and looked fearfully into my eyes. "It's okay, grandma," I assured her. "We'll take good care of you. Nothing to worry about." Waves of kindness and compassion overcame me as I met the gazes of people in pain, frightened by the sudden changes of recent days. This is how Whitman served in the Civil War. Isolated as I'd been, I didn't know specifically what had occurred but was certain my experience, if extreme, was typical of the intimate public drama currently sweeping aside all previous patterns of interaction. Some people had trouble absorbing the shock of such radical transformations, the overturning of the status quo raising all kinds of fears and questions. It was my job to calm people down, act as an ambassador of sanity, spread good vibes and await further instructions, it wasn't clear from where. Doctors were paged over the intercom system. I listened for a name that might be mine.

The building got busier as the day went on. I made my rounds like the rest of the staff. The fact that nobody paid me much attention reinforced my feeling that I was in the right place, doing what I was supposed to be doing, even if the goal was ambiguous. Like, was I supposed to report to someone? Were there more specific tasks for me than simply roaming the halls and wards visiting the wounded and helping to establish an atmosphere of normality? I didn't see anyone else wearing this kind of uniform, but if that was supposed to set me apart it didn't seem to matter. The patients, if that's what they were, for the most part welcomed my company, laughing with me at the subtleties of our shared jokes—"Waiting for the Rolling Stones to arrive?" I asked more than one person parked in a wheelchair—and gratefully accepting my earnest assurances that everything was working out fine, the concert was right on schedule. I was developing a bedside manner.

"Can I help you?" a handsome young black woman, apparently a nurse, interrupted my private conference with an old gray man on a ward with rows of beds.

I smiled. "Can I help you?"

"What ward are you on?"

"This one, I guess."

"No. I mean, are you a patient? Where's your wristband? Do you have ID?"

"I'm freelance," I said. "General practitioner. US Army. Unknown." Maybe she had my orders.

She gave me a long look, not unfriendly, did a doubletake on my bare feet, said, "Wait here," and walked away.

After a few minutes she returned accompanied by a large black man—my commanding officer?—in a white outfit crisp and clean as a blank page. He took me gently by the arm. "Come on with me." We rode an elevator to an upper floor, got out, and entered a locked ward. Down a long hallway lined with offices into a large open dormitory. We walked to the far corner of the dormitory, past the stares of the other residents, and my escort left me in a small room, locking the door behind me. Compared to the hole, this was luxury. There was a narrow plastic-coated mattress on the floor, wire-webbed windows that looked down on the street several stories below—it was getting dark—and a small rectangular thick-glass wire-screened window in the door that looked onto the ward. People were watching TV out there. I strained to see if I was on the news. Down in the street, cars were coming and going, lights were coming on, drivers were easing their vehicles in and out of parking spaces, negotiating traffic. From this perspective the rhythms of the movement, the graceful interaction of stops and starts, turns, lane changes, streams of red and white lights, the lights in nearby buildings, silhouettes of people in the windows, traffic signals changing, pedestrians moving through the deepening dusk, reflections off roofs and fenders in the parking lots, looping strings of utility wires and cables linking the power poles, invisible currents shooting through the wires—nervous system of the darkening sparkling city—struck me as a beautiful urban ballet, choreography composed as it occurred with the grace of the new order guiding its moves.

As I admired the view the door opened behind me and an orderly handed me a plastic plate with two thin pork chops and a slice of bread, no silverware. The greasy smell of the chops flooded my face like a storm from boyhood, dinners in the kitchen with Georgia, my other mother. Suddenly I realized how ravenous I was. No time for nostalgia. I sat on the mattress and devoured the meat, growling like a werewolf or a wild dog, shaking my own sense of human identity, wondering if I'd gone beast. Flashes of Fredric March in *Dr. Jekyll and Mr. Hyde*. I knew drugs were supposed to do this to you, but food?

Calmer after this feeding frenzy, I realized my hands weren't covered with hair. Yes, I was still human. But for a minute there . . .

Observing the activity on the ward outside, I saw that while most of the patients were "white," with a few Latinos mixed in, the entire staff was black. And they were cool. Bad. You know, good bad, not evil. There was an ease, an I've-seen-everything style to the way they handled those under their care. A casual understanding. Puzzled as I was by this latest phase of my incarceration, I felt I could trust these keepers. They weren't cops. In fact, if I read the coded messages in the plumbing correctly—calypso telegrams dancing through the walls with the latest revolutionary news—they were Black Panthers, camouflaged in white, and this was their headquarters. Evidently I was a resident head. Honored to be here. I was being groomed for something special.

Next morning I had my first interview. A Panther led me to a small office on the corridor where I'd come in. Behind the desk sat a young doctor, a guy about my age, maybe a couple of years older, who looked like any number of kids I'd gone to high school with—clean-cut, thick dark hair, neatly trimmed mustache, wire-rimmed glasses—a peer. The sight of him gave me confidence. Clearly I was in training for the profession—as other shrinks must undergo psychoanalysis before ascending to the ranks. If I stayed here long enough, they'd make me a doctor. Induct me into the Panthers. It might even be a higher calling than poetry. Not that they were mutually exclusive. William Carlos Williams had pulled it off.

"Good morning," said my interlocutor. "I'm Dr. Spitz."

Dr. Spitz. Give me a break. "What's up, doc?"

"Well, that's what we're hoping to find out. What's your name?"

He had me there. Trying to trip me out with a trick question. Hadn't I abandoned my name with the rest of my stuff at City Prison? If I answered with my ex-name it would be a setback, with who knows what consequences. What *was* my name? "Pickle," I answered. "R. D. Pickle." I'd named myself after my grandmother's best recipe. She used to keep gallon jars of kosher dills brewing in her refrigerator, sour enough when you took a bite to turn your face inside out. My nondomestic mother never learned the secret. Grandma had taken her pickles with her into the other world. Now I was bringing them back. Personified. "The R. D.'s for Ramblin' Dill."

Spitz smiled. "I see. And do you go by any other names?"

"Rambler. Nash Rambler." You are what you do, right? I'd been rambling. Sort of like a folksinger, without the folk. "You know, like Crosby, Stills, Nash & Rambler—Alvin and the Chipmunks on LSD? Or Mick Rambler, the Midnight Jagger? I'm not one of those."

"So you just rambled in here?"

"Right." Spitz was hip.

"Tell me, Mr. . . . Pickle. Or should I call you Dill?"

"R. D. is fine. Research & Development."

"Okay, R. D. What exactly brought you here, besides the rambling? I mean, do you know why you're in this hospital? Did you check yourself in?"

"I'm checking you out. Studying to be a doctor. I figure if I hang out here a while, talk to people, do the verbal jam, improve my powers of improvisation, eventually they give me a haircut like yours, glasses, trim my whiskers, trade me a white suit for this green one, and no more Pickle. Dr. Sambo White, or something like that. Dr. Joe Snow. Isn't that how you did it?"

Spitz was taking notes on a sheet attached to a clipboard. He looked up. "Not exactly." He studied me for a few seconds. I liked his relaxed style. Nonauthoritarian. We were working with a common script, developing our respective characters. "Aside from becoming a doctor, what are your other goals here? Is there any kind of help you'd like from us?"

"I want to help whatever's happening happen. I'll join the Panthers if they'll have me. I've always been on the brown side. Harry Belafonte. Willie Mays."

"Are you taking any medication?"

"Well, until the last couple days I was drinking a lot of water. Before that, grass, hash, mescaline. Nothing exceptional. I'd like a joint if possible, just to take the edge off. But I can handle it. You want me to drink more water? I'd be glad to if they let me at the fountain. Not much I can do, locked off in the corner. Can't complain about the room, though. At least it has a mattress."

"Do you know why they locked you in the corner?"

"I thought it was the presidential suite. Nice view. Especially compared to my previous accommodations. My guess was that I'd been promoted."

"Your previous accommodations?"

As if you didn't know. "I was a guest of the poetry police. A pickle in a pen. Or a pen in a pickle. Advanced composition workshop, Underground Man Chair, double solitude and the vicious circus. Intensive care. I passed with honors, right? A spitting image. Or should I say Spitzing? You know why I'm here, doc. I'm ready to be a healer."

"A good ambition." He nodded, smiling. Then he gave me a long earnest look. "Feel like telling me your real name?"

"Feel like telling me yours?"

"Spitz. Daniel Spitz."

"Dr. Spitz. That's really great. I can dig it. I'll be Dr. Kissez. Dr. Singz."

"It's hard for me to help you if I can't call you by name. It's so impersonal, you understand?"

Maybe I was being too eccentric, too individualistic. Too much a solo act. "Mann," I said. "Joe Mann." That generic enough for you?

Spitz looked skeptical. He set down his clipboard. "Okay, Joe Mann. Let's talk some more tomorrow. We're out of time for now. You can go back on the open ward. Just be considerate of the others."

We stood up, shook hands. I dug this doctor. Enjoyed our interview. Would like to have talked much longer, but I understood. We both had business to take care of. I stepped out into the hallway and made for the water fountain. Took a long drink. Felt the psychedelic refreshment percolating through the capillaries. This place was okay. I wondered how long I'd be here before trading in the pickle suit for a lab coat. I wondered what kinds of tasks the Panthers would set me.

Roaming the open ward within the confines of this so-called psychiatric unit, I made the acquaintance of Ramón Cordero, a young Chicano who assured me he was Jesus Christ. He had with him a photo album, which by way of documentation he displayed for me page by page, narrating each snapshot with an elaborate history of each friend and family member, all adding up inexorably to his identity as Jesus. Okay with me. I didn't follow all of his reasoning, the unconscious connections that led to his conclusion, but I appreciated the creativity of his tale. Like me, he was on some sort of mission—there were so many paths through the historic thicket we were in—and I could relate to his crusade, even if I wasn't sure what it was. We were both on spiritual journeys, had the same brown eyes, took our storytelling responsibilities seriously, understood we were part of a larger process. Ramón was a little strange, but he was gentle. One of the new breed.

Then there was Blue Jay, who presented himself as a Vietnam veteran and gravitated to my uniform, asking if I was a vet. I explained that I was a recent recruit in the consciousness brigades, had just completed my basic training, and would soon be receiving orders.

"I never really went to Vietnam," he said. "But I got napalmed anyway. Ha ha. Combat live on the tube was enough for me. Kachooey! Nuclear bazookas, booby traps in the brain. I'm fragged, man, friendly fire. My girlfriend's pregnant with a burning baby. Look what they did to my hands." He held out his hands. They looked regular but were trembling violently. "They wouldn't take me. I wasn't conscientious but they objected. They said I was unfit. Sick. My blood wasn't good enough. Fuck them. I'm no hippie, no commie, no turned-on turned-inside-outsider, sure I love-hate my country, contradiction's the name of the game, look at the news, count your own bodies, it's obvious. God, they're killing my babies. I can't save them. I can't serve." He started crying.

"It's okay, man," I reassured him. "They also serve who only stand and wait."

"Are you a spy? Neither am I. Ha ha. We're in this jungle together, aren't we, soldier? Nixon's gonna get us out. Ha ha. Nixon and Bob Hope and Lee Harvey Oswald."

Blue Jay's bright blue eyes and pink-white face reminded me of Jimmy Terwilliger, a high school friend of mine who'd joined the Marines as a way of avoiding college. He was a fuckup, a social and scholastic disaster who never accomplished anything in the highly competitive halls of Beverly High. He was a very sweet guy, not mean, not petty, not a suckup for popularity, just a bone-skinny, sincere, friendly, not particularly talented kid who hung around on the outskirts of the same crowd I frequented in my attempts to be "in"—guys with cool cars and cute girls who threw the parties everybody but the totally out-of-it brains and the really bad hoods wanted to be at. Jimmy figured if he enlisted, trained as a medic, served overseas and survived, he'd be able to come home and become a physician, something he'd have no chance of doing otherwise.

The night before he was to ship out for Nam—this was late '64, when I was a freshman at UCLA—he came by my house with a locked metal box, to be opened only "if something happens to me." He was wearing his dress blues, spiffy as the duds of any marching band, complete with white cap, gloves, red trim, gold buttons, everything but the sword. He looked beautiful, blue eyes ablaze under the crew cut, pink cheeks flush with the thrill of impending adventure. "Steve," he said to me, indicating the box, "when I get back we're gonna have some fun with this stuff." His handshake as he left was firm and cool, smooth as a piece of sanded hardwood. I'll never forget the look in his eyes. He'd done something with himself, had beaten the rest of us lazy shmucks to the real life beyond our enclave.

About six months later I got a letter from Jimmy enclosed with a note from one of his buddies. He'd been shot out of a helicopter near Danang as they flew in to evacuate the wounded. "Jim had a feeling the night before and asked me to send this letter if anything happened. He said you were a good friend and would know what to do."

Jimmy's letter looked as if he'd written it in the dark on a bumpy surface. "Dear Steve, I've got this funny feeling, so just in case, I want to let you know I always thought you were a good guy. Our friendship has meant a lot to me. I've seen some things over here I wish I could tell you about. You always were one guy I knew was not a 'mental midget.' Good luck with everything. Take care. Your friend, Jim."

I pulled the metal box out of its hiding place at the top of my closet and pried it open with a claw hammer. It contained dozens of tubes of morphine, Thorazine, other drugs whose names I didn't recognize, hypodermic needles, a sex manual, three or four pornographic paperbacks, and hundreds of rounds of ammunition for a high-powered rifle or machine gun.

As I listened to Blue Jay carry on about his noncareer in the military, his eyes shooting out blue flames of light through the greenish shadows of the psych unit, I kept seeing Jimmy's face superimposed over his, hearing Jimmy's voice, flashing on Jimmy's absent presence, as if Blue Jay were the negative space created by Jimmy's death, a deranged reversal of the self-respect I saw in Jimmy the night he shook my hand for the last time. I felt dizzy, nauseated by the mockery, half-encouraged by the thought that maybe Blue Jay was Jimmy come back to make fun of himself in the good-natured spirit of the wise, ego free, above and beyond the fiasco of his tragedy. Ha ha. A sobering joke. But what is death?

At night I observed the Panthers making their rounds, exchanging subtle signals and information under the guise of managing the ward. Staff would arrive on their shifts wearing black leather jackets and berets over the hospital whites, then switch into nursing or orderly mode, going about their duties as if there were no revolutionary agenda, as if this weren't the nerve center for operations that were changing the course of the culture. Blacks were assuming leadership in social and political styles as they had for years in music and sports, creating forms for the rest of us to imitate and emulate, absorb and adapt as we rejected the useless honky structures inherited from our parents and the putrid powers that be. These folks moved with the grace of cats, maintaining an easy control over their domain, keeping the patients or trainees in line with minimal effort, guiding us with hints and by example. This is the way the world is turned around.

But what if the struggle were not yet won? What if the other authorities—the pigs who had the guns—besieged this place or raided it in pursuit of the insurgent leadership? Had I become a target? A hostage? Bait to be thrown to the Man as a diversion? Had my imprisonment been just such a ploy, manipulation of a helpless head for reasons of realpolitik? Was I a bit player instead of a star in a story whose larger plot I couldn't fathom? These questions haunted me as I watched from my cot the comings and goings of my guardians, whose own motives and maneuvers I trusted but whose power in the bigger picture wasn't clear.

After all, I'd been brought up by black people. As a child I'd spent more time with the servants than I had with my natural parents. Endless hours in the kitchen with Georgia or Ruthie or Henrietta as they cooked and I listened to their stories and engaged them in discussions of everything from baseball to gospel music. Hours in the car with Leonard or Jerome or Walter as we ran errands for my mom. When I was little, three or four years old, Leonard would take me out with him at night and sit me on the bar in his favorite dive instead of babysitting me at home. Georgia, who raised me till I was seven, was more a mother to me than my mother. My folks were out building their underwear empire, flying around the country and the world on business, while I stayed home with the help and got darker and darker. I was as "colored" as the next person. That's what qualified me for this position.

A janitor appeared nightly on the ward, an old Chinese guy everyone called Flow Joe, who provided understated comic relief by rhythmically mopping the floor from one end of the unit to the other, nodding and smiling and mumbling some unintelligible mantra that the "psychiatric" staff cracked jokes about. But I in-tuited Flow Joe to be a much more significant player than he ap-peared, a transmitter or interpreter of cryptic communiqués from who knows where, essential messages of ancient wisdom or psy-chic transmissions from distant fronts. Lao Tzu's mouthpiece for line-of-least-resistance enlightenment. *I know the value of action that is actionless.* Such seemingly lowly figures were the secret force of the future, people who understood the underworkings of the world and had the power to reroute its energies.

By day, volunteers like sweet Sue came to see us. Sue, a whole-some blonde resembling Pam, my last ride back from Altamont a few days before in her pink VW, was a bright and cheerful girl who'd show up a couple of times a week to visit with us, walk us around the grounds, show us that kids like her were also part of the plan to undermine the crumbling order. All kinds of people had their roles to play in the raceless culture to come.

Every other morning or afternoon I'd be called in to talk to Spitz or some other young doctor assigned to see how I was doing. I'd always ask right off if I was a doctor yet, and the doc would find that very entertaining even though I wasn't being funny. If they weren't making me a doctor, and soon, what was I doing here? As the days wore on the novelty wore off and it began to feel like just another prison. I had more freedom to move around and talk to my fellow inmates, but if I became too talkative, engaging them in conversations that got somebody upset or agitated, I'd be removed to the corner room or to the solarium, a much larger space with windows all around but equally set apart from the rest of the population. And some of the people on the unit were so paranoid that if I even approached them they'd freak, warning me to stay back, threatening physical violence if I tried to relate. How come they weren't the ones who got locked away? Why was I being picked out for special punishment? I was getting tired of the rules and restrictions, wanted more inside dope on Panther procedures. The outside world was reeling with major changes and I was stuck in a place that, interesting as it was in many ways, felt removed from what was really happening. Maybe I wasn't ready for Flow Joe's wisdom. I wanted to check back in at the lodge, find out what was going on with Nona, see what Julie was up to, track down April, talk to my friends, take more control of my daily life. I wasn't suited for this kind of institution.

The holidays were approaching. Red and green lights glimmered across the cityscape visible from the windows. One day someone set up a Christmas tree, for chrissakes, in a corner of the open ward. I hated Christmas, the greediest, phoniest festival of all, the most reactionary, most materialistic ritual, the glorification of commercialism—and here it was invading what I thought was a cauldron of radical resistance. Maybe these people really were crazy. If so, what was I doing here?

One afternoon about ten days into my residency, during a conference with Spitz, I asked if I could use the phone. With his permission and a borrowed dime I dialed Misha's number. His deep voice answered on the third ring.

"Hi, Misha? It's me."

"Steve! Where are you?"

"At County General. Psychiatric unit. Can you come get me out of here? I'll explain later."

"Sure. Give me about an hour."

Misha showed up at the locked door to the unit, the most welcome sight I'd seen since the bread van picked me up in Livermore. Spitz came out to speak with him.

"You know this fellow?"

"I sure do. He's an old friend."

"Are you willing to take responsibility for him?"

Misha looked at me, my uniform, his eyes twinkling with good-humored curiosity. He looked at Spitz. "Yes, I am."

We both signed a paper, I thanked the doctor for his hospitality, said so long to the Panthers on duty and to Ramón and Blue Jay and the others, and we were out of there.

"What happened to you?" he asked me in his twinkly, mischievous way as we headed for his car. "Where'd you get that outfit? Where are your shoes? Julie's been calling me every day for a week. She's freaked. Nobody knew where you were."

"It's a long story. Can we stop and pick up some moccasins or something? My feet are freezing."

8

Love's Body

Sitting across from me at the kitchen table of his apartment on Dolores Street, just a couple of blocks up from where I'd been busted, Misha rolled a joint. We were kicking back after a savory fried-rice dinner Gloria had fixed to celebrate my return from zones unknown, and now we were sipping spearmint tea by steamy windows and relishing the pleasures of friendship. The tea was hot and tangy, sweetened with honey; my feet were snug in cheap new moccasins from a Mission Street discount store, and the army fatigues felt comfortably rough and warm. Gloria cleared away the plates. Misha passed me the skinny reefer—no bulges, thin as a knitting needle—his distinctive rolling style. I took a toke, filling myself with the cheery spirit of the season. I felt a soft light enveloping us. A moment's peace at last.

"Beautiful, isn't it," I said, handing the joint to Gloria; she declined and I passed it back to Misha.

He knew I was talking about more than the marijuana. "Hard to beat," he grinned. "How come you didn't call me sooner?"

I shrugged. "I thought if I stayed there a while they'd make me a doctor."

His dark eyes narrowed into crinkly slits as he laughed. He pounded the table with his palm, the tea mugs jumped. Gasping and wheezing through his wild beard, he tilted backwards in his chair, wobbling precariously on its two legs, then righted himself, regaining his composure.

I laughed along with him. "I'm not kidding. The doctors looked just like me, only straight. I could do what they were doing—sit around asking questions, have conversations—it's the oral tradition, my specialty. You should've heard my epic raps decking the halls of the Hall of Justice—I thought they'd give me a Pulitzer or something. Make me a Yale Younger Poet." I'd already given a condensed account of my fifty-odd hours behind bars. "I figured at least they were trying me out as an on-the-spot historian. You know, like someone who could call the apocalypse play by play."

Misha relit the joint. His Giacometti frame was loose, clearly relieved to take a break from law school studies. On the floor in the corner lay a pile of magazines and newspapers. The latest *Life* had a demented-looking hippie mug on the cover. Gloria picked up the magazine and excused herself, saying she was going to read in the other room, but Misha stopped her. "Wait a second. Did you see this? This is the guy they say masterminded the Sharon Tate murders in LA last summer. Charles Manson. Looks a little like you, doesn't he? They say the dirty work was mostly done by a bunch of stoned-out girls. Mondo creepo."

I looked at the picture. Manson. Man-son. How did people come up with these names? Son of a man. No relation, I hoped, to Joe Mann, one of my psychiatric pseudonyms. Those eyes, wired into voltage higher than mine, blazed darkly off the page as if from a distant star. I flipped through the article, unsure how to take it—as news, fiction, countercountercultural propaganda? Like the moon landing, it begged credulity. "It's enough to give hippies a bad name" is all I could say as I handed it back to Gloria.

She said, "If you ghouls will excuse me, I'd like to read about it too," and took the magazine away.

"It's weird," I said to Misha. "When I was in the Fillmore the other night—the night I was looking for you—this lady calls me 'Zodiac.' And that guy getting stabbed at the Stones concert. And these freaks on the rampage in LA. It's like people are taking Jagger literally—*I'll stick my knife right down your throat*," I did my Jagger imitation—"instead of literarily. I mean, knife-wielding flower children carving up movie stars? Somebody's got to be making this stuff up."

"Yeah: God. It's the Big Fiction, Steve. Like Mailer said, history as a novel."

"Life as legend. I'm hip. It's been happening to me."

"Entertainment as insurrection. Manson was supposedly inspired by the Beatles. Acidic messages in the music."

"Maybe he should have taken a few Rolaids."

"How about you? How are you feeling? Ready to face the outside world again?"

"Absolutely. I feel really good. Ready to improvise with any reality. I've been tested, Misha. I've learned more in the last two weeks than in a year and a half of grad school."

"So you want to go back to Santa Cruz?"

"Can you take me?"

"I have a ton of studying to do. But I could put you on a bus. Maybe Julie can meet you. We should call her."

On cue, the phone rang. Gloria picked it up in the other room. It was for me. My estranged wife.

"God, what happened to you?" she started out. "Where've you been? I've been calling everybody every day. Nobody knew anything. I'm so exhausted, I've been so worried, I thought you were dead, are you okay, the people at the lodge hadn't seen you, I even tried calling April, nobody had a clue, are you all right?"

"I'm fine. Try to take it easy. I'll tell you about it tomorrow. Can you meet me at the bus station?"

"Yes. Of course. Of course I can meet you. When? What time?"

"I'll check the schedule and call you back. I'm okay. Don't worry.

Just a little adventure. Give me a few minutes and I'll tell you about the bus, okay? Everything's all right. I'll call you right back."

We made the calls, made the arrangements. Misha and Gloria set me up with a quilt on the living room couch and we all retired. I lay there sleepless, wrapped in the quilt, consciousness charged, not reflecting exactly but reviewing in speeded-up time what I'd been through, the strange encounters, trials, conversations, hints and signs of what I was getting into, what I was into and going deeper with no clear destination. Was my journey ending or just beginning? Surely the revolution was still on. I had a role. Through the wall I could hear the sounds of sex—Misha and Gloria were getting it on, a pounding, groaning fuck that went on forever, bringing me into the apartment again, its funky smells and sensations. I imagined their climax to make it happen. Sex was so messy and scary, it complicated everything. Created such disturbances. But it was also the only source of peace.

"You sure you'll be all right?" said Misha as we rolled to a stop in the loading zone of the Greyhound station.

"No sweat. Thanks for coming to my rescue."

He handed me bus fare plus a couple of extra dollars. "Be careful. Stay out of institutions." His eyes gleamed, ambiguously ironic. "Call if you need me. I'll probably go to LA and see my dad for Christmas, but otherwise I'll be home. I'm way behind on my reading. Law school sucks."

"Later." I slammed the door of his rusty blue '58 Chevy, the *Chula Chonga* he called it for its resemblance to the lumbering wrecks that Mexican farmworker families navigated through the Salinas Valley. It handled like a tank. We'd driven it to Los Angeles last summer. Coming back at night up 101 we'd witnessed a fatal crash at Death Curve just above Gaviota and later been caught in a tumbleweed storm in killer fog north of King City, Misha asleep in the passenger seat and me steering with all my strength as the weeds stampeded across the road like buffaloes lurching through our headlight beams, a driver's nightmare but no big deal for Misha, who merely grinned in that cryptic way of his when I told him we'd almost died.

The *Chonga* pulled away and I strolled luggageless into the terminal, felt people's eyes on me, tested the ticket clerk's telepathy by walking up to the window and standing there waiting for him to issue me passage to Santa Cruz. When he played dumb I nodded knowingly and said where I was going.

"One way?"

"One way." The only way, way of the unwinding road, wherever it goes. Even the clerk was a philosopher, an accomplice guiding my mysterious journey. What was that Merry Pranksters slogan? Either you're on the bus or you're off the bus. Everyone was tripping now. And I was on.

Bayshore Freeway, headed south this time, leaving the driving to them, gazing out the window at the paved landscape, eyesore of SF International sprawling into the bay, huge jets soaring off spewing their fumes. The driver took the San Mateo exit and proceeded down El Camino Real, stopping in every suburb on the peninsula. The ride went on as if forever, this is eternity, passengers in the half-filled bus assuming a universal anonymity, we were anyone and everyone, no one, one another, rolling along together, separately, kept apart by the seat backs and some unspoken one-way rule of mutual reserve, sitting in rows, facing the same way, grammar school students subjected to a lesson, gear-grinding math or music of the diesel drone. I listened to see if it scanned, searched the sound for poetic undertones. Nothing came clear. Was this one of the institutions Misha had warned me to stay out of? Some kind of mobile nuthouse? Jails on Wheels? I'd seen those buses with the sad-faced inmates staring out through the mesh. This didn't seem to be one of those, but who could tell for sure, everything was changing. I felt restless, torn between staying "on the bus," which presumably would take me to Santa Cruz and Julie, or bolting for the exit at the next stop and god knows what.

As we pulled into Palo Alto I chose to play it safe, making a conscious effort to keep my seat. My body stayed there, by the window, about halfway back on the left, while the psyche, like Blake's "Mental Traveller" in that mind-blowing poem we'd vainly tried to analyze in one of my graduate seminars, wandered through many a thicket wild in search of something I couldn't begin to name. Quite a few riders, maybe a dozen, got on. One was a young woman, possibly a student, who placed her canvas shoulder bag and an instrument case—it looked like a mandolin—on the overhead rack and took the seat next to me. She was wearing blue jeans and a burgundy sweater and carrying a paperback copy of *The Possessed*. Once she was settled in and we were back on the road I said to her, "Are you really reading that, or do you just carry it around to impress people?"

"Most of the people you see on the street are not impressed by Dostoyevsky." She said "you see" as in UC, it sounded to me like a subtle putdown of California's public university system, where peons like me got our education while the cream of the elite ascended to Stanford. A clever cookie, quick on the draw. "Are you really in the Army, or are you just wearing that costume to depress people?"

"Actually I'm missing in action. I wear this outfit to confuse the authorities—parents, professors, all commanding officers. I bailed out of the ivory tower without a parachute. Landed in a barrel of pickles. It greened me. Good camouflage, don't you think?"

"Some camouflage. You look like what's-his-name. Charlie Manson. AWOL. If I were you I'd shave and get a haircut. You could get busted."

Who is this person? A guardian angel? Secret agent? For whom? What does she know? "You could use a haircut yourself. Let's ask the driver to stop at a barbershop. We can treat each other to a trim."

"No kidding," she said, looking at me through rimless glasses, thick brown hair draping over her right breast in a braid. "How come you have that uniform on? You're not in the Army."

"You're right. I got busted. Lost my clothes in jail."

"Busted for what?"

"You tell me. Disorderly consciousness. Disturbing the police. Aggravated surrealism. Unsafe changes."

Her eyes stayed on mine, amused, intrigued. As if to herself she muttered, "What a trip."

"Yeah, well, anything to serve my country." We both laughed, I'm not sure at what, exactly, maybe just relief at the ease of our rapport, delight in the hip swiftness of our banter. I liked her. She was sharp. An improviser. "What about you? What's your trip?"

"I'm a musician. Songwriter. Been holed up with my band at our place in Portola Valley. All-woman group. Psychebilly bluegrass. The Kickass Sisters. We're not into the flower-child thing. Mostly just playing music, tightening our licks. Writing songs. Laying low before we get famous."

"How come you're on the 'hound?"

"Oh, I'm paying a courtesy call to my folks for the holidays. They live in Los Gatos. Where're you headed?"

"Santa Cruz. Under the Boardwalk. I'm subterranean homesick. A poetry addict. My head's a jukebox of modern verse. I might have been a musician if not for baseball. Was always a banjo hitter anyway. What do you think of Dusty Essky, the balalaika-picker from St. Petersburg?"

"He's got me in his clutches. Really messing with my head. Roman Polanski meets the Rolling Stones, if you know what I mean."

I knew what she meant. Pity and terror in the public domain. Stories within stories. Everything returning to the theater of current events. This is the way the world was spinning, intricate swirls of interconnection, no individual detail without its web of associations, a natural continuity yet dangerous too in its revolutionary resonance, multiple waves of implication spreading with every beat, with every note, with every word and image, and we were in it and of it, riding this wild world's allusive waves, up to our wits in history, in fiction. Everything burned with meaning, glowed, radiated risk and urgency, a kind of magical contamination. Anything you touched or said or did could make you a mutant, a monster, an immortal. You lived and you took your chances. My companion understood.

Los Gatos. Bobcats. She closed her book, gathered her gear, said, "See you 'round," and was gone.

The bus climbed into the mountains, winding slowly over 17, hugging the right lane. My eyes drank in the sunny green light angling across the hills, that naked solstice low-lying sunlight sharpening everything it touched. Even in the crummy stuffy bus poisoned by its own sick fumes I could taste the freshness of the sky outside, the redwoods whipping by. This is what I'd missed. The earth and its air, breathing and growing. Emanating serenity. For now.

Julie was waiting for me at the Front Street station, the black Porsche parked across the street. She looked superb, bell-bottom hiphugger denims, green turtleneck sweater to match her catlike eyes, fringe jacket just like mine (now warming some smack addict in City Prison), brown zip-up boots on her long legs. Long wavy hair, parted in the middle. Our problems aside, she was one fine woman. Impossible to ignore. And she knew it. She'd calmed down since our telephone conversation. Was playing it cool. We hugged, crossed Front, got in the car. She drove.

"You want to come home with me?" she asked.

"Sure. For a while. I've got to go up to the lodge at some point soon and check on my stuff."

"I was up there a few days ago. Everything was fine."

She'd taken over. "Okay. Anyway." No point in discussing that.

We drove to the cottage in Rio Del Mar, our honeymoon house, now hers, where the freight train rumbled by twice a day, and at night from the back porch you could hear the surf breaking half a mile away, just beyond the sewage treatment plant. The hillside between the house and the railroad tracks was covered with hot-poker plants, those asparaguslike spears with red-orange tips, and pampas grass, which resembled wheat—or what Julie and I thought wheat should look like, never having seen it except on television. For the first time since our split I was her captive, counting on her for transportation, grateful that she was there to bring me back into the familiar world after my excursion in purgatory. I gave her as simple a synopsis as possible of where I'd been, what happened to my clothes and my car, and why she hadn't been able to track me down. "I went down the rabbit hole. Through the looking glass." I had to translate my story into code, testing her revolutionary intuition, scoping her responses for what she knew. I felt uneasy trying to explain what I didn't fully understand myself, and wasn't sure what to reveal of recent insights. Julie was hip but she was so excitable; I wasn't convinced she could process the information.

A lot of my things were still at her place; I'd change clothes there. Before I could get the fatigues off we were kissing, cupping each other's buns, teeth clacking, pressing our pelvises together. We paused long enough for her to put on a record. Quicksilver Messenger Service, one of her favorites. *Oh God, pride of man, broken in the dust again*, my cock throbbed to the rhythm and she was all over me, licking and nibbling, rubbing her gorgeous body against mine, both of us naked on our former bed, clothes thrown everywhere. Over the past few weeks I'd felt that sex, omnipresent as it was, was somehow secondary to the larger changes embracing all of us, that erotic energy propelled our lives but sexual fulfillment was a detour or distraction from the absolute transformations at hand. Except for an occasional encounter with Julie, I had almost transcended sex, more by circumstance than choice—it just didn't seem convenient or available—no woman would have me, or I couldn't stay in one place long enough to have a woman. But people were doing it, I knew that much. Jesse and Tanya at the lodge on Thanksgiving, giving that exhibition for their guests. Misha and Gloria last night. And now it was my turn, our turn, sliding through Julie's wetness with an aching load, her legs locked on mine, hips whipping, rocking together, brimming, both of us sobbing with relief as the tears flowed, juice and come poured forth in hot sweet spurts, the pungent funk of our sex surrounding us, an aura of gratitude and satisfaction.

After an interval she said to me, "Stay, Stephen. Let's get back together."

Oh, no. This isn't what I had in mind. "I don't know. It may not be possible. There's so much going on. I need to get my orders."

"Orders?"

"I have responsibilities."

"What do you mean?"

"I've been called up. Drafted. Active duty. Dig?"

"What? *Drafted?*" She didn't dig.

"Everything that's been happening to me. It's basic training. Like when you're tripping or really stoned and somebody puts on Zappa or Lenny Bruce or *Blonde on Blonde?* A major mindfuck, only more intense. Way more important, not just in your head but in the world. Haven't you noticed? You were the one who said so first: 'Sixty-nine is gonna blow everybody's mind.' We're chosen."

"What for? By whom? How do you know?"

"That's the whole thing: it's a riddle. A mystery. Slow-motion revelations. We have to pay attention. It's happening, everything's coming together. We're part of it."

"Maybe you should talk to Dr. Hopkinds. Just tell him what you've been through, what you're thinking."

"Are you kidding? Lightning Leo? He's probably CIA. He'd just pump me full of Stelazine, neutralize my native electricity. He hates me. He thinks I fucked you up. Anyway he's your shrink, not mine. Last thing I need is a shrink. That's why they let me out. I'm lucid. Clearer than ever. Pure."

"But look what's happened to you. You lost your car. You lost your clothes. You lost *me.* Everything that defined you is disappearing. Who knows where you'll get locked up next time, or what kind of shit you'll wander into. You can't live like that. It's dangerous."

Fuck. Just when I thought I'd cut my mother loose I'd got this other one. "I can take care of myself. You don't know what I've been through, how I handled it. I don't need the protection. People are looking out for me. The bus, the clothes—I'll deal with them, don't worry."

"But I can help. I can help you, like I always have. I'm the one you can count on, not these mystery people. Two years ago when you were sick at Bard, didn't I fly back there and nurse you?" I'd had an attack of gastroenteritis that almost did me in. "I got you to the hospital, didn't I? I emptied your fucking urinal. Sat by your bed with an eye on the IV, watching to be sure it didn't run out and stop your heart with an air bubble. Even your mother almost blew it on that one. You could've died. Haven't I proved my love? So what if you fucked that little bitch. It doesn't matter. We're married. You're mine."

It was a rerun of the argument she'd made last January for getting married in the first place. I lay there entangled in guilt. I'd gone from public institutions—the university, prison, hospital—to intimacy central, the slammer for runaway husbands. Wedlock. It was ridiculous to think that I was free when I was dependent on her for getting around, for shelter, for sex. Even for comradeship. She was the closest thing I had to family. Who did I know that I could really talk to? April, but she was shacked up with her physicist. Misha, but he was in San Francisco struggling through law school. Who was the new Norm? And who and where was Norm? Did he exist, or had he too been an agent playing a role, an angel—or a phantom, someone I imagined, filling my own need. I couldn't respond to Julie's words. She had me. I was stuck. Domesticated. What was happening to my epic quest? Penelope's web was a trap.

She said, "You got so skinny. I'll make sandwiches."

We ate. Smoked. Talked all afternoon. I showered. Put on some other clothes. Faded cords, old desert boots, longsleeve T-shirt under a loose cotton sweater with a burnhole over the heart. My black denim jacket would replace the hip fringes. A spiral of de-stylization. I was adaptable.

In the morning we drove to the mountains together—I took the wheel this time—to check in on my cabin at the lodge. Julie had been there in my absence asking about me, so everybody knew who she was, no introductions needed. But if anyone was there they weren't visible. Nona's car was parked in front, but she must have been in the main house, maybe upstairs. We drove back and parked by my cabin. There was no lock on the door, but everything looked exactly as I'd left it, books lined up on the mantel, sleeping bag on the bed, typewriter on the table, Altamont newsphoto tacked to the wall, clothes in the dresser drawers. Julie said I should collect my things and move back in with her. How would I get around without the bus? It was getting colder. Rain was overdue. These cottages weren't meant for winter habitation. Living up here would be a major hassle. Musty dampness. Mud. And isolation.

I walked back out on the porch. Stood there surveying the terrain. The two big maples were naked now, dead leaves littering the ground. The air was good, filling my lungs with fresh green power, always a perfect complement to the pot. While Julie was inside puttering, organizing my stuff to get me moved (on the assumption I'd see it her way), two kids, young boys about eleven or twelve, came up from the riverbank and past the cabin. Their names, if I recalled correctly, were Bobby and Tim—they'd stopped and talked to me a few times before on the way to or from the river, friendly little guys. They seemed to admire my so-called lifestyle, a hang-loose longhair rocking on the porch. Who knows what the appeal was? Maybe they wanted to smoke some dope. I never offered them any, but that didn't discourage them.

Bobby was bigger and a little older. He walked right up and said, "Hey, merry Christmas." I'd forgotten it was the twenty-fourth. Tim echoed the greeting.

"Yeah, what do you know." The Christmas bullshit made me sick.

Bobby reached into his pocket. "This is for you. We found it stuck in a tree over by the river." It was an old Case folding knife, probably a fisherman's, about six inches long, heavy, its antler handle engraved with a roughly handcarved V. Somebody's initial or V for victory. Peace. The boys' gift to the hippie in residence. As if they knew I'd lost my knife in jail.

I felt its weight in my hand. Opened the slightly rusty blade, still pretty sharp but well worn. Smelled the steel, intoxicating in its strange cold way. "Wow. Thanks, guys. Have I done something to deserve this?"

"We thought you'd moved away," Tim said. "You haven't been around."

"Yeah, we missed you. You're the coolest old guy we know around here. We thought you'd like the knife. See? It has the peace sign."

I was speechless. Touched. Julie came out on the porch. "This is my wife. Julie. Bobby and Tim. Check out this knife they gave me." Julie examined the knife and handed it back, not overly impressed. Tim and Bobby gawked.

After an awkward pause, "Well, merry Christmas."

"Yeah, merry Christmas. "

"Same to you, gentlemen. Thanks a lot. Hope you get some good stuff. Stay loose." They walked on out toward the road. I handled the knife a few more seconds, admiring its feel, its heft—its character—then slid it into my jacket pocket.

Julie stroked my hair with her left hand, pressed her breasts against me, said in her sexiest voice, "It would be so easy to move you out of here. Come on. Happy Hanukah." Kissing me on the mouth, she slipped her tongue in, slid her right hand down my sweater, under it, into my beltless pants. My penis stood at attention. Everything else went soft.

I said, "We should discuss this."

"Let's."

We went inside for a conference, closing the door behind us.

9

Return of the Native

By the time we emerged from our meeting it was midafternoon. Nona's car was gone. I left her a note saying I was back, I was okay, I'd be paying rent through January but probably wouldn't be spending much time up here, just using the cabin as a retreat, a place to write, to think. Julie had persuaded me to give our marriage, such as it was, another shot.

That night we were expected at a Christmas Eve tea party at the home of Carolyn Corday, who lived with her kid, Siddhartha, in a cottage in Beach Flats. Carolyn was smart, independent, tough and cynical—qualities Julie admired. She'd gone back to school after a few years in the world to get her undergraduate degree. Julie'd been hanging out with Carolyn quite a bit since my departure, and also with Carolyn's boyfriend, Kevin Bannister, one of my colleagues in the literature program, a blue-eyed Brit with low-key charm who rolled his own cigarettes in dark brown paper and from whom I'd now and then scored some grass. Both Carolyn and Kevin seemed to me more experienced, older, more worldly than I, and in their company I felt naïve, as I had with my older brothers and sister.

But now I'd come of age, seasoned for having survived the past few weeks, not just survived but thrived on the ordeal and risen to new heights of psychodramatic accomplishment. A party at Carolyn's was cool with me.

It was an intimate group; the four of us and another couple, Ray Martino and Lena Holloway, graduate students in history of consciousness, sitting on pillows on the living room floor around a low cable-spool table covered with jars of green and red candles, a secular concession to the holiday. No sawed-off tree, but sticks of jasmine incense mixed with cigarette and marijuana smoke perfumed the atmosphere. The Beatles' *White Album* on the stereo, the volume low so as not to disturb the two-year-old asleep in the back bedroom. Carolyn brought out a pot of hot tea and a heaping basket of homemade biscuits, butter and honey, knives and spoons and mugs. A wholesome spread, and sensuously tasty, textures and flavors of the butter and honey mingled with the flaky dough of the biscuits filling the mouth with a drippy sweetness completed by the heat of the jasmine tea. Candlelight, the ember of a circulating joint, good-looking faces in a circle.

"Polymorphous perversion," said Ray. "Like Nobby Brown says in *Love's Body*. The intellectual's duty is to reintegrate the brain with the body, resensualize the intelligence, but most of the people in the HistCon program, faculty and students alike, are totally stuck in their heads. They practically can't think without first detaching their heads. It's tragic. Because they go to all this trouble to get Brown up there and they completely ignore his philosophy. Fools."

"Graduate school should be a series of orgies then," said Kevin. "Am I correct?"

"Absolutely," Ray said, laughing.

Julie said, "It sounds beautiful, but how can you think with the body, how can you reason when the body has its own logic, it takes off, sexually I mean, on its own trip, takes you into another place, a whole different state."

"That's the idea," said Lena. "Philosophy should be as transcendent as sex."

"For the eye altering alters all," I quoted Blake. "What you see is what you are. The people in HistCon, Lit for that matter, can't think past their own sexless brains."

"I think brains are very sexy," said Carolyn, whose striking feature was her gaze. Her eyes pointed in different directions, so you couldn't tell what or whom she was looking at. Her dancing glance ricocheted off the rest of us. "They're so contoured and convoluted."

Lena agreed. "All those nerves all over the body picking up all those sensations and shooting them up the spine into the brain—it's like a river of continuous orgasms."

"The brain is electric," Ray said. "It's a transformer and a generator, and a receiver too, like a radio."

"The body's electric too," I added. "Walt Whitman said that."

"I dote on myself," Julie quoted Whitman. *"There is that lot of me and all so luscious."* She picked up my habits, my poets, would sometimes cite them during our fights. Now she was doing something else, suggesting something.

Carolyn's peerless eyes were playing games. As she acted the role of hostess, seeing to the needs of her guests, she scanned the group in a way I found unnerving, as if, no matter whom she focused on, her other eye was aimed at me. It was a turn-on, but also intimidating. Something was brewing here, I was getting hard and worried at the same time. What had Carolyn and Kevin and Julie, and maybe even Ray and Lena, been doing together in the months since I'd moved out? Sexual juice suffused the air. *Do you don't you want me to make you,* Ringo chanted from the stereo. Was this supposed to turn into a six-way swap, mixing and maximizing our fuck fantasies, our brilliantly polymorphous perversions? Or was I the pervert, reading sex into everything—paranoid, repressed, obsessed, possessed.

"Does anyone need anything?" said Carolyn.

"I need to get some air," I said, turning to Julie. "Let's go to the Boardwalk."

"The Boardwalk's closed."

"All the better. We'll have the place to ourselves. Excuse us." I got up.

"What was that about?" she asked as we strolled down Riverside toward the rollercoaster. "Is something wrong?"

"I just got restless. I couldn't sit still. Carolyn was looking at me funny."

"Carolyn looks at everybody funny. That's the way she looks. She's cross-eyed. You just have to get used to it."

"But it was more than that. What have you guys been doing?"

"What do you mean?"

"I mean you and Carolyn and Kevin."

"I don't get it."

"Bullshit. You know what I'm talking about."

"If something's bothering you, just say it."

"I am saying it. What kind of sex scenes have you been having?"

"How can you be jealous after what we've been doing the last two days. I'm yours. Isn't that obvious?"

"That's not the point. Are you telling me that you and Kevin and Carolyn haven't been getting it on? That something wasn't supposed to happen tonight? Why was everybody talking about polymorphous perversity and looking at each other like that?"

"Where have you been? I thought you were an intellectual." She wasn't denying anything.

"Are you saying nobody was looking at each other that way?"

"What way?"

"A sexual way. You know, bedroom eyes."

"*The eye altering alters all.* You're the one with the bedroom eyes. You're projecting."

We walked onto the Boardwalk, under the enormous darkened frame of the Giant Dipper, one of the last wooden coasters still running, though not on winter nights. Whipping along its rails, climbing, plunging, banking, was a therapeutic thrill, a cathartic mixture of fear and fun, shades of eternal teenage summers. Now shut down. How could we be adults? "Who else have you been fucking?"

"Stop it, will you? You're the one who's been coming around for a quick fuck and disappearing. Can't you accept the fact that we're back together?"

Maybe I couldn't. I didn't know where I was supposed to be or what I ought to be doing. At least in jail and in the nuthouse I'd had the sense I was there for a purpose, was being readied for some grander role. The very strangeness of everything, that feeling of a dream, made it all mythic in some way, much bigger than just my life. But this? Tamed into domesticity again by wild girl-woman? A woman whose body did the thinking for both of us. What about my soul? Had my adventures been hallucinations? Impossible. These last weeks had been the realest time of my life. My soul had begun to come into its own. Jail, County General. Unreally real. Superreal. Realer than this empty amusement park. We walked down steps and onto the beach, across the expanse of sand to the surf's edge. The water settled my mind, rushing up the packed sand and retreating. Julie lit a roach and passed it to me. We sat down, quietly smoking, facing the bay. Stars overhead. Sea lions barking under the wharf. I sucked in gulps of iodine-rich air, pulling the darkness into me, I wanted the night inside me, wanted to vanish into it, be absorbed in its immensity.

"Why don't we take a trip tomorrow?" she said. "Drive down to LA. Visit people. Maybe your parents have forgiven us."

"I don't know. Even Don never eloped." My oldest brother had been the family delinquent, but I was surpassing him in all-around badness.

"But couldn't you make up with them?"

"How, by divorcing you?"

"Maybe you're right."

"Even that wouldn't do any good," I said. "Don was a rebel, but in that fifties way, just out to have a good time, race cars, get laid. I've got the big ideas—they hate that, it's a threat. *Yonder stands your orphan with his gun.*"

"Well why not just go in there and blow their minds? If they're that hostile, what's the difference? *When you ain't got nothin' you got nothin' to lose.*" Julie could always match me in a bakeoff of Dylan's Familiar Quotations. I loved that more than I hated it. She could be me in an emergency.

"I guess we could just call them and say we're coming. What are they gonna do on Christmas, tell us to get lost?"

"It'll be trippy, that's for sure."

"I bet we could stay at Don's place." When he wasn't directing television shows or exploitation movies he liked to go deep-sea fishing. His home in Benedict Canyon was the perfect bachelor pad, a cottage hidden on a little dead-end street. "You could try to see your dad, if he has the time. And your mother, if she's not too smashed."

"Or we could just trip around the city, it doesn't matter."

It doesn't matter. That was her mantra when things went bad. Dad and mom for both of us were bummers. "Yeah," I said. "We'll blow their minds. Return of the freaks."

"Revenge of the runaway sex fiends."

"Dangerous fucking maniacs."

We laughed and laughed, pleased with the prospect of putting our parents through changes. Suddenly life seemed promising again. Full of possibilities. An open road.

It was on Christmas morning, two years earlier to the day, that I had been driving west on US 66 out of Winslow, Arizona, in this same black '64 Porsche coupe en route from school in New York state to a reunion with my family in Los Angeles, accompanied by fellow student and poet Jean Claude Roget, a wild Belgian adventuring in America, when at seventy miles an hour the car hit a patch of ice, skidded into a roadside snowbank and rolled three times, leaving the Porsche crumpled but right side up some twenty yards from the road and, miraculously, neither of us hurt. Either that or we'd been killed instantly, coming to in some other dimension identical to this one. The moment I knew I'd lost control, hands on the wooden steering wheel and right foot pressing the accelerator, I felt completely relaxed, giving myself over to fate with a so-much-for-that attitude, nothing-I-can-do-about-it-now-so-what-the-fuck. The car's back window had blown out and our books and manuscripts were scattered over the snow. Crashing, I'd followed in the fading skid marks of both my brothers—Don, who'd survived three flaming wrecks as a professional racing driver, and Hank, who'd rolled *his* Porsche, a '57 Speedster, on Mulholland Drive when he was sixteen, almost killing his best friend, Danny Hirsch—not to mention my mother's head-on with a telephone pole on Airport Boulevard in '54, totaling her brand-new fire-engine-red Oldsmobile Rocket 88 convertible and throwing my sister Gena and me to near-oblivion on a nearby sidewalk. (I'd been spared injury in that one, I was sure, by the silver St. Christopher my second-grade girlfriend, Ursula Rank, had given me.) Smashing up cars was a family tradition, but somehow we were all still alive. Don was supposed to have been riding in the most famous Porsche of all, James Dean's '55 Spyder, the day Jimmy died on the way to the races, but Don had changed plans at the last minute and driven with another friend, Conrad Rothmeyer, boy millionaire, in his Mercedes 300 SL. *I ain't goin' down to no racetrack to see no sports cars run*, Dylan had sung long before his famous motorcycle crash, *I don't have no sports car and I don't even care to have none.* Maybe he was alluding to Dean, or unconsciously foreshadowing his own disaster, but Bob and I differed on sports cars, I loved the speed, and its feeling of freedom, the edge of danger, the distinction of surviving if you were lucky enough to walk away from a crackup.

This mental collage of automotive associations, cultural legends and personal calamities, especially my Christmas flip in this very car, which placed me in the same league with Dean and Dylan, swirled through my consciousness as Julie and I tooled south on 101. The car had been resurrected by Junior's Body Shop in Flagstaff, and now I was at the wheel again, back in the saddle, wildly alive, fueled by the aromatic marijuana and the cool clear California end-of-the-year air, privately inspired by my fantasia, finding its imagery exhilarating, its accident-wracked violence bracingly mythic, as if imagining terrible events—or recreating them in memory—could prevent them from actually happening, or happening again. Jeffers had said of his stormy poems, his "bad dreams," that they'd been written "to magic horror away from the house," like gargoyles staring down the scary powers ruling the coastal ranges. Jeffers country was just west of us, over the Santa Lucias, and my thoughts served a similar purpose, chasing the phantoms from this splendid day as we sped through the fields of the Salinas Valley.

I couldn't speak to Julie of these things. Her brother Tony, after all, when she was just a child, had steered his Triumph into an oncoming truck at a blind curve on Sunset Boulevard. To her, the mention of catastrophe was the same as making it happen. We could discuss all sorts of exotic topics—alchemy, astrology, parapsychology, psychedelic chemistry and its applications, witchcraft, black and white magic, occult sexual practices—but to raise a subject that might apply to what was going on here and now in any way that might invoke the darker powers was forbidden; she was too suggestible, it freaked her out. If I were to note, even casually, that this was the anniversary of my Christmas crash, a date I looked on fondly as a personal milestone, she would protest, Please! Don't talk about it. Do you want to get us killed? So I kept the visions to myself despite my desire to share them and the attendant happiness I felt to be free again, driving, digging the sky, the surrounding hills, the windbreak rows of big eucalyptus, the speed, the smells of the rich soil, the humming feel of this precision machine sailing over the road. I kept alert for the highway patrol, constantly checking the mirrors, those cats could be on your ass in a second, you never saw them coming, just all of a sudden that hot red light behind you, pulling you over. The last time I'd been stopped was in my bus, a few days before Altamont, a "routine check" of license and registration. The clean-cut picture, I explained to the officer, was taken while I was still doing business with barbers. "I can see that it's you," he said. "There's love in your eyes." That's what I mean about the CHP. These motherfuckers were so bad, trained to deal with the most horrible emergencies imaginable, able to handle those souped-up black-and-white sedans with the grace of race-drivers, skilled with deadly weapons, they could afford to be gracious. But when they nailed you, they nailed you, politely writing out the ticket. However beyond the law I knew myself to be, I didn't want to press my luck today. I had no ID with me, for one thing, and wasn't sure how to explain that my wallet was still in jail in San Francisco. All I needed was to have to call my parents to bail us out in Santa Maria. Or maybe they'd just throw me in the madhouse at Atascadero. *Atascadero*, literally a place to get stuck, like Mobile with the Memphis blues again. Even LA would be preferable to that. I wasn't ready for another incarceration. I had to kill my parents first, as one of the current gurus had insisted. Figuratively, of course. I guess. Just cut them loose. I hated LA but it was part of me—driving was more natural than walking—and hard as it was to face the native city, it got my adrenaline going. Same for my lame-duck parents. I looked forward to the encounter.

From early on my mother had told me, in her warmly ironic way, that I'd been "an accident"—not that I'd been conceived in love, in the spontaneous embrace of passion, but that my existence was accidental, like her crashing the Olds. Soon after I arrived she had her uterus removed. While they were away on business I was bonding with the help. Maybe that's why the civil rights movement meant more to me than the Six Day War. Despite the lectures I heard on the importance of Israel, whose emergence as a state more or less coincided with mine as a person, I found it easier to identify with the "colored people" I knew than with my alleged relatives in Zion. Unconsciously I felt more black than Jewish, a faith the family never practiced anyway in any sincere form. Don, calling me Pancho, reminded me I might be Mexican. And another running joke in the family, that every fourth child in the world is Chinese, that I was the fourth child and therefore Chinese, increased my special sense of otherness, my place of alien honor as the late arrival. In elementary school I was a discipline problem, bored with conformity, impatient with the childishness of my peers, shooting off my mouth to set myself apart, demonstrating that the art of the wisecrack was more entertaining than the dull routine of obedience. For such disruption I spent hours standing in the hall, exiled. Notes were sent home to my parents, and the citizenship part of my report card had many checks in the "unsatisfactory" column.

Mom and Dad couldn't understand it; after Don's early adventures in delinquency, Hank and Gena had been model children. What had gone wrong with me? Later, in high school, my mother seemed pleased with my early attempts at poetry, but she was busy with her own nervous breakdowns, my father was distracted by his collapsing business, and we all sort of lost touch with each other. The closest we'd been in recent times was the night four or five years ago, when I was still living in their house and commuting to UCLA, that they'd expressed concern about my moodiness and I thanked them for their interest but explained there was no point (I couldn't figure out the meaning of life), and walked out the back door and burst into sobs. I felt miserable not only for my own distress but because they couldn't touch me, just like now, but now it was with more rage than grief because we'd written each other off. I'd resigned myself to exile. There was no going home, they'd moved to another house, but somehow I needed to connect with them, everything was so unsettled, unresolved. At my age Don was off racing cars, Hank and Gena were both married and starting families; just because Julie and I hadn't gone through regular channels with a straight wedding, why should that make us outlaws? The hassle, the hypocrisy, the formality, the relatives— that's what we were trying to avoid. Why should my parents care? Julie's mother and father didn't object. Going to see my folks was either a way of making peace or telling them face to face to fuck themselves.

We pulled into their Bel Air driveway early that evening, dusk just fallen, fuchsia light flaring in the west. We'd called that morning; they were expecting us. My mother opened the door, elegantly informal in a long satin shift, deep blue, presumably to match her mood. A stiff uncomfortable smile, a peck on the cheek for each of us. She led us across the teak floor of the living room, Julie's boot heels hammering the planks, into the den, where my father was watching the news and smoking a cigar. The smell of his Grade A Cuban contraband reminded me of autumn Sundays in the fifties, driving in his Caddy to the Coliseum to see the Rams, thick smoke pouring out the wind wing, our happiest—practically our only—moments together, just the two of us, sharing the aroma of quality tobacco.

He had on his soft yellow cashmere cardigan, white dress shirt buttoned at the collar, brown gabardine slacks, silk socks, Italian loafers, casual at-home attire. His bald head fringed with silver gray gleamed under the light of the table lamp. He took one look at me—my hair, my thickening beard, my baggy clothes—and said, "What do you want to look like that for?" It wasn't a question but an accusation.

"What do you mean? Look like what?"

"Like some kind of criminal. A madman." He was talking about Manson, the hippie from hell.

"Same reason you look the way you do." I wasn't eating any of this abuse. "There are plenty of criminals in business suits, you know. There's blood on the hands of a hell of a lot of respectable-looking executives, not to mention the fucking president and most of the politicians."

"Watch your tongue, boy."

"You watch yours, *man*."

Julie was cowering in the doorway, ready to flee, and my mother was standing half-paralyzed, unable to seat herself or speak. My father, the meek one, was on the offensive, and she, the articulate matriarch, was speechless. However many tranquilizers she'd taken to brace herself for this get-together, it wasn't enough.

I wasn't doing so well myself. My legs were trembling. My chest was holding back sobs. "Jesus, Father, I walk in here and the first thing you tell me is that I look like shit. Thanks a lot. I look the way I look, can't you accept that? I'm not a fucking banker."

My mother attempted to intervene. "Stephen, don't use that language in this house. It may be right for you and your friends, but not here."

"Right. And it's okay at the racetrack, huh, among all those colorful characters my dad collects, but no fucking at home. I'm sure you guys don't. Why do you want to make me feel like shit? Oh, sorry. Drek, how's that? Nice Jewish word."

"You know, Steve," my father said, trying to sound reasonable, "you dress like that, the hair and everything, the beard, and people are gonna get a bad impression. This Manson character, his picture's everywhere. You don't want to be confused with him."

"I'm not confused. That's their problem. People are so hung up on appearances. Just because somebody has a nice neat haircut doesn't make them respectable. And who wants to be respectable anyway, what's to respect? Why be a hypocrite? I don't give a fuck what people think. Don't give a darn, I mean."

"But darling," my mother, motherly, "you used to be so well groomed, you were so handsome. Why do you have to be so wild looking, hiding behind all that hair?"

"I think he's handsomer now," Julie interjected, "long hair and beards are beautiful. It's a new style. It's natural."

"It's all so superficial," I said. "What difference does it make? Some guys think it's embarrassing to be bald. I don't see you wearing a hairpiece, Pop. People should feel free to be the way they are. That's what makes horse racing, right? It's a free country—or it's supposed to be, according to the big liars."

"You bet it's a free country." He leaned forward for emphasis. "You think they'd let you look like that in Russia? It's because of this free country that you can live the way you are. There are guys your age right now fighting to keep it that way. Or maybe you'd rather surrender to the Communists."

"Oh, man, don't give me that shit. Are you saying the Viet Cong are building tunnels under Bel Air, just waiting to take your TV set away? Or are you scared of the spades coming up from Watts to loot the lox from your refrigerator? Just because you were free to make a million doesn't mean the system's fair. I'm not playing the same game. What the Vietnamese want to do with their country is their business. I don't suppose you'd want me dying over there?"

"Of course not, dear," said my mother. "But someone has to stand up for freedom. It's no secret the Russians want to conquer the world. Better to stop them in Vietnam than here."

"That's what we're doing," Julie said. "Standing up for freedom. Freedom to be ourselves, to not be conquered by anybody's propaganda, to do our own thing."

"Nixon's the last person I'd take orders from. At least Ho Chi Minh writes poetry."

"And Hitler was a vegetarian," my mother said cuttingly.

"Don't worry, Mom, I'm no vegetarian. But by the haircut logic, if I were, would that make me Hitlerian? I mean if it's not the Commies it's the Nazis, for godsakes. Or the blacks, or the Manson gang. You people must be scared shitless. Even harmless hippies like us are a threat. And the funny thing is, we are. There's a revolution going on, right here, and it's not little guys with rifles and black pajamas running through the jungle. It's in the air, it's consciousness that's changing, and there's not a fucking thing you can do about it." I turned to Julie. "Let's get out of here." Then to our hosts again. "Thanks for the warm welcome. Merry Christmas."

Julie's boots rapped out the rhythm of our retreat. I slammed the front door, the brass knocker banging one extra time with the impact.

A minute later we were speeding east on Sunset. I was fuming. "Can you believe that motherfucker? Telling me I look like a murderer? What do they think they're trying to turn me into? Fuck. I drive four hundred miles to try to relate to them for once and they treat me like a war criminal. What's the fucking use. What are we doing in this town?"

Julie, who'd been on the verge of tears, had steeled herself. "It doesn't matter. They're so far out of it they'll never find their way in. I think you're right. They're scared of you. Did you see the look on your mother's face when she opened the front door? She looked like she'd seen a ghost."

"Or creatures from some cruddy lagoon."

"Forget it, it doesn't matter. Here. Try this." She handed me a joint. A couple of tokes and another mile or so and I was cooling out. The dry Los Angeles desert winter air streamed through the car, soothing me with its soft electricity. We'd entered Beverly Hills, silently passing the curve where Tony had died, her brother's memory flashing through us both, someone I'd never known but felt I had by way of my own brothers, either of whom could easily have perished in similar crashes. Mangled bodies and blood seemed so incongruous with these manicured streets, fragrant, meticulously landscaped, depopulated. Immaculate lawns and imported shrubbery blindingly green under the burglar-discouraging floodlights of lavish homes. Colored Christmas lights lined some roofs or draped an occasional tree. Peace on Earth. A star is born. "Let's get something to eat. I'm starving all of a sudden," Julie said.

Hamburger Hamlet was reliable. The red carpets, red upholstery of the booths, soft-but-not-dim lighting, black waitresses and cooks in black-and-white outfits (always a white cashier) made for a comfortable setting. An orderly establishment, efficiently managed, almost serene no matter how crowded it was. We seated ourselves in a cozy booth, looked at the menu. Our waitress was a woman who'd worked there forever, Jeanette—they all wore name plates—she'd served me scores of burgers since I'd started coming here as a kid. I was glad to see her. "Jeanette!" I said. She looked different, older, more weary than she had a few years ago.

"Hello. Nice to see you." Vaguely. No telling whether she really knew who I was.

"How've you been?"

She looked at me as if I'd asked the worst possible question. All she'd wanted was to take our order, and I'd gotten personal. She held my eyes with hers. Her voice was flat. "I lost my son in the service."

"Oh." I held back a surge of tears. A surge of guilty rage. "I'm sorry. I'm really sorry." How could I be alive when her son was dead? How could any of us? Who deserved to live anymore when all these kids were *wasted* for no reason?

Jeanette smiled understandingly. "What can I get for you?"

Don was out marlin fishing and had left us the key to his house in Benedict Canyon. Eleven years older and always off adventuring one place or another, he was the brother I didn't see much of as I was growing up. It was Hank I followed around and copied when I was little—Hank or the help. By the time he was seventeen Don was racing cars, moving in faster and faster circles, running with Jimmy Dean, Steve McQueen, and other Hollywood speedsters. I was thirteen when Hank got married, moving out to start his own family, which left Don as a much more promising hero to emulate through adolescence. He was the one with the glamorous international itinerary—"fast cars, fast girls," as he put it—roaming the country and the globe on the professional road-racing circuit, earning a reputation as one of the fastest drivers alive. Little Lead Foot or, since Jews were so unusual in that field, The Rapid Rabbi. He'd met his best friend, Conrad Rothmeyer, heir to the Rothmeyer department store fortune, at a school for asthmatic boys in Arizona when they were kids. Conrad, too, used to live in the canyon when he and Don were young playboys back in the fifties, around the time I'd begun to regard them both as handsome examples of what it meant to be a man. Conrad had been married to the actress Jean St. James, whose presence next to me as a guest at our dinner table sent rushes of sexual excitement through my pubescent loins, her perfumed breasts practically poking me in the eye as she passed the applesauce. Don and Conrad, as they came and went from our house with their gorgeous cars and gorgeous women, assumed near-mythic stature for me and my high-school friends; they were the kind of men that we could only dream of being.

Letting us stay in his place, sleep in his bed, was a brotherly gesture of solidarity, an acknowledgment that I'd come of age, was stud enough to shake the sheets with the big boys. Julie was a beauty worthy of his attention—she still bore a scar on her right calf from the exhaust pipe of his motorcycle—and perhaps he was taking vicarious pleasure in imagining what we were doing together here. But even as Julie and I sexually exorcised our anguish over the day's frustrations, temporarily obliterating the all-pervasive universe of fear and death, the distance between Don and me had grown unbridgeable. I was no longer in awe of his powers as a playboy, had been long since disillusioned with the Hollywood mystique, had seen the emptiness and desperation behind the great-looking faces of some of his friends. Despite his encouragement to write for the screen, I wanted nothing to do with scripts or producers or starlets. The world was much more serious than anyone in movieland wanted to acknowledge. The inward motion of poetry, its soul-changing revolutionary imperative, was pulling me deeper and deeper, into *what* I didn't know.

Don's bed took up most of the tiny bedroom. Lying there with Julie, both of us too distraught to sleep, exhausted from dope and sex yet wired from the evening's encounters, I tried to let my brother inhabit me, let his physical, who-cares attitude overcome my excessive reflectiveness, wipe out introspection, bring me around to my senses, the feel of the clean sheets, smell of Julie's body, shadows of moonlit foliage pressing against the windows. But nothing was simply what it was, the leaves and vines were faces and hands, a tangled jungle of writhing humanoid shapes crawling over each other to smother us, crush us, implicate us in every prevailing atrocity, innocents being slaughtered far and near, we the victims, we the perpetrators, possessed by poisoned blood. Just uphill from here Gena and her husband Dave and their three kids slept behind locked doors, and less than a mile from there as the raven flies Hank and his wife Carol and their four kids were securely tucked away, living in a world of station wagons and new appliances and life insurance while only a few short months ago, a mile down the road and up a hill, Sharon Tate and her friends had met their killers on a quiet night, one of the dead a man who had run with and styled the hair of some of Don's showbiz cronies, all the connections much too intimate, my father's judgments, Jeanette's dead son, my black car parked outside like a coffin, private and public histories haunting my every breath and heartbeat. What were we doing in this doomed town?

Two long days of driving around and getting stoned, fragmentary meetings with friends and family, awkward abbreviated conversations as if talking across vast distances, we were coming from another world, speaking another language, our points of reference didn't match up, Julie and I in our smoky cloud encapsulated in the little coupe inventing a floating island of necessary mutual understanding by virtue of our helplessness to deal with anyone else. Thrust together, as in the days before our marriage, like stunned survivors of some calamity we never saw until it hit us, we clung to each other, endured the strain of our shaken psyches and agreed to keep each other going. Physically the city was not so bad, the four-day holiday weekend thinning the traffic and the smog, and we kept moving, driving, letting the radio serenade us with reassuring rock'n'roll, stopping to visit, paying respects, explaining we couldn't stay, escaping, staying on surface streets, no freeways, tracing a zigzag path across a landscape I knew by heart like lyrics to songs I'd gone to sleep with as a kid, the vast violated terrain spreading every which way in endless replication, a monstrous anonymous embrace of aimless chaos. Something was keeping us here, we couldn't go home until we'd finished our business, but we didn't know what that was. We had to complete some cycle, close some circle, tie a final knot.

The house on Camden Drive, where I'd lived for sixteen years, remained to be revisited, even though it had been torn down to make way for whatever was under construction; I needed to see it, know that it was gone, my childhood razed along with it. Camden was the town Walt Whitman died in, only now did I understand this rhyme between his life and mine, how it had marked me early on as his offspring. Lined with magnolias, the street on spring nights reeked with their intoxicating smell, and I would breathe deep, thinking as I walked, the only pedestrian for miles, looking in windows for signs of life, wondering. That house held so much of me, I hadn't wanted even to drive by and find it vanished, supplanted by some new reality. But that's what I had to do, shut the gate on that kid, slam it in his face, kill him, just like I'd killed my father and mother. My ex-ID was still in San Francisco. For all I knew it had been assumed by some other inmate. Who we all were was in a state of flux. Now I could face my death fearlessly, we were constantly reincarnated, I could kiss my ass good-bye like a schoolboy ducking under his desk to dodge the H-bomb and still survive to describe it, I mean I could die and live on in other forms. So Sunday before splitting town we drove down to Camden, where both of us had lost our virginity one night in high school when my folks were away. Maybe we could screw in the ruins.

We pulled up across the street and parked. The same magnolias, same thick-trunked towering palms where the front yard used to be, now littered with lumber and concrete blocks and lengths of pipe and rolls of roofing and stacks of ceramic tile. There were two big houses in progress side by side, packed together like boxes on a supermarket shelf, where the old place had once stood alone with plenty of room around it. I remembered pictures I'd seen of the neighborhood in the twenties, aerial shots that showed the house standing all by itself amid vast undeveloped blocks, one of the original Beverly Hills mansions, in the colonial style, white and stately. So much for history. We walked across the gouged dirt lot that used to be a lawn, stepped over and around the construction materials and miscellaneous debris, and through the skeletal frame of one of the new houses. We found a spot to sit on the foundation, facing the back yard, almost unrecognizable now except for the drained swimming pool and the big fir tree that had stood guard over my room when I was little. Julie lit up a ceremonial joint.

In its way this presumably familiar terrain was stranger and spookier than anyplace else I'd been this month—Altamont, jail, the hospital. "I can't believe it's gone," I said. "I lived most of my life here, almost everything that happened to me happened here, I can't believe they just took the place apart, it's like it never existed."

"It's a gift. You can be in the present now."

"Memory sucks." I started crying.

She put her arm around my shaking shoulders, set down the joint, and tried to wipe my tears. A feeling of love and gratitude welled up in me, she was all I had left, a comrade, we were stuck with each other.

Behind us we heard a car pull up and stop. The Beverly fucking Hills police. Julie instinctively brushed away the roach. The cop got out of the car. We let him come to us. "This is private property," he said.

I've got more right to be here than you do, asshole. "Yeah, we know. You see, I used to live here, and, we were just, sort of, paying our respects."

"We came on Sunday," Julie said, "so we wouldn't bother anyone." She smiled at him.

He was disarmed. Almost apologetic. "Well, you best get going now."

The three of us made our way through the scattered scraps and stacks of building materials back out to the street. He warned us about trespassing, got into his patrol car and drove slowly away, checking us out in his mirror as we climbed into the Porsche.

"Good thing he didn't ask for my ID."

"Good thing he didn't search my bag." We laughed. "Let's get out of here. This is getting weird."

"No shit." I started the engine.

We drove directly west to the nearest freeway—405. North-bound.

10

Cat Man

Back in Santa Cruz on New Year's Eve, which we celebrated by barbecuing a couple of steaks in the fireplace, getting stoned and listening to records, we received a visit from the Rum Tum Tugger. The Tugger was a local stray, more likely runaway, handsome mongrel tomcat, a collage of gray and brown and white and black short smooth fur that rippled rhythmically as he cruised our back porch for handouts. We'd fed him some tuna one afternoon several months ago, and ever since he'd come around regularly, a reticent and claustrophobic visitor, probably abused or locked in by his previous keepers and therefore shy about getting too close or coming indoors. Eventually he'd grown to trust us, and now he would come inside for a while provided we didn't shut the door behind him. He was not ours, but in a way we were his, and when he showed up at the kitchen door we welcomed him by opening a can of cat food. As he slinked around the kitchen cautiously checking us out after our absence, he eyed me with the expression of someone who understood me, was like me, cool but edgy, ready for a quick getaway. I studied his moves.

But I was running out of things to run from. Nor could I go home, wherever that was. The LA trip had been a disaster, shattering any idea I had of reconciliation with my history. The lodge was not really fit for habitation now that winter dampness would be seeping through the cardboard walls of the cabins. The cottage in Rio Del Mar where Julie and I now tried to reconcile by staying high and fucking our anxieties away felt to me like a temporary shelter, a tent of last resort in my manic wanderings. I was finding it impossible to sit still, except when rolling or smoking a joint, I had to be moving, preferably on the street. But without wheels of my own, yoked to Julie in the Porsche, incapable of taking off without her, I was stuck. Which naturally increased my claustrophobia, cranked to unprecedented sensitivity by the recent stay in City Prison. But tonight was a time to kiss off the decade, to exorcise the old year and its psychic pollution of body counts and bad faith and governmental gangsters and ecocidal oil spills and airplane highjackings and promiscuous tear-gassings and acid-driven massacres and Chappaquiddick. A time to blow smoke in each other's mouths and supersede the news and history itself with music and sex and the sweet green leaf, ritually transform public pain into soothing waves of intimate sensation taking us someplace else. Until the tone arm lifted, clicking us back, revoking whatever reveries.

I rose from the big floor cushion to change the record, felt sickly dizzy for a flash and passed out backwards. When I came to, a few seconds later, Julie was leaning over me, dread in her eyes. "Are you all right? God, you almost hit your head on the table. You could've killed yourself."

"Yeah, sure. I just, uh, got up too fast. I'm fine."

"That was so scary, Stephen. Tugger went darting out the door, you freaked him completely. Don't move. Just lie there a minute. Are you sure you're okay? Don't try to get up."

Julie calmed down after a couple of minutes, and I got up and took my place on the cushion. Strange to just faint like that, blood draining out of my head as if somebody'd pulled the plug. The year was ending with a slam, like the front door at my folks' house, and I guess my head got caught. I was troubled that the Tugger had split. He was a comforting touchstone, nonelectronic animal reality, music without the sound. I missed him. So much easier to relate to than a wife, though Julie's gray-green eyes were also remarkably feline. The cat in his way resembled us both, like a child.

Without knowing why, around midnight I went to my jacket hanging on the back of a kitchen chair and pulled out the Christmas knife the boys had given me. Julie was standing in front of the stereo, about to flip the record, and I approached her, opening the blade, and with my left hand held her gently by the waist, pulling her to me as she turned around, and with my right hand held the open knife against her face. Neither of us spoke, but we looked in each other's eyes with the deepest, tenderest bond, some understanding way below consciousness, a shared submission to terror. She was so beautiful, with those Cherokee cheekbones inherited from her mother, her smooth olive skin, straight nose, soft lips—lovely and vulnerable with the knife on her flesh, surrendering serenely to my power. That's what I wanted to know, I suppose, that she trusted me, and after an eternal few seconds with the steel pressed to her face and my loving gaze locking hers with a bottomless longing, I lowered the knife, and stood there looking at it, and after another long silence, said, "I was going to stab you with this knife."

She didn't say a word, just looked at me.

"I was testing you. You trust me, don't you."

"Of course. Can you put the knife away now? You're scaring me."

I folded the blade, set it down next to the stereo. Then, while we still stood there, held by the spell of a new and spookier intimacy than we'd known in all our years as lovers, I kissed her, breathing the comfort of her heavy smell, our tongues blending, hips pressed tight, I was so high, I felt such tenderness, I wanted to cry, my cock was throbbing, her tears ran into our mouths, we melted, slowly slipping to our knees on the rug in front of the free-standing sheet-metal fireplace, undressing each other, caressing, licking, biting, conquering the year's agonies with the force of our gorgeous muscles and skin and spit and all our dripping and shooting juices.

Once we'd erased ourselves and everything else, I lay there floating in space, face up on the floor, letting the grain of the open ceiling boards come through my closed eyelids mingled with the patterns of blood vessels pulsing and twisting in serpentine swirls. Julie got up and moved around in the room, and next thing I knew the front door opened, her voice said, "Bye," the door shut, the Porsche started, and she was gone.

I rolled over on my stomach, the shaggy rug scratching my naked torso, and took a cat's eye view of the room, tacky vinyl floor over plywood, costly and useless electric baseboard heat, cheap veneer paneling, hollow doors—a summertime guesthouse like so many other student rentals—nobody ever thought they'd be staying all winter. Even year-round homes around here never had enough insulation to keep out the damp cold of January. A draft blew across the floor. It must be about one. First hour of the new year, new decade. A change of times. Could '70 be any stranger than '69? I put my pants and T-shirt on, threw a few sticks in the fire, felt loose yet sinewy, catlike, solo, abandoned, trapped but satisfied, wily as Steve McQueen in some prisoner-of-war movie. But I was running out of Steves too, throwing away my names, turning them over to the other inmates and moving anonymous into new cells, new selves. I prowled the room, scrutinizing our temporary possessions, all so unfamiliar, insubstantial, alien. Nothing belongs. I'd be better off naked if it weren't so cold. Truer to the naked truth. What can I burn? Purify to the bones. Warm this empty space. I went to my little study in the corner, a small room painted pale blue echoing with Sheetrock acoustics, its loud walls muffled by crooked full bookshelves I'd built myself with brackets and boards from the hardware store. Under the shelves along one wall I kept two cardboard boxes full of memorabilia—old pictures, poems, journals, letters. I carried the cartons into the living room and started feeding the contents into the fire—letters I'd written to my mother from Europe which she had later returned to me following some blowout between us, photos of me in my baseball uniforms posed in rows with my teammates (how many of them dead by now, drafted and sacrificed to the war gods?), rhymed sub-Wordsworthian poems I'd written in high school to relieve my romantic angst and attract some girl's attention, piles of pointless nostalgic debris I was pleased to be free of, warming my living blood and bones by the flames—a simple ritual to expunge history. I watched the faces of my former childhood curled black around the edges and consumed. I felt cleansed, giddy with anonymity, high on the freedom to be whatever. Freedom to be nothing and nobody.

Before dawn the phone rang. It could only be one person. My slut. Maybe her orgy had ended early. I let it ring five times, then grabbed the cord and ripped it out of the wall. No need to put up with anything anymore. I'm the Cat Man, King of the New Year, time's executioner, killer of dead kids coddled too long then dropped by their moms and dads. Liquidator of a wasted life I hereby bury and disclaim. Nothing can touch me. *For he will do as he do do*, as Eliot said of his original Tugger, *and there's no doing anything about it.*

The coals glowed. A psychedelic flaming pink sun came slowly rising over the sewage plant and all the birds in the neighborhood started babbling. I stepped out on the back deck to breathe the brilliant new air, wearing some old rags I didn't recognize. A triangle of odd lights, not an airplane, hovered a few hundred feet above the ocean less than a mile away, then streaked off silently northwest. Interplanetary visitors? Why not? We need another dimension. Other worlds. Signals to the initiated. Around the corner of the house came the Rum Tum Tugger, strolling onto the deck as if he owned it. Maybe he did. The landlord. Lord of the land. King of the jungle. The antipet.

"Hey, Tugger," I whispered, "what's happening, man?" He approached and rubbed coolly against me as I crouched. He wouldn't let anyone pick him up, that was understood. Comrades. Always leave each other plenty of room to move. The basis of all trust. "Hungry again already?" We still had scraps, the fat from last night's steaks, which I collected for him on a little plate. I left the back door ajar.

It wasn't much later when I heard the Porsche pulling up outside, followed shortly by another car, it sounded like a VW bug. My heart was pumping overtime. What if they catch me as a cat? Boot steps rapped on the porch, the front door opened and in came Julie with Carolyn Corday, one of her crossed eyes skewering me and the other taking in the room. Cardboard boxes, scattered papers, clothes were thrown around. It looked like—what? A cat on acid had taken laps around the walls, ripping things up. I felt my adrenaline racing, coursing, practically lifting me off the floor. Carolyn smiled at me, or at something, a sympathetic smile, kind and knowing, in control.

Julie said, "Will you let us take you to the hospital?"

"I'm the Cat Man. I don't need to see no stinking vet."

"Stephen, please, you're being really freaky."

"Come for a ride with us," said Carolyn. She was radiant, emanating a warm power that totally dismantled my self-protection. Suddenly I felt helpless, tired from having been up all night, relieved, ready to give myself over to someone else's care. Carolyn's presence calmed me, gave Julie confidence, united the three of us in a way that made me want to go to bed with both of them. They both came over and held me, then gently guided me to the door and into the back seat of Carolyn's Volkswagen, where I curled up with my head in Julie's lap.

The purring sound of the motor soothed me. Julie stroked my head. I felt frightened but safe, out of control but totally entrusted to these two women, my rescue squad, midwives of the birth I was going through, or death, or reincarnation, all the strands of my psyche violently coming unwound, weightless, flying apart to be rewoven in a fresh form, a being I could be freely, no explanations or expectations, no apologies ever. This must be what Dylan meant by *Everybody must get stoned*—everyone has to come unglued and be reconstructed, shattered potheads pieced back together and refired.

Julie's long smooth hand on my face consoled me as we pulled into emergency. I didn't want to look. Just take me. Do what you have to. *He not busy being born is busy dying.* Somebody put me on a gurney, it started rolling, Julie walking alongside talking to me, saying I was doing fine. Being born was so hard and horrifying. I'd come out bloody and screaming, get slapped around, have to start from scratch, learn everything over. Dying was even worse, impossible, a sleepless waking into vacant space, no thing, no body, vertigo. I lay curled on the moving gurney. Hands on my body. Voices. I kept my eyes squeezed shut. I was wrapped in a sheet and rolled through corridors, into an elevator, up, out again into another corridor, through double doors. When I opened my eyes I was on a bed in half of a private room divided by a folding screen. Julie was sitting on the bed with Carolyn standing behind her.

"You're going to be okay now," Julie said. "Everything's fine. You're safe." There were tears in her eyes.

Two North, the experimental psychiatric wing of Franciscan Santa Cruz Hospital, was directed by Dr. Leo Hopkinds, Julie's shrink, the county's ranking psychiatrist, a high-powered post-Freudian from West LA who'd come north to try his short-term intensive technique on his own little unit, a collection of less than two dozen patients that now included me. The ward housed some pretty strange people—Leona the moaner, so inconsolably miserable she was kept in isolation, her cowlike lowing echoing through the antiseptic halls in a pathetic parody of Muzak; manic-depressive Madeleine whose obsession with Hollywood celebrities convinced her, when she wasn't withdrawn in the darkness of her private theater, that the rest of us were movie stars in disguise; a middle-aged man named Frank whose boozy-faced good humor was a transparent mask for vast hostility and bitterness; Frank's inseparable sidekick, Norton, a former boxer whose aggression smoldered rather than flickering up in bursts of insipid patter; evil nurse Phyllis, who seemed to be working out some kind of power complex on the customers, dictating every arbitrary command and prohibition she could think of; Harryette Pulliam, a motor-mouthed black woman who walked the floor rapping to no one in particular a nonstop commentary punctuated by choruses of "Three Blind Mice"—but for my money none was stranger than Hopkinds himself.

The doctor's round expressionless face, vaguely reminiscent of Charlie Brown's if you can picture the cartoon character as a human adult, had a disquieting assortment of nervous tics. He always seemed to be in a hurry, even during private consultations, and his impatience shaded into animosity when discussing with me my recent behavior—as if he were not a healer but a judge. "Julia tells me you threatened her with a knife."

"Julia? You mean Julie?" We were sitting in his personal conference room, a privilege, I was given to understand—I'd been on the ward for several days before being granted this audience, interview, arraignment, or whatever the fuck it was.

"Your wife. Can you tell me why you did that?" His eyes were twitching.

How could I explain that the knife was no threat but a gesture of trust and love, a seal of our intimacy? "You mean our ceremony of innocence?"

"Innocence?"

"You know, like in Yeats. *The best lack all conviction, while the worst are full of passionate intensity.* We were turning that around. Sex is purification."

"I'm afraid I don't follow your reasoning."

Reasoning? This guy's a shrink? "It's poetry, doctor. *The lineaments of gratified desire.* Innocence by association. Didn't they teach you how to mix metaphors in med school? Coming is dying and arriving at the same time. Knife rhymes with wife. It's a trope."

"A trope."

"A trip. A way of getting from one place to another."

"Or an evasive action." His grim mouth quivered. "I'd like to help you." He wasn't convincing. Fear and contempt were what I picked up. I saw myself reflected in his twitchy eyes as some kind of homicidal hippie he'd heard about on the news and was seeing in his nightmares: STUDENT POET SLAYS PSYCHIATRIST.

"I'd like to help you too. Why don't you start by telling me about your childhood?"

Not even a flicker of a grin. He was unreachable. The interview ended in a standoff, a hung jury. As the days went on I could hear their voices endlessly debating the truth of my testimony, commenting on my thoughts, they were inside me and everywhere, talking to me, about me—judging, praising, badgering, kibitzing, mocking. I asked Ken, one of the psych techs, why they were doing that and he told me that those voices belonged to people so wrapped up in themselves they'd completely lost touch with the world around them. I wondered if he was talking about me.

As a supplement to the steady diet of Stelazine I started smoking Camels, which I figured were the next best thing to marijuana and at this stage of the revolution were surely laced with strands of hemp. Not only was the strong unfiltered smoke a powerful rush, the package, with its palms and pyramids, its domes and minarets, was emblematic of the holy city, the new society, the creative oasis I and my fellow insurgents were building out of the arid wreckage of the old order. Smoking a cigarette with a fellow patient was like pausing to share a joint, a meditative break in history while the grass-enriched nicotined blood flooded the brain. Stelazine couldn't stop me. I was still freelancing as a jammer, taking laps around the rectangular ward, walking and talking, tangling up my trip with those of people oblivious to the larger changes. They were on their own bummers, riding their own highs, dealing with their private apocalypses. And yet we were all being blasted with the same drugs, subject to the same experiment, Lightning Leo's laboratory rats. *"Three blind mice, three blind mice . . ."* Harryette was on to something.

Julie came to see me almost every evening. One night she brought Carolyn and Kevin along. Carolyn was cool as usual, criss-crossing her gaze around the place with knowing composure, but Kevin, ordinarily Mr. Nonchalance, was in a state: his teeth were chattering, his lips pulled back like an anxious chimpanzee, incisors on edge; he had trouble looking me in the eye until I offered him a smoke, which he declined, rolling one of his own instead, and that seemed to calm him down.

He spoke to me in low tones as we smoked. "Last night at College Five there was a poetry reading. Anthony Christensen. You know who he is?"

"Of course. Saint Anthony. The poet-priest who couldn't resist temptation. Decided God rhymes with bod and defrocked himself. Became a beatnik. Doesn't he live in the mountains around here?"

"Right. I didn't realize how famous he was. The dining hall was filled, hundreds of people, everyone was just hanging on his words. Everything he read was about sex, sex and God, intense stuff."

"That's what celibacy will do to you."

"I suppose. But it was his presence—his presence was even more intense than the poetry. He hardly even read that much. He spent half the reading just staring at the audience, pacing the stage in his moccasins and fringes, white hair, white beard, bushy white eyebrows, and that gaze—just penetrating, really. Those long silences." He took a drag on his cigarette. "He was you."

I didn't have to ask him what he meant. I understood. All poets are part of the same conspiracy. Even though I was here I was there also, wherever one of us engaged others in the improvisational drama we were all living. Our job was to remind the civilians that everything was poetry.

"It went on for more than two hours," said Kevin. "There was something ritualistic about it, yet also unpredictable. By the end of the reading he was crying, people in the audience were crying, some were squirming, others were just entranced. Really a strange night. As if everyone was tripping." He flashed me a blue-eyed glance.

Why had Julie brought Kevin along if not to confirm my understanding that inside and outside people were equally crazed, that being in here was part of the creative continuum, my work continued on all fronts, there was no stopping the process. That's why Lightning Leo couldn't quit twitching, he knew somehow it was hopeless to try to control the minds of guerrillas, we had a built-in resistance to lightweight pacifiers like Stelazine, our metabolism was geared to a higher-powered chemistry. Vanguard psychoactivists like me were setting new standards for sanity. Mental health was a political definition established by people like Hopkinds with his Mickey Mouse nuthouse, who were incompetent to judge. Saint Anthony and his kind were the new doctors. Sex was the sacrament. Poetry the prescription. Julie, tuned in to these transformations, helped channel the flow from outside into my psyche.

She also arranged for my brother Hank to fly up from LA to visit. It was always encouraging to see Hank. In his understated way he was the sanest person I knew, a stable point of reference, someone to test reality by. One afternoon he took me on a pass to Lighthouse Point. It had been raining hard and the surf was high and wild, walls of white foam smashing the rocks and sending up salty explosions that sprayed our faces as we walked. There were hundreds of people out that day watching the ocean, a special event as if staged for us, nature putting on a demonstration. The keys to Hank's rented compact car had what struck me as the astounding power to open its doors and start its motor—keys were magical instruments capable of triggering crucial changes, keys were freedom and authority—the act of someone who wasn't on the hospital staff having control of a key amazed me. I was in awe of Hank's ability to use keys that didn't even belong to him. He acted as if there was nothing to it, as if anyone could use a key. We had lunch at Javier's and headed back to Franciscan. Hank said he'd come see me again next week.

The morning he was supposed to visit he called me from LA to say the airport was fogged in and that he'd fly up later that afternoon. I hung up the telephone certain that this was a coded way of saying he was waiting outside and that I should come down and meet him and he'd take me out of here. One of my favorite breaks from the ward was to walk downstairs to the chapel and sit in the peaceful stained-glass light absorbing the silence and the soft bright colors of the windows and studying the series of wooden carvings in relief along the walls, the Stations of the Cross, or the Stations of Sisyphus as I saw it, a man lugging a cosmic burden uphill eternally in a circle, the neverending existential curse of consciousness, knowing we're doomed to suffer and die and doing it anyway with grace, with dignity, with the understanding we can't escape, we have to carry that load, Christlike, climbing the walls. Usually someone came down to the chapel with me, a nurse or a psych tech, but the day Hank called and I asked permission to visit the chapel they let me go unaccompanied. I sat in a pew for a few minutes, nobody else in the small sanctuary, breathing the odor of a holiness I couldn't quite feel except through the hint of stillness I found there every time, a quiet interval free of all the raging information I couldn't get away from otherwise, a safe place to think, or not think, to be calm, temporarily contained.

Instead of returning upstairs to the ward I went out the other door, to the street, a loading zone where I looked around for Hank. He wasn't there, so I proceeded on out to the main drag, Soquel Drive, and walked in the direction of Rio Del Mar, three or four miles down the road, where Julie and I had our house. Maybe Hank was waiting for me there. It felt good to be outdoors again on my own. This must be what I'm supposed to be doing, they wouldn't have sent me down without an escort otherwise; it was an invitation to get away. Escape therapy. I was feeling the benefits already. A spring in my step, rain-refreshed air and January bus exhaust in my lungs, I strode optimistically along, turning back over my left shoulder now and then to float a thumb at a motorist, content to walk or ride as destiny determined.

An hour and a mile or two down the road, passing Cabrillo College, I had a cramp in my left foot that crippled me in my tracks. It must be a signal from someone at Cabrillo: stop here. The closest building was the gym, so I limped through the roadside iceplant and hobbled inside. The foot began to relax as basketball practice proceeded, a harsh-voiced coach putting the team through a tough workout. Hershey Horvitz, a poet I knew who taught English at Cabrillo, had been a high school basketball coach in San Francisco some years earlier. The coach on the court looked nothing like Hershey but what difference did that make when, as I'd learned in my travels, some people could shift shapes at will, assume various forms, human and animal, in the course of creating the new reality. The coach was barking commands at his players, who were running, dribbling, passing with military precision, that varnished-floor-and-sweat gymnasium smell enveloping me as I crouched by the sidelines watching, evidently unnoticed. Whatever Hershey was trying to tell me, his drill-sergeant style was the wrong approach. I waited for my foot to come back, waited for anything resembling instruction or information that might be coming from Hershey, then gave up, left the gym, and crossed the bridge to the main campus.

Not knowing my way around Cabrillo and having no destination in mind, I simply rambled, ignorant of my mission but certain I'd been led there for some purpose. I wandered in and out of several classes, teachers lecturing or conducting discussions, nobody paying me much attention, if anything seeming to welcome my arrival with barely perceptible gestures, glances, oblique acknowledgment that I was getting warm, must listen closely for hints. One young instructor, a rugged-looking guy in his early thirties wearing jeans and workboots and a flannel shirt, interrupted his talk to point me out as I entered—the whole class turning their heads—saying I illustrated his theme, that it's impossible to waste time. He had a half dozen marking pens clipped to his breast pocket, unsheathed one with the grace of a master swordsman and drew on a large easel pad with bold sure strokes a Möbius strip, image of continuum, one side fits all, a surface over which I could slide forever in abstract imagination never leaving the loop, Sisyphus on a roll without the rock. The strip was a sling that flung me out of the classroom into another orbit, past young girls earnestly carrying their books, and clusters of kids sipping juice and soft drinks in a snack lounge, and rigid administrators glimpsed through institutional floor-to-ceiling windows as I sailed past. An art studio caught my peripheral vision with a colorful collage that covered one whole wall, pictures clipped from magazines and patched together into an eclectic kinetic portrait of culture in transformation, athletes and industrial workers, aircraft and architecture, soldiers, musicians, dozens of multiracial faces leaping off the wall to seize me. I entered the empty room to the sound of some blues man singing *Packin' up, gettin' ready to go* on a record player and a black instructor emerging from a hidden office saying to me, "Yes, sir, what can I do for you?" It's done, I thought, getting the message in the song, it's time to split. In the campus parking lot I saw a car that somehow pulled me to it saying steal me, a red Karmann Ghia, beautifully maintained, unlocked, parked in a loading zone. I got into the driver's seat certain it was the right thing to do, that it was Bob Dylan's car, that Dylan was following me around, another one of my angels. There was no key in the ignition so I looked for some clue toward starting the engine, and on the gearshift knob thought I read "on" for one of the positions. I shifted the transmission into "on," but nothing. Tried again. Nothing. Refusing to be discouraged, I unscrewed the knob and took it with me as a talisman. Then I resumed my stroll down Soquel Drive.

The stretch of road between Soquel and Aptos was almost rural then, wild weedy hills and spreads of country space still claimed by insects, animals and birds, spears of grass and mud where later driveways and tract homes would seal the earth. Like the rest of the county it was hawk country, lots of tasty little rodents scampering through those fields. The sky was silver-gray, no claw tracks exactly but a fox-colored field of vision streaked with streams of spiritual purplish-pink, translucent veins pumping gods' blood through the air, wisps of their cold breath floating around the clouds, traces of rain suspended, shades of silent unanimous praise for the great day shimmering over me in this friendly wilderness. At intervals homes appeared, and little businesses: shoe repair, glass, real estate, antiques. I looked at my shoes to see how they were doing. The afternoon deepened. I kept on.

In Aptos Village I saw a girl walking twenty or thirty yards ahead of me. All I could see was her back, but from this angle and distance she looked exactly like Denise Millan, a sweetheart of mine from Bard. "Denise!" I called, and the girl turned. As I got up close to her I saw she was not Denise. And yet, and yet.

"My name is Monica," she said to me. Her face was wide open as if expecting, welcoming my arrival. "How do you know me?"

"I'm your guide," I said, "from another life."

"This is a special day." Was she on acid? Our interaction was dreamy, both of us floating as we walked, comfortable in this sudden familiarity. Maybe she was Denise, her journey aligned with mine, our paths converging for mysterious purposes we'd understand only by proceeding.

"It's good that I found you. I wondered where I was going." Like the meeting with Norm at Altamont, this instant sense of connection was meant to be accepted, no questions asked on either side, a gesture of trust in the universe, faith in the perfectly unfolding story, the inevitably inventive drama of our amazing lives. Forces beyond and within us were setting our course through unprecedented times and spaces charged with magic. We placed our steps in harmony with these powers. In twenty minutes we were at the cottage in Rio Del Mar.

No Porsche parked in front, therefore no Julie. I found the hidden key, kept around back under a loose board. YALE, it said, as in Yale Younger Poet, as in the Yale from which Herb the Hot Dog Frankfurter had come with his colleagues to the West Coast to sabotage my imagination with the notion that poetry was "self-indulgent," an onanistic exercise for those too frivolous to do criticism. Incredible. The key turned comfortably in the lock. Monica/Denise and I entered the house.

It was quiet inside, a still gray in the darkening afternoon. I kindled a fire to warm the place up and, confirming that Dylan was with me, placed *Bringing It All Back Home* on the stereo, side one, band one. "Subterranean Homesick Blues" rumbled and twanged and sang through the house, clear and loud as if the band were literally playing in the basement. Our chaperones, troubadours, guardians, enchanters. Above the kitchen was a sleeping loft with a ladder leading up there from the living room. To be here with this young woman was the blessing I'd been granted on this special day—my twenty-third birthday, I realized—of course, this was my gift. I took the little ceramic jar where Julie and I kept our stash and climbed into the loft with Monica. She looked young but also ageless, a plump girl-woman with lovely pink cheeks and straight blond hair and clear blue eyes and an utter willingness to go along with me into whatever experience. I had appeared as her pilot at precisely the right moment, her partner in adventure, her initiator.

"You look like an angel," I said.

She said, "You look like God."

I rolled a joint, took a puff, passed it to her, music rising from beneath the floor played live for us by our troubadours. The light through the little window was silvery, mingling with the silver smoke to encircle Monica's face and fine long hair. I kissed her mouth. The house began to shake—it was the daily freight train headed south along the coast. We lay on the bed. The whistle blew. Dylan sang, *The bridge at midnight trembles* . . . I felt her breasts through her smooth white blouse, then started undoing the buttons. My hand was on her back, feeling the firm shape of her flank, the curve of her yielding spine, unhooking her bra, when the front door opened.

"For godsake, what are you doing?" Julie shouted. "Excuse me," she was addressing Monica, "this is my husband. He escaped this morning from a psychiatric ward. I'm sorry. Please. You'll have to leave now. I can't believe this."

Denise or Monica buttoned her blouse and climbed down the ladder, apologizing. "I'm sorry, I didn't understand, I'm only sixteen. I'm really sorry."

Julie took her outside, spoke to her on the front porch for a few minutes, and came back in alone. "Jesus, Stephen. How can you do this? Do you realize what you're doing?"

"Do what? It's my birthday. I was supposed to leave the hospital, wasn't I? What else were all those signals trying to tell me?"

"God. Please. Just wait here, stay here, will you? Hank is flying up from LA. He'll be here pretty soon. Please wait with me so I won't have to call an ambulance."

I tried to calm her, embrace her, my erection looking for a safe place.

"Stop it! I can't take this. It's too much. Just sit. I'll make some tea, okay? I'll make some tea."

I sat. She made some tea. Put some less festive music on the stereo, John Williams playing Bach, solo guitar. *Johnny's in the basement mixin' up the medicine*, just as Dylan had declared. Everyone was present. Witnessing.

We sipped the tea. I didn't understand why she was so upset. It was I whose trip had been interrupted. But what did it matter? The day had been wonderful, exhilarating. Free. I felt refreshed. Everything was perfect.

After about an hour Hank arrived.

11

Moon Shot

"It'd probably be a good idea not to say too much about your travels this afternoon," Hank advised as we drove back to Franciscan. "Sorry I couldn't get here earlier. The fog was so thick in LA the planes weren't taking off."

"I thought you wanted me to meet you outside."

"What made you think that?"

"I don't know, just something in your voice, the inflection, the undertone, like you couldn't come out and say what you meant. Maybe someone was listening in. I had to interpret."

He half-smiled, keeping his eyes on the freeway. "I can assure you I'll say what I mean. You can take me literally."

"How long are they going to keep me in there?"

"Only as long as they have to. So you don't get hurt."

"Get hurt?"

"Some people think you're acting a little strange. It disturbs them. You could get hurt."

"Sorry if I fucked up." I still wasn't sure that I had, but felt it was important for Hank's sake, in case we were being bugged, to

170

go along with this law-and-order song and dance. As if all rules weren't now subject to revision, as if authority were linear and uniform rather than swirling in diverse spirals, as if the world's Hopkindses could lay down limits for beings like me. Hank had to play it straight, so I went along with the act, looking for openings, reading between the lines, outside the lines. Reality was up for grabs.

"Don't worry about it."

"Do the parents know I'm in the nuthouse?"

"They left for Israel last week. Hopkinds advised me not to tell them. He said there's nothing they could do. I think he's right. Why worry them. Unless you want me to say something when we talk—they'll be calling soon, I'm sure."

"Yeah, tell them to give my regards to the Jews."

Back in Two North I was half-blackballed, half-respected for my escapade. Everybody knew they weren't supposed to encourage me, but they also—the patients anyway—admired my chutzpa to just take off like that. Something they wished they could get away with but wouldn't dare. The staff's new strategy, no doubt handed down from Hopkinds, was to ignore me as much as possible, offering minimal counsel, and wait for the drugs to straighten me out. I took some pleasure in knowing I was screwing up Lightning Leo's know-it-all treatment, placing his theories in doubt, thwarting his command of his domain. As in graduate school, I enjoyed playing the role of the guerrilla, sabotaging institutional intentions, sniping at the big guns. Honchos like Hopkinds needed agitators like me to keep them honest, challenge their dogma, reverse their expectations. The trickster. An honorable tradition. I was just doing my job.

I let the voices play in my head, talked back in multiple dialects, trying to scramble their signals, mash their fantasies with barrages of repartee, sitting on my bed in my room with the door closed spewing out a stream of jive, taking several sides of the same imaginary argument, or playing it safe in the group at meals, muttering unspeakable comments directly into the collective subconscious, silently injecting my thoughts into the dialogue currents, shredding and reconstituting conversations. I didn't know what else to do. As in City Prison, it was the only skill I could offer. I wanted to be useful. I wanted to advance change.

The doctor had other plans. One afternoon I was standing in the hall outside my room getting a drink of water when I looked around and saw coming through the locked door of the ward, in the rippling slow-motion haze of a Western movie where the posse advances toward the camera warped by the heatwaves rising from the trail, my brothers Don and Hank, my sister Gena and her husband, Dave Tannenbaum. At first I thought I was hallucinating. What were they doing here? Happiness mingled with apprehension. Was this some sort of family reunion, or a conspiracy to outnumber me, coerce me into obedience? Don looked bloated, edgy, contact madness penetrating his crust and playing wicked tricks with his composure. Hank seemed more jittery than usual too, avoiding eye contact with me, as if the gang force and Don's seniority undercut our one-to-one trust. Gena was warm with sisterly affection, putting her most compassionate face forward, clearly uneasy but kind. And my brother-in-law Dave, the eternal big shot, walked with his tight-assed duck-footed stride, looking around with inflated authority as if trying to impress the staff with his mastery of the situation. A curious cohort as far as I was concerned. Definitely abnormal.

Don walked up to me and said, "Hi, Panch. We're taking you out of here."

"What do you mean? Where to?"

He didn't answer, but Hank said, "We need to have you closer to home, so we can keep in touch. You can't stay here."

"We're going to LA," said Gena. "All five of us."

"Bullshit. I'm not going to LA. It's not my home. I hate LA." It wasn't just the lousy few days I'd spent there two or three weeks ago, it was the whole horrific wasteland I'd just succeeded in fleeing, the money-driven movie-deluded smog-coughing flash-in-the-chrome syphilitic philistine hamburger drive-thru whorehouse that had done its best to wash my brains already and barely failed. Why hadn't anyone consulted me? That's what rankled. Even if I was allegedly crazy I could have told them going to LA would only make it worse. My whole trajectory was out of there, I was finished with that trip, finished with my fucking self! This was no time to go back to where it all started.

Big brother Don, ringleader of the abductors, was not the kind of person to argue with—wasn't even the kind to reason with—he was impulsive, impatient, stubborn, recalcitrant like me, and when he'd made up his mind there was no room for discussion. "Sorry, Panch," was all he said to me as he directed the junior siblings in the act of subduing and removing, capturing and transporting the wild little Mexican Jew, the outlaw baby with the drug-stained brain whom they were duty bound to take away. The doctor couldn't handle me anymore and didn't want the bother.

The same could be said of my parents. Where were they? In Israel. Perfect. Israel, this Jewish Utopia where trees were planted in my name, had always been more important than I was. The year after I was born it became a state, and all my life was a kind of rival, the perfect idealized kid who could do no wrong. The Nazis had made Jews morally superior by victimizing them, driving them out of Europe into a desert full of irate Arabs. In my mother's view it was Israel *über alles*, a cause above and beyond all others, but I never bought the idea that the Jews were more important than everyone else. I felt closer to the people in our kitchen than to some cousins I'd never met in Tel Aviv. As a child it was hard for me to understand the importance of a Jewish state on the other side of the world—Beverly Hills was like a Jewish state right here, what's the big deal? At school, where I was warned by my mother I might be made fun of or otherwise picked on because I was Jewish (and therefore superior), Jews outnumbered everybody else. We tried to make some of our gentile friends feel less excluded by calling them honorary Jews. Luckily for me, my parents weren't religious, but that didn't keep them from sending me to Sunday school. I should at least know how to go through the motions. I got to ask the questions at Passover. I knew by heart some of the more rhythmically seductive riffs from the prayer book—*Thou shalt love the Lord thy God with all thy heart, with all thy soul, and with all thy might . . .* —they had the same mysterious kick that first turned me on to Shelley's lyrics. I liked the Exodus story, Moses was a revolutionary. But Israel? I couldn't get excited. That my parents were there and as far as I knew ignorant of my situation was fitting geophysical evidence of the distance we'd put between us.

So here was Don trying to take control of an uncontrollable freak who was resisting with all his heart, with all his soul and with all his might the effort to deliver him back to the scene of his former crimes. I was still the outlaw, the rebel, demanding respect and autonomy.

My demands were ignored. The four of them herded me out the door, down the hallway, into the elevator, through the hospital lobby into the gloomy gray light of a rainy afternoon. They were acting more coplike than the actual cops who'd busted me and hustled me around last month—it seemed an eternity ago, a movie I'd seen, a dream. Protesting all the way, I was lovingly shoved into the back seat of their rented car, stuffed between Hank and Gena. Don the director rode shotgun in front, turned with his left arm over the seat back to keep an eye on everybody, and Dave took the wheel. The tension inside the car was sharpened by the rain outside: the windows were rolled almost all the way up, squashing us in the pressure of the weather, steam fogging the glass and dark clouds bearing down from above. But rather than claustrophobic I felt cozy, squeezed on either side against Gena and Hank, like in that old black-and-white photo of the three of us on the couch when I was an infant and they were four and eight, both of them smiling genially and me with terror on my face as I faced the camera. Now the fear was on the other foot, they were the scared ones and I was reclaiming the righteous low-down self-possession of the seasoned prisoner of war, certain that justice was on my side and getting comfortable with my kidnappers. Dave pulled cautiously out of the hospital parking lot and onto the freeway north. Nobody spoke. Rain played its lugubrious music steadily on the car roof as what light there was dimmed with sundown, slate-gray sky darkening into solid sheets of black liquid lashing the packed compact moving through late-afternoon traffic, all of us placing our lives in Dave's hands as he negotiated the famously fatal Highway 17, its high-speed slippery curves twisting over the hill toward San Jose. Gena held my right hand, our fingers intertwined, trying to calm herself as well as me. Hank on my left assumed an unobtrusively neutral but friendly presence, yielding to Don's dictatorial authority. Dave had his hands full behind the wheel; even on their home turf LA drivers regarded rain with terror, and here the skiddy road conditions were aggravated by unfamiliarity, on top of the shaky state of psychic affairs. His usually talkative lips were zipped, he had more important things to do than impress us all with how much he knew about mental illness or art or politics or whatever expertise he claimed this week on account of having read *Time* magazine; he kept his eyes on the road. Gena slipped the simple turquoise ring she'd worn for years onto my pinkie in a gesture of solidarity. I was still distraught to be shipped out against my will but physically I was snug. It was Don who needed help. He kept looking back at me nervously, blankly, as if I was an object, then at the road, then at Dave driving. His left hand clutched unconsciously at the seat back. I hadn't seen him in a while and though I knew he was overweight, his body looked blown up like a basketball, his face grotesquely swollen by a beef-heavy diet and anxiety. His roguish days as a great young racer had long since given way to the sorry complacency of a prematurely middle-aged TV professional who'd scored big in the industry and become a victim of his own success. He was contemptuous of his work, "grinding out the shit," as I'd heard him describe it. He was having problems with his current girlfriend; maybe she'd left him lately, or was about to. He would have been better off taking my bed at Franciscan than try-ing to run this ridiculous operation. He looked at me as if he didn't know who I was, had no clue how I'd gotten like this, how I could be so irrational. Here was a guy who'd driven Ferraris hundreds of miles an hour racing and never lost his cool, even when crashing, but creeping over 17 in the rainy redwood darkness with his little brother trapped in back was agitating him no end. Maybe because he wasn't behind the wheel. Maybe I should have been driving, at least I knew the road, unlike my captors.

When we finally reached the airport, the plane to LA was de-layed on account of weather—not just the rain here but fog down south—so we all had to wait in the busy terminal with hundreds of other travelers milling around. I couldn't sit still, despite the fact that they'd doped me up with Thorazine before we left Franciscan; so I milled with the masses, trying to engage assorted strangers in spontaneous verbal jams as Hank or Gena followed me around both to be sure I didn't slip away and to signal not too subtly to the people I approached that, well, excuse us, my little brother's nuts, don't let him bother you, thanks for understanding. As we waited for news of our flight I circulated through the terminal trying to gather intelligence on what was really going on. My escorts were upset at the delay, but for me it was a reprieve; maybe it meant we would not be able to go—the gods were intervening on my behalf. In Santa Cruz I felt somewhat grounded, familiar with the terrain, at ease in the local culture, but LA—even though I'd lived there eighteen years—was just too vast, too overwhelmingly chaotic to reenter and feel oriented. It was like going to another planet. "Why are you doing this to me?" I kept protesting. "I don't want to go. I belong up here. How can you make me do this? What are you doing?" We're taking you home, to another hospital, Gena or Hank would answer, and that was that. Don sat in one of those anchored airport seats, looking left and right, rocking his fat crossed legs one over the other, as if holding back an urgent need to urinate. If the energy in the car had been strange and strained, the atmosphere in the terminal was feverish—frenzied passengers rushing back and forth with their bags or waiting, like us, impatient to board their flight. I wasn't exactly hallucinating, but the near-delirious activity in this large space-age building was giving me a trippier feeling than I'd had at any time since Altamont, a sense of imminent apocalypse, as if everyone in the whole place were on acid, which I continued to assume was in the water supply, and so kept sipping from the drinking fountains, certain that my experience under the influence equipped me to handle whatever crisis might arise, perhaps even serve as a stabilizing influence on my siblings, who didn't seem to be handling the scene so well.

At last our flight was announced. Bummer. I'd thought it might be canceled. My abductors steered me toward the boarding gate, while I made one last desperate effort to state the case against taking me. As we hustled along the corridor Don suddenly put an end to my complaints, lifting me off the floor with both arms—he must have outweighed me by eighty pounds—and slamming me against the nearest wall. My head bounced off the paneling, slightly cushioned by my untamed pageboy. Stunned, I looked him directly in the eye and said in questioning disbelief, "Don?" My tone said, What are you doing? What happened to you? Time froze for a moment as passersby watched the drama of a large meaty balding man recklessly brutalizing a skinny hippie. Don couldn't hold my gaze, let go of my arms, and lurched away, obviously more freaked than I was. Hank went after him. Dave and Gena led me outside through the drizzly night and up the metal stairs into the aircraft.

Gena ushered me to a window seat and sat beside me on the aisle. The plane was crowded, and the delay along with whatever else was in the air had the passengers frantic. Finally everybody settled down, the routine announcements were made, we pulled away from the terminal building, taxied to the runway, the jet revved up to its bone-crushing takeoff speed, and we were in the air, soaring out of San Jose, clearing the fog, climbing into a deep blue night illumined by a full moon. Jesus, I thought, we're going to the moon. Gena clutched my hand. I wouldn't say anything, didn't want to alarm her. Maybe we're supposed to start a colony up there. I flashed back to last July in the Haight, scoring the lunar hash while the astronauts were landing—it was prophetic, a personal message to me. I'd be following in their smokestream. The moon might be spooky as a destination, but it was no more desolate than Los Angeles. At least my parents wouldn't be there. But "Israel" could be code for anything. Zionists in space? There were too many possibilities, no need to speculate. A rumor circulated that the flight might be diverted to Ontario. What difference did it make? Time and space were constructions, convenient fictions. We were here and now. I'd find out soon enough where else I was headed.

A long hour after takeoff we descended through dense overcast into the unmistakable glittering sprawl of the LA basin. As the wheels touched down on the runway at LAX, the passengers applauded. Everyone but me.

12

St. James Infirmary

So under duress I signed myself in at St. James Hospital in Santa Monica—a full-moon lunatic turned in by a search party collecting the reward on my head by delivering me alive to the care of Dr. E. Leonard Silverman, my latest healer. For someone who'd been abducted I was in pretty good spirits, joking with Gena and Hank as I followed their instructions. "This is my contract with the Dodgers, right? Big-league bullshit from here on." Looked at as an expansion of my adventure, the transfer was a promotion to where the action was, the actors and other players in the powerful imaginary industry that had popular vision in its grip. The revolution of course would have to include Hollywood, electronic force fields must knit new understanding among cultures, ordinary life would assume an improvisational ritualistic primitive artistry, an endless jam of amateur actors bringing to reality previously unseen drama. Julius Trailerman's theatrical strategy and Morgan Hurst's democratization of creativity combined. LA was the center, the laboratory studio out of which images sprang that infected everything— why not turn it to higher purposes, let loose subversive conspira-

tors to shoot visible fresh juices through the spiderweb of connections that had hold of so much imagination, and at the same time
in every intimate encounter let individuals exchange acknowledgement of what we all knew was coming, all meaning those of
us charged with the good news. It was a blessing and a psychic
virus, like poetry, a disease you wanted to spread for the way it
could make every minute more interesting. The world could be
turned around through naked innocence, absolute candor and
openness exploding, blowing away all deadly conventions. I was
too hot to handle, had to be contained until the outside world
caught up. St. James was not just Jean's last name to make me feel
at home at a holiday dinner breathing the fragrance of that famous
body, but more important the infirmary of blues legend related by
gospel to John the Revelator, illness and visions linked in an earthy
cosmic continuum, wheels within wheels. It was prophetic to be
imprisoned here, a post-Alcatraz Devil's Island for outcast angels
lost and found in the deepest circles of Inferno-Paradise, El Lay, or
as Silverman called it, Loss Angle-ease. I was dizzy with the realization that I'd been called up to the majors. My performance here
would have a vast audience. I was being asked to bare myself even
more completely than in San Francisco. LA was everywhere, and
everywhere else was just the outskirts of LA.

E. Leonard Silverman, or Lenny, or E.L., or, as I called him, El
Silver Man, who loomed over me with his prematurely gray hair
and Freud-like silver beard and heavy-lidded eyes as if he too were
taking Thorazine, was presumably the one shrink Hopkinds knew
who might be able to handle me. Silverman too, it turned out, was
from Beverly Hills, even though he now lived in Malibu. His father
was a famous surgeon, Louis Silverglade, and Lenny on opening
his psychoanalytic practice had changed his name to Silverman
so as not to be taken for any relation to the old man. His Edipal
thrust was right up front—he'd killed off his dad by dumping his
name. But I was to learn all this much later. What first impressed
me about El Silver Man was how tall and slow and silver he was for

a guy who couldn't have been over forty. On his big-boned frame seemed to hang the case histories of so many out-of-control youthful maniacs and undersea depressions of the overprivileged that his posture suffered; he walked with a slouch that belied his size. Yes, in some ways Silverman appeared to be under water, moving and speaking in deep slow motion, as if to be sure he'd never alarm you with a sudden gesture, you were paranoid enough already. His drug of choice was Thorazine, the walking lobotomy designed to put the lid on any manic acid-ravaged schizophrenic or otherwise overactive consciousness too astonished to eat or sleep or stop pouring out the cryptic tickertape engraved with poetry received uncensored from unknown transmitters. Thorazine was supposed to suppress all that with tons of lead, or a chemical equivalent, loading the bloodstream with its dead weight, wrapping up the patient like a wet straitjacket but invisibly, simply drugging you to a stop. Funny thing was, though it was fed to me in large doses four times a day, it wasn't even slowing me down.

Silverman could see this. He knew also that he personally wouldn't have near enough time to follow all the trails of my inner wilderness to their sources in subconscious history; would be able to see me less than an hour daily, and therefore assigned a special nurse to baby-sit me eight hours a day. His name was Isaac Odom, independent RN from South Central, a small broad-shouldered father of four who walked with a slight limp due to a wound picked up in World War II. He contracted out to individual patients and did shifts at several area hospitals, mainly the VA. Isaac, or Ike as he said to call him, looked a lot like Malcolm X, only shorter; his face was the same shape, his expressions similar to Malcolm's in photos I'd seen. He had a space between his front teeth and his left eye wandered outward when he was tired, giving him a strangely sinister and powerful countenance behind his taped-together horn-rimmed glasses. So Ike was Malcolm come back to take care of me on the ICU at St. James. The immortals never died. ICU stood for intensive care unit, but also for I see you: you're being watched. Ike was my guardian. It gave me a feeling of pride and fear that such a historic figure had been assigned to me by whatever occult commanders were observing my every move from some underground headquarters. Could I live up to such a standard? Would I too wind up zapped by assassins' bullets only to return as a guide for some young initiate? Or was I the kind of lone nut who might be programmed to perform some momentous deed? My man was Isaac, son of Abraham, sacrificial lamb who survived by the grace of a burning bush; was Ike, benevolent general with the stylish jacket whom only my gramps and I, of our whole family, had backed for president in '52, Ike who'd warned us wisely of the military-industrial complex now roundly denounced by radicals; was Malcolm, revolutionary leader with the terrible swift tongue who talked his way into his own murder and immortality; and Odom, like Om in some African dialect, a meditative name with a bass beat embedded in it, holding the song down, anchoring it so the lyrics and melody can soar securely—that's how I deciphered my special's identity there in One North on the I See You.

"That's right, Steve, drink lots of water; it'll keep you cool. And eat what's on your plate, especially the meat; you need those amino acids."

Amino acids, lysergic acid, battery acid—it's all the same to me, more electricity for my blazing brains—I could absorb as much as they'd give me, whatever was necessary, by any means. The megadoses of Thorazine must have been a test to see what I could withstand, and I was holding up better than most, still rapping and raving while some of those around me were reduced to zombies and others had submitted to the random tyrannies of the staff and its medicated commands. The Thorazine thickened my tongue, made it impossible to focus my eyes thereby precluding reading, softened my cock so I wasn't so sexually excitable, prickled my skin with a ferocious itch if I had the good luck to step out into the sun, and made me sleep each night like sludge at the bottom of the sea. One morning I awakened to ask Ike, "Is it still 1970?"—so deep and dreamless had been the unconsciousness into which the drug had plunged me. At the time I was in restraints, strapped to my bed by wrists and ankles, a clever technique they had devised for keeping me in one place, though I yelled my head off as much as I could through my bloated tongue and blackened vocal chords. Malcolm had said you've got to make noise if you want to get anyone's attention, and as I made my case for freedom I sounded black, my accent picked up unconsciously from Ike, who'd originally come from Arkansas. "Am I still white?" I asked him once when I couldn't believe the sound of my own voice. Ike laughed, assuring me my race had not been changed. Not that it mattered to me. In fact I felt that to change races, like shifting among human identities of any kind, or human to animal and back as needed, was a skill to be mastered by the highest spirits. I'd never been really white. More like a warm ambiguous shade of brown. And I was feeling darker all the time. Georgia, who raised me in the early years, was the same color as I was. No wonder I'd always felt I was hers. As I hung out with Ike our kinship deepened. He was the teacher I'd been seeking, but working under his tutelage wasn't easy. His power scared me. He took on this curious hypnotic look when his left eye wandered that made me think he was trying to control my mind. Insights like this sharpened both my fear and my affection for him—nobody could be so purely good you'd trust them unconditionally, an edge of paranoia was healthy, realistic, as Misha always maintained. Ike was grooming me for something crucial, with the tough compassion of a coach; the toughness was necessary to keep me competitive. Basic training. Also brainwashing? It was a risk I had to run. My heart responded to him. When he came through the door in his whites at the start of his shift and walked up with his slightly lopsided stride and gave me the Black Power handshake—"Hi, Steve, how you doin'?"—his voice resonated in my sternum and I welcomed him as an ally, someone working with me even as he might be working me over.

Outside the window of my room on the ICU was a thick old magnolia whose trunk writhed when I watched it closely enough, its roots gripping the ground with cosmic strength. I felt I could see it growing. Nature, the world itself, was so alive that even if you knew you were hallucinating you also knew there were physical forces people could perceive if they paid attention. The acidic water in the drinking fountains helped cut through distractions and let you zero in on the deeper powers. Human faces openly revealed everything you needed to know about them. Most people just never stopped to look, couldn't take the intensity. If I was seeing things, it was only because they were there. Same for the voices. What I was hearing were the undertones of actual conversation, the internal asides and interjections and subterranean marginalia that constantly accompany talk whether the talkers are conscious of it or not. The speakers I heard may have been in my head but the microphones were planted on everyone around me and that's how I picked up what they were really saying.

Since the Thorazine had rendered my eyesight worthless I was unfit for occupational therapy, those kindergarten sessions in the dining room when cheerful volunteers helped the inmates string beads or tool belts or do needlepoint or play with blocks or whatever the fuck exercise they could think up to take people's minds off their boredom. So during OT I'd hang out with Ike while he played solitaire—the two of us taking turns reading the cards like a Tarot deck, telling stories by association—or just roam around while other nurses and patients were building and taking apart and rebuilding enormously complex thousand-piece jigsaw puzzles that I couldn't begin to sit still long enough to start much less finish putting together. My most useful therapy was self-prescribed. Ike helped me track down pads of blank white paper, which I carried in my back pocket along with a pen and scrawled out all sorts of poems, letters, speeches, aphorisms, greetings and gifts for fellow patients, invocations and incantations, songs, prayers and sermons. I printed these texts in large letters so I could read what I was saying—what some other force or source, like Cocteau's radio, was saying through me; I was merely an amanuensis.

The blade draws more blood than the pen,
elicits a quick response and isn't prison.
Must we bleed out loud to reach the white limits,
the self divided against the self
at the eleventh hour, day brief and breaking against salt rocks,
granite, not like a still life, sunstroked foreheads
hammered together at the front lines.
Trenches weep muddy and mess up their tenants.
What landlord, wished upon like a lead-off star at night,
will spread his wings and say we're safe at home.

There were endless supplies of this stuff spilling out of me, I didn't know what it was.

It breaks my ripped heart to see a man go down defeated.
He is the plain top notch from anywhere,
the tough intelligent genius in disguise.

In blue ink I scribbled:

This page for a badge of blue courage.
A cougar caught fighting every cat in the alley
has a weakness for pantheism.
Just like Long Tall Sally, the witch doctor loves to ball
and is loose on the women's ward waving his totem,

What do you make of that, o mighty Silverman? Everything was there, war and baseball, sex and poesy, fear and death and the punished rage of the incarcerated.

Bead games, end arounds and bunts aside
someone is asking where the hell he is.
Is it a cave with drawings on the wall?
Is it an aquarium crawling with sharks?
It may be rather a brotherhood of nuns
all clad in the snow-white habit of their work.
Pack up your tablets, Moses, and go uptown.
Your neon last name gives off a loud glare.
A cluster of dust like a lynched whiteboy

hangs in my throat to choke off memories
of dreams on flying red horses at the wire.
Success is the means to a short-lived finish.
Any resemblance to actual persons
living or dead is purely synchronistic.

I saved these scraps of paper—the ones I didn't give away—until they filled my pocket, then turned them over to Ike, who turned them over to my editor/critic, Silverman. He'd engage me, or try to anyway, in discussions of what they "meant," as if I knew. As if they didn't mean what they said. I wasn't trying to hide anything. I wanted everything revealed and this was the only way I felt it could be done—words—not the pedestrian discourse of therapeutic prose but the poetry of the unknown shooting up unexpectedly from nowhere. "Look," I lectured the shrink, "isn't the idea to say whatever comes into your head? Weren't Freud and Breton on the same trip? Just let the unconscious rap on."

Then one afternoon, out of context and unlike anything I'd said to him up to then, I declared: "I hate my mother."

Silverman's eyes lit up like a scoreboard when the home team hits one out of the park. The spirit of Groucho's duck dropped from the ceiling: I'd said the secret word. "Let's go into that thought a little further," he said with restrained enthusiasm. It was the first of many conversations exploring that simple statement of filial malice. *How sharper than a serpent's tooth is a thankless child*, my mother used to misquote Shakespeare every time I took some unspeakable step toward liberation, ungrateful brat that I was to dare grow up and reject their protection. One thing that made me so mad was the feeling of being cheated, kept from knowledge of the outside world by the insular security of our privilege. It was shocking to learn belatedly that Beverly Hills was not representative of what was going on at large. It was disconcerting. Why didn't everybody have a trust fund? What gave me the right? And wasn't it a handicap? *I'm trying to read your portrait but I'm helpless like a rich man's child*, Dylan had wheezed in one of those songs composed on speed in the studio while recording

Blonde on Blonde. So I was mad at my dad too, he was the one who'd busted his ass so his kids would never have to worry about where the next meal or car was coming from. But he had fewer expectations, made fewer demands than his wife did; he was detached, with nothing to prove, he could take me or leave me. Discussing possible futures and ambitions when I was little, he'd say to me, "If you want to be a bum, be a bum—that's fine—as long as you're a good one." And he meant it. But my mother, hearing of my writing plans: "Why can't you be a lawyer and write poetry on the side?" This from an English major fond of dragging out literary quotes when it served her guilt-pumping purposes. We actually argued when I was ten years old the wisdom of my being a professional baseball player. "Do you realize they can trade you like cattle?" she admonished, invoking those other cattle cars I'd been told the Jews were taken to the death camps in. Wow, baseball as the Holocaust, I guess I'd better hang up my cleats. But she did take an interest in my early verse, listening to my discoveries during those first years at UCLA. No, as a mother she wasn't that bad when she happened to be around, but they were off on business a lot, and her dominating edge really bugged me when she turned it on Pop. He had devised over the years ways of ignoring her, but sometimes at the dinner table she would correct his grammar or some other meaningless mistake, asserting her authority. As he told me privately one time, "She can't be wrong."

Silverman listened patiently to my monologues, alert for the stray clue that led to whatever he was looking for, so I tried to keep the material coming, like a nightclub comedian. Held over. Talk, with luck, could be my ticket out. The instant poems I was composing made me one with Wilfred Owen writing his sonnets in the trenches on the backs of ammunition orders in the War to End All Wars. I was allied with Lenny Bruce in paranoid paradise. The Tokyo Rosebud of my time, seething with subversive communications. Sending headlines along the hotlines. Burning the wires with my revelations. But where did it get me? Nowhere. My sentence was indeterminate. El

Silver Man might tamper with my dosage, adjusting it to see what happened, but obviously I wasn't going anyplace.

Pacing the halls with Ike one morning—though I still slept on the ICU, I was free to circulate among the civilians most days— I stepped into one of the little offices used by the doctors for private interviews. I sat behind the desk in the swivel chair and put up my feet. Ike sat across from me. "So," I said to him in my most authoritative tones, "you'd like us to consider you for a job?"

"Yes, sir," Ike smiled self-effacingly.

"Well, tell me, son, what are your qualifications for this position?"

He paused for a second, reflecting. "I can work long hours without a break. I can tell fortunes with a solitaire deck. And look, I have white shoes."

I passed my pad of notepaper across the desk. "So far, so good. Now. Won't you write us a short essay—it can be a poem if you prefer—encapsulating your philosophy?"

Ike wrote with some effort, the pen clutched in his left hand: *Life is a gift to be lived one day at a time, and plans for tomorrow is as good as our hopes. Though alterations or change of plan sometimes come when we are the least prepared.*

I read it slowly, as it had been written, actually printed, on my pad. Its simple wisdom humbled me for a minute. Made me wonder what all my verbal performances were for. Reminded me who he was. A mentor. "You're hired, my man." We stood up, shook hands and walked back out on the ward.

Silverman was looking for us. "Oh, so there you are."

"Hello, Dr. Silverman," Ike said.

"Doc," I declared, "I recommend we hire this guy. He can handle the job."

"Sounds good to me," said the medicine man.

"Well, I thank you both," said Ike. "I guess I'll leave you to yourselfs awhile."

Silverman nodded and led me back into the conference room. I took the doctor's chair. No problem. It didn't matter to him where we sat.

"So," I began. "Where would you like to begin? Your child-hood?"

"Yours," he said in that slow, loose way of his. Downers, or some kind of contact low picked up from his patients. But he wasn't down. Even, rather. Even Stephen. "Your mother is back from her trip and she'd like to visit. Do you want to see her? Shall I tell her to come?"

"Sure. Why not. Maybe she'd like to check in." My mother had her own impressive history of hospitalizations, at least two mem-orable episodes, when I was about fourteen and eighteen. She'd flipped into a manic mode much like mine, wouldn't eat or sleep, called friends long distance and talked all night in streams of in-comprehensible revelations. Both times she'd received electro-shock therapy, various medications, been kept on ice for a while, and then released. One time she reportedly punched out a nurse. She was a veteran. Send her on in.

Next afternoon she arrived, on schedule, smelling like a depart-ment store, tastefully attired in beiges and browns as she pecked me on the cheek, careful not to smudge her makeup. Her skin was tanned, but she looked older than I expected. "Hello, darling," she said to me shakily, apparently scared of some Mansonoid response. "Are they treating you all right? Are you getting enough to eat? You look so thin."

"I don't need to eat much, Mom. I'm running mostly on electricity."

"Oh," she said.

"How was Israel?"

"It was wonderful. I'm sorry we weren't here when you went into the hospital. We didn't know. We would have canceled the trip if you had asked for us."

No thanks. I wasn't getting into this. "It doesn't matter, Mother. I didn't want to see you. I was on my own trip. I'm sure we all had a better time."

We looked at one another, looked away, out the window, around the room, a private lounge of immaculate anonymity—space-age plastic furniture, easy to clean in case of matricide.

"Your father and I are glad that you're in town. It will be easier to stay in touch."

"I don't see why we have to. What good do you think it would do? It's a little late."

She looked at me very sadly. "Stephen, you know we love you."

"Yeah, I know. Thanks, Mom." How much longer must this last? We were both squirming. What was so hard about being civil? She was so . . . concerned. Polite. Trying to understand. And I, as usual, the serpent's tooth.

After a few more awkward exchanges she gave up. "Well, if you want to see either of us, just call. I'll be happy to come over whenever you feel like it. And your father would also like to see you. All right? Try to eat more, sweetheart."

I watched through the window as she made her way to her Mercedes parked on Arizona Street. She had her hanky in her hand.

Julie came later that same week. Hank had told me they'd been in touch and that she was repairing some of the wreckage I'd left up north. She wore a short black skirt, black tights, black leather boots, and a dark green sweater that hugged her luscious torso. A dimpled smile. A glimmer of our high-school spark. Postadolescent sexual electricity. My penis overcame its sedation. Sex, the consummation of desire, was relief, communion, a place of peace. Intimacy had healing powers. She looked so ravishing. Where could we go? Nowhere. I was in prison.

"Stephen, you're so lucky you're here. I've been checking up on your doctor. He's supposed to be really hip."

"I wouldn't go that far."

"Hopkinds told me he's the best in West LA."

"Groovy. We know how with-it Lightning Leo is."

"Don't you see he was doing you a favor getting you out of Franciscan and down here?"

"Yeah, this is a much more interesting scene. It's just his police-state tactics I can't relate to. Especially when I'm the designated criminal. But no hard feelings. El Silver Man's pretty cool."

She briefed me on the stuff I'd left scattered all over Northern California, my van (repaired and fetched from Livermore), my clothes and books (collected from the lodge), my personal property (wallet, hanky, and 47 cents change recovered from City Prison—forget the clothes), and said she'd be staying in LA for a while. The woman had stamina. Loyalty. The John Henry principle in action. *He drove so hard he broke his poor heart,* and Polly Ann picked up the hammer. *Polly Ann drove steel like a man, Lord Lord.* "That's what you're doing," I told her. "Taking care of unfinished business. You're heroic."

After she left, my erection lingered.

When she returned a few days later she told me we had a pass. I'd earned points for good behavior on my outings in Santa Monica with Ike, walking through public parks and along sidewalks just like any other citizen, admiring the merchandise in antique shops, checking out the car lots for my next Porsche, privately scouting for a getaway car. But where would I go? I was still awaiting instructions. Julie suggested dinner and a motel. I said motel first, then dinner. She brought me back within the allotted four hours.

Pretty soon others could come and take me out for little excursions. Gena was my date for a walk around Westwood Village, harmlessly shopping in the Friday night stores, holding hands and gossiping about the family. Don, she told me, was very upset about the airport incident and wanted to visit but wasn't sure how I felt. Send him along, I said, no sweat, I'd be glad to see him. So he came, apologized—"Sorry I got so worked up, Panch"—and took me to a movie, M*A*S*H, a wartime hospital comedy? Please. It was about me, in some way, I knew, trying to make me laugh at my situation, but it wasn't funny. The audience was laughing at *me*. I sat there absorbing the humiliation, felt I had to sit through the whole thing, submitting to Don's authority while at the same time understanding I would hurt his feelings if I told him the movie sucked. Mash. That's what he'd do to me. He was freaked enough as it was. I didn't want to provoke him. He's trying to be nice to me, I told myself. He's atoning for his attack. Unless he's rubbing it in.

Hank came by with my Master's degree, sent by the lit board at UCSC, complete with the autograph of Ronald Reagan, the mad-dog governor I so admired whose bloodbath in the streets of Berkeley was a watershed in my political education. I asked Hank to take me shopping for a Porsche; I wanted to get out of here and head north. He said we could get a car when Silverman cleared my release. I was doing well. "Just keep playing by the rules and you'll be all right."

"It's about time you showed up. I've been looking for you for twenty-three years."

My father laughed at my opening salvo as we sat across from each other at a table in the basement cafeteria, a large low-ceilinged room with fluorescent light, bunkerlike in its underground security. It was early evening, after dinner hour, and just a few staffers were scattered around us smoking and drinking coffee and sipping soup. Fat Jack was fresh back from Santa Anita and was wearing a handsome deep-brown cashmere sports jacket and charcoal-colored wide silk tie, plain white dress shirt, light brown slacks, and alligator loafers. Tasteful, conservative, top-quality threads. The old man had a keen ear for the honest word and an eye for the authentic. He understood exactly what I was saying and could dig the irony. He seemed relieved that I should start our conversation with a joke, even though I was kidding on the square. I knew at some level he admired me for dropping out, walking away from the piles of pretentious horseshit steaming in the streets of Beverly Hills— the self-promoters, the big talkers, the deal makers, the operators, Don's fast-life buddies who came over flashing their cars and their babes and their great plans, schemes, scams—the public display of all the ambition money can buy. Though it puzzled him that I'd chosen such a strange profession as poetry, some part of him respected the independence.

"You know, Steve, when you get out of here you're gonna see all this as a real learning experience. You're gonna be better for it."

"I'm already better, Pop. I'm better than ever except that I'm stuck in here. And these drugs they've got me on. Kind of takes the edge off. But that's cool. If it makes them feel better."

"You comfortable? You need anything?" He was so much looser than my mother. Except for one thing. He kept reaching inside his coat with his right hand, as if he had a pistol in there. Long before I was born he'd hung out with gamblers and gangsters in Seattle—he frequented pool halls as a kid and later was in the liquor distributing business—and early on I had a sense that he was a heavyweight from the way I'd seen people treat him at the track, at the club, in restaurants. Carrying a gun could be in character. Especially if he felt his life was in danger. With a drug-crazed son who looked like this Manson guy you couldn't take any chances. I watched the hand go into his coat unconsciously as if checking his wallet. A gun. Far out.

"I'm all right." I didn't mention it. That would be indiscreet. It was okay with me. We were starting to understand each other. I respected the fact he'd kill me if he had to.

"I hear you got your Master's degree. Congratulations."

"Yeah. Thanks. I think they're trying to get rid of me. Like settling out of court. They give me the Master's so I won't come back. You think it'll do me any good in the real world? I guess I could insist that people call me Master."

He laughed again, the right hand moving into the coat. "Someday all these books and things are gonna be useful to you. All this study is gonna pay off."

"It's already paying off, Pop. I'm a poet."

"Well, maybe you've got the right idea. Your own way of doing things. You don't take any"—(he lowered his voice)—"shit from anybody."

"Sure. Except in here. They try to turn you into one of the herd. Who knows if they'll ever let me out."

"Don't you worry, boy. I've heard about your doctor, Lenny Silverman. Supposed to be a very good guy, good doctor." From his box at the track he could get background on anybody just by asking a few questions. "His father is Lou Silverglade. Very respected guy. Top surgeon."

"Cool. As long as he doesn't try to cut me."

"These guys know what they're doing. You're gonna be all right." Like taking your Cadillac to the factory-certified mechanic, delivering your head to the right shrink ought to inspire confidence—another one of the old man's favorite words. All you've got to sell is confidence. Zen of a salesman. The hand went into the jacket.

"So how are you doing? Picking any winners?"

"Oh, I about break even. I tell ya, if it wasn't for the racetrack I'd get tired from doin' nothin'." He'd sold his company and retired five years ago. "I go into the office every day, but Hank's got everything under control. He doesn't need me in there. I just get in the way." No self-pity in this assessment, just facing facts. "But those characters at the track, they're really something. That's the greatest show on earth, for my money."

For someone with his money he didn't have much ego. He'd shed pride on the way up. Without training in any monastery besides marriage and the manufacturing business he'd reached a self-lessness born of an understanding of life's basic toughness and of how lucky he was to have done as well as he had. He credited his success to the people he worked with, claimed only to be a jockey of others' talents. Even though property was evidence of his accomplishment, whatever he'd accomplished was not his property. I liked this philosopher side of my father.

It was the materialism I couldn't take, the translation of everything into money. When he and my mother had visited Santa Cruz and we drove by the wild empty field at Lighthouse Point—acres of weeds and wildflowers and birds and eucalyptus and cypress trees—all he could say was, "That piece of property must be worth a lot of money." He read the papers and the *Racing Form*, they were connected to facts; but poetry? Too abstract. As if the glint of light on insect wings playing over that real estate meant less than its potential for development. I wanted to wake him up to the world's gratuitous beauty, demonstrate that business isn't everything. He just couldn't help converting whatever he saw into cash. Money was not an end in itself but a cushion, insulation from the outside world, which he saw not as beautiful but ruthless. Abandoned by his own father as a kid, he had gone to the other extreme, providing for his offspring way over and above whatever we needed to get along. It was as if he thought none of us were competent to take care of ourselves. He wanted us to be independent—"so you never have to go begging hat in hand"—but the effect was to make us dependent on him. And in providing so well for his family he'd worked so much he hardly ever saw us. Yet his generosity was general. Don used to say a person could make a decent living picking up his tips. He believed credit was a deadly trap. His mind spoke the language of cash.

"This stay here must be costing you a fortune," he said. Hank was paying the bills out of my savings account. "It's a good thing you can afford it."

When I'd turned twenty-one I instructed Hank to please sell all the stocks they'd bought in my name when I was a kid. I wanted to divest myself of all those killer corporations. After I'd sold my shares the stock market collapsed and my father thought me a financial genius. It was those revenues that were going into the coffers of St. James and into Silverman's beachfront house.

"Yeah," I said. "I guess." It was as good a way as any to unload the money. "But that bread could buy a lot of baseball cards."

He laughed again. The hand went into the coat. The gun was to let me know he saw me as dangerous enough to take seriously. We could face each other man to man. I was confident he wasn't going to kill me. He got up. "I should be going. Let me know if you need anything."

"Okay." I wondered what kind of gun.

13

Escape Artists

April caught me by surprise. I hadn't seen her since November when she got weirded out by the vibes at the cottage and I wouldn't take her home and she ended up hitching into town herself. I'd stopped by her garage a couple of times last fall, once interrupting a love embrace with her physicist boyfriend, but we'd lost touch after Altamont. She walked onto the ward like any other visitor, showing up as if she belonged there, white face shining, gray eyes ablaze, for all I knew she was tripping. "Hi," she said in her low voice, smiling.

Even accustomed as I was to the surreal, my mind was blown. "What are you doing here? Are you crazy?" We both laughed, giddy to see each other, unsure what was going on.

"Yes."

"Too bad," I said. "I can't stand crazy people." Then I hugged her and she hugged me back, pressing her body hard against mine. What a unit. Her lean frame fit my physique precisely. I let my left hand slide down over her butt. Kissed her on the cheek. We pulled apart. "Really, what are you doing here? Are you you?"

"No, I'm you. Who are you?" More laughter. She was staying with family friends in Pacific Palisades for the weekend. She'd heard in Santa Cruz that I was in the hospital down here and just thought she'd stop by and say hi. She was still with the physicist but she'd left him up north.

"You told me I needed to do something with myself, remember? Well—" I gestured toward the ward in general, as if it were my personal domain, as if by being here I had accomplished something.

"Very impressive," April said, and we laughed some more.

"Listen. Maybe we can get a pass, go out for a few hours."

"I don't have a car. I got dropped off."

"It doesn't matter. We can take the bus or hitch. I'll call my shrink."

It was Saturday. Ike was off. I got through to Silverman by way of his exchange, and he talked to the charge nurse. They gave me a four-hour pass. I said we were going to a matinee. *Butch Cassidy and the Sundance Kid* was playing in the Palisades. Shades of Neal and Kerouac, or the Hopalong of my childhood. We could catch a bus up there, have something to eat, see the movie and be back by dark.

From the start I liked April's willingness to say or do unspeakable and unexpected things, like calling me at home when I was still with Julie and asking me to meet her downtown, or seducing me for the first time that afternoon at her friend's place in the mountains with other people partying in the sunlight right outside the abandoned cabin, or just coming out of nowhere with comments like "Our dialectic is approaching synthesis." She spurred my daring. Her boyish body and unladylike style—so different from Julie's femininity—made her more like a sidekick than a sweetheart, or like the bratty little brother I never had. Her antiromanticism complemented my Keatsian indulgences. Yet she was more adventurous, less conventional than I was. Some kind of alter ego. Once, on acid together, we'd traded faces.

Inside the theater we saw ourselves on the screen, our outlaw partnership, a couple of quick-witted easy riders cutting a stylish swath through the wild West. The sunlight flooding the cinematic landscape mirrored the wide-open enlightenment of our alliance, the territory beyond good and evil where we took our existential chances. The world was teeming with stars—that's one of the things I'd realized at St. James, which after all was named after a star, and where the ward swarmed like a psychodocumentary with thinly disguised incarnations of Robert Redford pretending to be a nurse and Frank Sinatra playing a patient named Tony Cantwell who played cassette tapes of his own recordings over and over in his room, or Joan Baez and Mary Travers making guest appearances as outpatients or occupational therapists, Dustin Hoffman as a visiting shrink and Sharon Tate returned from the murdered as a nurse, Norman Mailer and Willie Mays coming and going as staff or inmates, and the supposedly dead Kennedy brothers showing up as a couple of business-suited middle-aged women, well-groomed hospital administrators—history might make anyone a major actor in events, inspiring exploits that only later became legendary. April and I watched our story loping across the screen, and this time when the audience laughed at the protagonists' predicaments I took it personally in a positive way, as if everyone understood the absurdity of my struggle, appreciated its weirdness, encouraged my perseverance, saw this dream through which I was living as the dramatic ordeal it was and were grateful for my taking on the risk as their stunt man. My burden was philosophical, like Sisyphus Christ's in the myth on the sanctuary wall back at Franciscan.

Though I couldn't read the texts through my Thorazine glaze, I was constantly scanning the bindings of the volumes in the library on One North, looking in their titles for clues to my destiny. Signs, coded instructions, objective correlatives to intuition were everywhere. A black-covered pocket paperback had flashed its fat yellow type at me: *From Here to Eternity*. A dark green clothbound volume said *Northwest Passage*. I understood my course was being charted, directions given in subtle hints it was my responsibility to interpret. I felt myself up to the challenge, reading between the ambiguities, prepared to follow whatever route, even if it contravened official restrictions. Surely my training as a poetry analyst, on top of whatever cryptogrammatic instinct I had, was being tested. Newman and Redford as Butch and Sundance were spilling information all over the place. Their names alone were laden with implications. New Man—obviously a reference to my neo-humanity. Red Ford—perhaps an allusion to the make and color of my getaway vehicle. The simplest words, if you opened them up or broke them down to their components, revealed more meanings than you could use. That's why most people just ignored them. April and I were different. Alive with visionary attention.

As we came out of the theater into the dance of daylight we were elated for having seen our lives given back to us with interest. Confused as we may have been about the larger chaos, April and I felt anchored in the certainty that we could do no wrong, that we were artists lacing our braided paths through each other's creations. We knew the four-hour pass was a formality. We were outside and we were on our own. A cool bright winter afternoon on the wild West Side of LA. Anything could happen.

We decided to hitch out Sunset toward the beach. It had been weeks since I'd seen the Pacific. A rusty maroon Continental convertible resembling the model the president was killed in—a red Ford historically enhanced in translation—emerged from the flow of late-day traffic, pulled over and stopped for us. Sitting three across in the front seat were two men and a woman, not typical hippies in appearance but clearly not average citizens either. The driver, a clean-shaven man in his mid-thirties with close-cropped, prematurely white hair (maybe it was bleached), looked both of us over as we climbed in back. The woman, in the middle, had short dark red hair, very pale skin, dark eyeshadow and lips painted a bluish maroon, voluptuously thick like Mick Jagger's. Riding shotgun was a younger, thinner man who had a certain grace or poise detectable even just sitting there, probably a dancer, or ex-dancer, as this trio didn't look exactly athletic. They looked tired, not so

much physically, but tired with a jaded we've-seen-everything de-
tachment, an attitude beyond cool. We exchanged perfunctory
greetings as we got comfortable, the Lincoln gliding away from
the curb and back into traffic like an ocean liner.

"We're going to Malibu," said the driver. "My name's Harry. This
is Mary and that's Larry."

We told them our names. "Malibu's cool," I said. Northwest
passage.

The top was down. Larry hunched over in the passenger seat,
struck a match, then turned and handed April a burning bomber.
She took a hit and passed it to me. I savored the taste of the marijuana, a bulging surfer-style joint, my first pure smoke in nearly
two months. The Camels I'd started smoking at Franciscan were
too harsh, the high was intense but the tobacco scorched my wind-
pipes. The smooth sweet taste of the grass was medicinal, a fresh
high spiraling lightly into my psyche, triggering acidic sensations
and unspoken understandings, the motor's animal vibration purring through the leather upholstery, high clouds sailing pink-tinged
through the sinking sky, April's wiry reliability beside me reinforc-
ing our common strength, our benefactors' bohemianism putting
us at ease. I blew the smoke out slowly and passed the joint to
Mary. Harry flicked a knob on the dashboard and warm air came
rushing around our legs like water in a Jacuzzi.

"You guys going anyplace in particular?" asked Harry, exhaling a
double lungful of smoke that swirled back over us, aromatic.

"Anywhere at the beach is fine," I said.

"Why don't you come to our place at Corral Canyon? The beach
is right across the road. You can come in and hang out with us for
a while. We've got everything."

Larry seconded Harry's invitation by tossing us a stoned grin,
and Mary, gazing straight ahead, repeated, "Everything." The joint
made one more trip around the car, Harry taking the final hit and
flicking the roach into the wind of the Coast Highway as we entered the long strip of land called Malibu. Corral Canyon was far

enough down the road to be out of town, halfway between the Colony, where Silverman lived among the movie stars, and Point Dume, where my family owned a bluffside lot with a little one-room beach house wedged in the hill. The place was abandoned last I heard. Maybe we'd wind up there.

The Continental turned right onto a gravel driveway and up a hill, its tires crunching to a stop in front of a weathered ranch house. With the engine off and the dusk wind sweeping over the Santa Monica Mountains, the bay air was quiet and rich with that soft Southern California perfume of a desert coast uncorrupted by smog. The house had the austere, half-monastic feel of an art studio, sliding glass doors, pine paneling on the walls, rough plank floors, bedrooms in back, a simple one-story structure. Larry fetched some eucalyptus logs and built a fire in the flagstone fire-place. Mary brought some Mexican beers from the kitchen and Harry pulled a black lacquer cigar box out of a wall cabinet where the stereo stood. Mary lit candles. Larry put Blind Faith on the stereo, Stevie Winwood's haunted voice wailing over the hypnotic tickling of his and Clapton's guitars, *and I'm wasted and I can't find my way home.* Outside, the bay darkened through a progression of blues and pinkish purples. The house smelled salty, damp with the sea but spiced with eucalyptus smoke.

Harry sliced some hash and passed a pipe. We sat in a semicircle around the fire, the flagstone wall flickering pink and yellow as the kindling caught and the dry logs flared hot. April took off her cape and let it fall on the couch behind us. She was wearing tight jeans and a dark blue wraparound top whose belt went behind her back and tied in front. Harry came over to her and pulled the V neckline apart, just like that, and took a long look at her chest. Her breasts were wide apart, beautiful as baseballs, nipples erect. Unfazed, ex-pressionless, she looked him straight in the eye as if to say, What the fuck are you trying to prove? Her reaction or lack of one blew his mind and he pulled the knit top back together, laughing. That April. I felt a wave of love.

The mixture of grass, hash, beer, and the absence of food and my afternoon blast of Thorazine, which I'd skipped by going AWOL, was giving me a certain buoyancy, pumped further by lingering feeling from the film and the strange stimulation of Harry's demonic comedy. He was creepy and charming at the same time, an experimentalist, obviously the ringleader of this rhymed threesome. I focused on the fire to keep my mind from flying around the room or out the roof.

Harry said to me, "Did anyone ever tell you you look just like Charlie Manson?"

"All the time," I said. "Did anyone ever tell you you look just like Timothy Leary?"

"Who looks like Dennis the Menace," April added.

Harry chuckled and regarded us. "Are you two tripping?"

"All the time," said April.

"That's a groove," said Mary. "So are we."

April was speaking figuratively. A mystic metaphor. Life is so naturally trippy that acid merely clarifies what's already eternal. All the time. From here to eternity. Being with her was like swimming around deep in the subconscious, it hardly mattered whether she'd actually dropped any drug or not. And I was tripping too, even though Altamont was the last time I'd eaten a psychedelic, I was still traveling on that trajectory, getting tremendous mileage on the momentum, drinking loaded water as a booster, wondering if or when I'd ever come down.

"We knew Charlie before he went bad," said Larry. "He was an interesting little guy. Too bad his power trip got away from him."

"Yes," said Harry, still fixing his gaze on April. He grinned. "Power corrupts."

Mary got up from her cushion on the floor and sat beside me. She took my head in her hands and kissed me on the mouth, her tongue massaging mine with startling agility. I wondered what kind of test this was, what were our obligations, how far should we go and which way, the scene was starting to feel wrong, as if we'd wandered into a drugwarp of unknowably distorted dimensions, I was excited by Mary's mouth but also scared, turned on and uneasy, even a little sickened, yet wasn't the reigning demand to seize sex at every chance, use it or lose it, April didn't care who I fucked, she had a man, but what about these other guys, whose holes were they eyeing, or did they just want to watch, that was possible, was it a free-for-all or a carefully choreographed orgy in Harry's control, his trip, my resemblance to Manson turned him on because he had Manson fantasies, charismatic love king of hippie hitchhikers, in his mind maybe April was the next Mary, and I another Larry under his power. Harry smiled approvingly at Mary's move, his canines flashing like fangs, a draculoid glimmer in his firelit candlelit eyes.

"Sorry," I said, getting up, extracting myself from Mary's clutches. "We'll catch you later."

April had already grabbed her cape.

"Thanks for everything, but we'll skip the rest. Let's boogie," I said to April.

"Don't rush away, sweethearts," Larry said.

"Yes," said Harry, "there's no reason to leave. How will you get anywhere? It's early. Stay."

"Maybe in another life," said April.

We were out the door in the fresh night, a quarter moon high over the water. As we hiked down the driveway to the coast road I wiped the lipstick off my mouth.

We could have crossed the highway and hitched into Santa Monica, getting me back to St. James just a couple of hours late, but instead we stayed on the northbound side, waiting for a ride to Point Dume, breathing that tangy canyon air and watching the moonlight sparkle on the dark water. I tried to kiss April but she turned her head, saying, "Yuck, not after that slut had her tongue in your mouth."

It wasn't late, maybe seven or eight o'clock, but this far out of town there wasn't that much traffic, even on a Saturday night. We waited patiently, putting our thumbs out whenever headlights approached. Soon a car pulled over, one of those round-backed Volvo coupes. We climbed in behind a young couple who looked familiar in the dim green dashboard light, not personally but culturally, subconsciously, as if emerging from a myth or a movie. He had a thick head of blondish locks, shaggy but not as long as mine, the beginning of a beard softening his sharp profile. She was darker, dark eyes and hair, handsome in an unglamorous way, like Natalie Wood in *Rebel Without a Cause*. Could this be her and James fucking Dean come back to give us a lift? They were warm, friendly, almost wholesome next to the trio we'd just escaped. "Where you guys going?" asked Dean.

"Point Dume," I said. "Just a few miles up."

"I know where it is."

Natalie turned around in her seat, flashing her black eyes and white teeth at us. "Isn't this the most incredible night? It's so clear. Look at that moonlight. Smell the air." Her shaded face shone with a fierce exuberance, radiating electricity, wind whipping her long hair, wrapping us all in its cool embrace and letting go, flowing out as fast as it could pass through, a stroke was enough, time in motion, nothing to hold, a streaming eternal moment, two pairs of strangers bound instantly in the intimacy of adventure, hurtling out Route 1 toward Dume, that mysterious triangle of land at the northwest edge of Santa Monica Bay, like Lighthouse Point on Monterey Bay, even the geography rhymed, my turf was everywhere, I was at home in the flow.

After Paradise Cove the coastline curved south and the road went straight on, leaving the point on our left. I saw up ahead the little real estate office, its painted sign lit by a floodlight, and said, "You can drop us right up here."

"If you want, we can take you where you're going on the point," said Dean. "We've got nothing to do."

"Okay," I said and directed him through the three or four turns—Wildlife, Fernhill, Grayfox, street names laden with loaded associations—that would take us to the gate of my parents' property, bought as an investment in the late fifties but used only occasionally since then as a place for a Sunday outing or a Friday night party for me and my high school friends. When I was in college a young couple had talked my father into renting them the place, promising to fix up the ramshackle one-room beach house and act as caretakers. They had moved on and the house was empty now as far as I knew. The gate was padlocked. "Come on," I said, climbing up and over the chainlink fence, my monkey fingers tasting the rusty metal. Natalie and Dean followed April.

We walked out across the empty lot under the enormous sky, looking down the coast and across the bay at the rim of lights lining the water. Even with the moonlight we could see hundreds of stars swimming overhead. We made our way down the path through iceplant and little scrub pines toward the bluffside house, breathing the heady smells of the night sea mixed with those of the vegetation spiced with fireplace smoke. Although we were still in Los Angeles County it felt as if we had broken out to the far side of civilization. Exploring dream territory. Making our way through the essence of our own invention.

The house was locked, but with a small stick I reached through the crack and unhooked the latch on the door of the outdoor shower the tenants had enclosed, entered and opened the wood-framed French doors to the living area. "Won't you come in?" I said to my guests, who were standing on the patio spaced on the vast view. There was one electric lamp, which worked, illuminating the room with a dim yellow glow. The place smelled stale, shut up too long, airless and taken over by resident mice. Their scat was everywhere. There was no firewood. One wooden chair to sit on, and a moldy mattress on the raised platform in the corner. "Excuse the mess."

"Are you sure it's okay for us to be here?" Natalie asked.

"Oh, yeah," I assured her. "My folks really own this place. How else do you think I knew about it?"

"You could've imagined it," April said.

Dean laughed. "That's hip. Just imagine things up as you need them."

"Far out," said Natalie. "Now what?"

"How about this," I said. I picked up the chair, carried it outside, and smashed it on the concrete patio, loosening two legs, then pounded its shaky joints against the cement until I had a pile of sticks and boards, which I carried back inside. "Firewood." Intuiting my plan, April had found a couple of grocery bags and sheets of newspaper lining a cabinet and placed them by the fireplace set in the stone wall abutting the bluff. I built a fire. Dean provided the match.

With a frazzled broom she'd found in the closet Natalie swept the floor in front of the hearth, clearing away the mouse turds so we'd have a decent place to park our butts. We sat and watched the remains of the chair go up in flames. I introduced myself and April.

"I'm Dean," said Dean. No shit.

"I'm Willow." Natalie would have been too obvious—she was still alive, wasn't she? Names didn't matter anyway. We were beyond such bourgeois conventions. Identities were mutable, like the disposition of moonlight on the bay, we were all flecks and sparks and bits of each other and of everything, constantly dancing, changing, breaking apart, exchanging energy, interpenetrating, trading places, faces, physiques, that's why no one could die, life was continuous transformation, if you got crushed in a car crash you showed up elsewhere in another form, always evolving, recombining, spirit springing surprises into flesh. Pick any name, it was temporary at best. The flesh, I mean. Some names on their own could last forever. Connected to certain works and deeds, to certain legends.

What we were doing here was more obscure. We looked at the fire as it burned down, exchanging glances in the yellow light. We'd left the doors open to air the place out, and the salty geranium breeze was chilly. I waited for a sign.

No sign.

The night got colder. The fire was dying.

Driftwood. There'd been enough rain that there should be plenty scattered along the tide line. There were wooden stairs that led to a path that led down to the beach. April and I could take a walk. "We'll go collect some wood," I said. "Wait here. Make yourselves at home."

At the bottom of the path we removed our shoes. The sand was cool and smooth between my toes. We agreed to split off in different directions, collect an armload of wood and meet in a few minutes.

I gathered my armload fast, feeling the sexy wave-hewn shapes, savoring the weight of the mass soon to be heat, smelling the salt. Brought the load back, dumped it on the sand, and headed off down the beach to intercept April returning. She looked miraculous in the icy moonlight, a flash of magic.

"Hold it," I said. "I mean drop that stuff." She dropped the driftwood. I put my arms around her, ran my hands through her short hair, kissed her left temple, the side of her neck. A curve of the bluff hid us from view of the house. I kissed her mouth and she responded, thrusting her hips against my member. "Let's do it now," I said to her.

"Cut it out. I didn't come for this. I can't."

"What do you mean? It's only everything."

"I have my period."

"Let's get in each other's blood. It's our one chance. Look at this night. It's destined." I slipped my hands inside her cape, caressed her ass, inhaled her milky smell, the musk oil she wore, pulled her against my erect cock, drank from her open mouth. She was getting hot.

"What about Dean and Willow?"

"They can take care of themselves. They're probably getting it on. We can meet them back at the planetarium."

"Huh?"

"Forget it. Let me take the cape," I said, unfastening the button at the neck. I led her by the hand to the base of the bluff and spread the cape on the sand. Drew her down onto me. My cock was aching.

"I can't fuck you, Stephen. Really," she said, opening my jacket, running her hands down over my chest, my belly, stroking my cock, unbuttoning my pants, unzipping them, sliding down me, pulling my pants and shorts around my thighs, holding my penis gently in her hand, then licking the length of it, running her tongue around the tip, taking it into her mouth. I could feel her warm saliva, the smooth wet tongue slipping playfully over me, soft lips moving up and down, her fingers fondling my scrotum, I saw a shooting star, felt my juice rising, her mouth working wet, my back arching, hips writhing, I groaned, the hot semen shooting into her mouth, heard her laughing, gagging, swallowing, gulping my come.

I stroked her head as she lay between my legs. Saw another meteor falling, flaring out. "Oh, April, you're amazing. You made the sky come too."

She looked up at me and grinned, her lips still glistening, then slithered into my arms and kissed me, sperm spilling into my mouth, slippery and tart. "I give cosmic blow jobs."

Then I heard hoofbeats, horses approaching, galloping up the beach and past us, two girls bareback on their animals out for a moonlight ride—shades of Butch and Sundance, another variation on our adventure, thunderous rhythmic accompaniment to my interstellar ejaculation.

When we got back up to the house our guests weren't there. Probably gone to find Sal Mineo—Plato in *Rebel*—echoing April's platonic act of fellatio. Everything connected. Revelation by association. If this was madness, fuck sanity, I felt this pitch of consciousness as a gift, a meteor shower illuminating meanings deeper than the speed of light, the universe ringing with pinball poetry, explosions of correlations, orgasmic correspondences igniting minds with blinding unspeakable understandings, a music of passionate unity, Blake's lineaments of gratified desire coming and coming like electric guitars in an endless cadenza pouring its power into the open soul.

We built a fire with the driftwood, warmed ourselves, and watched the movie in the flames. After a while we climbed onto the mattress on its platform, but for me the bed was too scuzzy with mold and dust and the smell of mice to sleep on. April didn't care, she was tired and spread her cape and zonked out peacefully while I just lay there squirming and watching the sky through the windows, watching the fire's shadows, watching her face. I was married to her in spirit as much as I was to Julie, maybe more. So many different forms of love, powerful affinities, passions, alliances, friendships. How could you choose just one exclusive partner? It made no sense. Marriage, monogamy, was just another form of state repression. If freedom had any meaning it had to encompass love, open up love's possibilities, dismantle the apparatus of illusion that pretended to wedlock people together. Legal sanctification meant political control, artificial restraint, perversion of nature. Humans were animals, enlightened creatures. How could you keep the spirit from forming fresh associations, spreading light?

Something ran by my head and April screamed. "Ow, it bit me! The little fucker!" The place was crawling with mice. There must have been a nest in the mattress. We were surrounded. The fire was down to coals. It was deep night outside but it was too creepy to stay. We scampered from the platform, shaking ourselves off, brushing the dust and crud off each other's backs, shivering with cold and disgust. I scattered the coals with a stick and we hiked back up the path, alert for packs of attacking rats or other marauding monsters in the iceplant. We hopped the fence on the strength of our fear and began the long walk out toward the highway.

It took about half an hour to reach Route 1, walking the streets of this rustic neighborhood smelling of horses and ocean, the houses dark, no humans about, it must have teen three or four in the morning. A large white cat dashed across our path from left to right a dozen yards ahead. Good luck. I breathed a little easier. My heartbeat calmed but my mind was beside itself. I felt fatigued, oppressively sleepless, yet somehow still had energy to spare, whatever was necessary to get to a clean bed, take a break from the intensity. April said she was hungry. We were both wasted. Wired. Alive to the wild night.

At that hour the Coast Highway stretched endlessly desolate in both directions. The moon was down. We stood by the light of the real estate office and waited. Every so often a set of headlights came up out of the northwest topped by a little row of yellow lights, an all-night trucker, roaring past us, some of them giving a little ironic toot on the air horn as if to taunt us. What are you crazy hippies doing out here at this time of night? One of them slowed, though, pulled over and brought his rig to a squealing stop some fifty yards up. We ran after him, climbed into the high cab. Thank god he was going into Santa Monica. Across the bay a red glow slowly rose over Palos Verdes. The driver went a mile out of his way to drop April in the Palisades.

I was back at St. James by the time the sun was up.

14

From Here to Eternity

Boy, did I catch shit for that field trip. The charge nurse had me put in restraints the minute I checked in, and to tell the truth I was too wiped out to object. They fed me a devastating dose of Thorazine, snapped into place the bars alongside my bed, strapped my wrists and ankles to them and I was gone, instantly falling into deep captivity, falling and falling through layers of dreamless sleep.

When I awoke Ike was in the room, sitting quietly in a chair. My arms and legs were still strapped, the leather cinches expertly secured to the bed rails, my arteries throbbing. That was the day I asked Ike if it was still 1970. I felt as if I'd been out for years, decades. I started to cry. Why were they doing this to me? All I'd done was to take a little break, a leave of absence. I'd come back, hadn't I? I wasn't trying to escape. I wasn't violent. Why did they have to tie me down like some psychopath? My feelings were hurt. Ike stood by my bedside and put his hand on my shoulder as I sobbed.

"It's okay, Steve. You scared some of the people, that's all. They was afraid you wouldn't come back. I'm gonna see if they'll let you loose now."

Ike left the room and returned a few minutes later with the charge nurse and a psych tech, one of the goons who'd rigged up this torture contraption. As he undid the straps the nurse asked, as if speaking to a five-year-old, "Do you think you can behave yourself now?"

Behind her back Ike nodded to me. "Yes," I said, thick-tongued from the drug, suppressing the rage I wanted to spew in her face.

When the torturers left the room and I could move my arms and legs I lay there for a few minutes just enjoying the sensation of my circulating blood, the ability to move my limbs, the comfort of Ike's comradeship. He was my human shield against the institutional forces attempting to break me, crush and reconstitute me into a model zombie of obedience. As my special nurse he had limited authority in the hospital hierarchy, but at least he saw me as an individual. Though sometimes I feared his power over me, I knew he was with me. I trusted him.

"How come these people hate me, Ike?"

"Oh, they don't hate you, Steve. They just don't have the time to understand you. They got so many other peoples to look after. They got their rules they has to go by. They don't see how you might be different from some of these other folks."

Yeah, I might be different, like from another world.

"Everybody tells me I look like Charlie Manson. Why can't they just see me for who I am?"

"Well, you know, Steve, some folks can't help thinking who a person looks like on the TV or in the papers, that's just the way people think. A lot of peoples tell me I look like Sammy Davis, but I just let that go by, I know they don't mean no harm."

"You look to me like Malcolm X," I dared to say, watching for his reaction.

Ike lowered his eyes modestly, then looked at me. "Now I consider that a compliment. He was a very great man. But you know, Steve, I'm just Isaac Odom. Your special, here to look out for you." He wasn't copping to anything. Invisible Malcolm.

"Maybe I should cut my beard off. What do you think?"

"I think you'd look real handsome, Steve. And maybe some of these nurses and folks would see you different, wouldn't be so scared. I can shave you if you want."

"Let's do it. I'm ready for a change of face."

Ike fetched some scissors and a straight razor, shaving soap, a portable basin and a towel, and went to work, standing over me as I sat on the edge of the bed. Working deliberately, like a sculptor carving a bust, he shaped my new face, wielding the blade with grace and confidence. I could feel the strength of his powerful shoulders attuned to this delicate task, could smell his cologne, observe his concentration. I had to contain my love and gratitude, couldn't start crying with the razor by my face. This man was saving my life, keeping me human through this interminable trial.

"There," he said, wiping away the excess soap. "A new man. I'll go get us a mirror." There were no mirrors on the ICU, nothing that might be converted to a suicide tool. Once when a razorblade was found in a toilet Ike had retrieved it quickly with a coathanger as if defusing a bomb. Emergency surgery, search and rescue, crisis prevention. A man of action. I felt my face with my fingers. Three months unshaved, now strangely smooth. When Ike came back with the looking glass I didn't recognize myself.

"Who is this guy?" I asked him.

"It's you, Steve. You look fine, if I do say so myself." He laughed, taking credit for my transformation.

Not that the shave changed the way I perceived my habitat. The dreamlike psychofantasia of my surroundings persisted in the way the characters on the ward continued to play their multiple roles, doubling their identities as stars and strangers, provocateurs and co-conspirators, friends and aliens, shapeshifters and unreconstructible squares, their faces a flow of screens on which emotions ran and retreated like a Jackson Pollock Rorschach-in-progress, streams of compassion and paranoia mingling and muddying each other, swirling currents of frightening confusion and soothing assurance like acid trippers flipping from states of grace to fear to horror to humor and back in a flash, everyone's identity a hoax or a joke, a gift, a curse or blessing in disguise. The TV set on the main ward watched us all, the convex screen collecting our reflections and sending them back to control central where our thoughts were monitored, ambulance sirens from emergency attempting to mask the drone of the sinister machinery in the walls recording our conversations, our coded dialogues in schizophrenese that secretly spelled release. I'd been swimming around in this psychedelic soup so long it was my medium, the world had kicked over into a permanent state of lysergic acidity, hallucination made real, it was exciting and tiring at the same time because it never let up except when I slept, as if realities were reversed and the only way I could emerge from the dream was by losing consciousness completely. I began to want to wake up, to escape from nightmare's responsibilities. I wanted to come down and be relieved of the load.

The people around me saw my beardless face as the sign of a changed man. Everyone, from nurses to fellow patients to my shrink to various visitors, commented on how much better I looked, how much younger, healthier, how handsome, etc. until I was sick of hearing it implied how horrible I had appeared to them before. Silverman kept my medication heavy, gradually dragging my physical energy into a thickening swamp where my every act was leaden. This new slow-motion mode was perceived as a sign of mental health. My resistance to authority weakened. I didn't have the strength to respond to the madness in which I still felt imprisoned—no madness of mine but of the institution, the prevailing madness, the artificial normality. The oppressiveness of everything—the drugs, the rules, the expectations, demands to conform, to be invisible—began to have the effect the doctor desired. My manic symptoms subsided as my spirit drooped. My clean-shaved well-behaved subdued persona began to convince my keepers that I was recovering.

After a week or so in this brought-down state I said to Silverman one day, "So when can I get out of here? Aren't I sane yet? What more do I have to do to prove I'm not crazy?"

"Do you really think you can handle it now outside?" he asked in his low, slow voice.

"Listen, Doc, the longer I'm in here the madder I get. Can't you just test me to see if I'm . . . to see how I do? This place is making me sick." I'd been in St. James two months. It was almost spring. I needed to get away. Take my show on the road.

"How can I trust you not to run away?"

"I can't run away if I'm released already."

"What about your medication? Would you take it unsupervised?"

"Whatever's necessary."

"Let's see how you do without Ike for a few days. Okay? Tomorrow will be his last shift. How about it?"

A good test. El Silver Man was shrewd. Could I deal with the daily scene and my private visions of its permutations without Ike's stabilizing company, his encouragement, his protection? "Cool," I said, knowing I had to make the sacrifice, had to prove I could do it.

Next day as his shift ended Ike shook my hand in both of his. "You take care of yourself now, Steve. You're doing just fine. You get out of here and you just play it cool, you know what I mean?"

"Sure, Ike. Thanks a lot. I'll see you."

"You need me for anything, you let me know, all right?"

He gave me his home phone number. "Bye, Steve." I watched his white-suited shoulders pass through the door of the ward and down the hospital hall.

All I had to do was cool it and El Silver Man would set me free. I made a major effort to be dull, not challenge anyone to test the stupid reality of the ward, keep my mouth on a short leash, be meticulously inconspicuous, polite, cooperative, calm. I consciously chose to ignore hallucinations of any kind. I wouldn't be provoked.

The strategy worked. The following week Silverman signed me out into the care of Hank and Julie, who came to take me away.

Julie had rented a small apartment in West LA. Lacking any other local home, that's where I set up camp until I could get a car and head north again. Four mornings a week at eleven o'clock I went to see Silverman, but all I could talk about was getting out of town. "Neurotic patterns are not geographically endemic," he said to me. "Why don't you stay and work a few things out?" But even the relative freedom of being on the loose with Julie in Los Angeles was making me claustrophobic. It was partly the proximity to my parents, who were giving me the creeps just by being in the same city—their nearness was antimagnetic, I felt repulsed by the prospect of seeing them even as I knew they expected some contact, our power struggle was still too complicated, no one was sure just who owed what to whom—and partly the city itself with its blue-brown smog and its vehicular tyranny, its solitude on wheels, its speed, its slickness. Julie and I drove around, sped up to Malibu and back, cruised through the Hollywood Hills along Mulholland looking for a little beauty, something natural or real beyond the anemic palms and imported flowering hothouse tropical foliage like pancake makeup on the landscape, expensive perfume to obscure the actual desert. We played the radio for traces of musical truth, smoked the pot she always had in plentiful supply and rolled with such fastidious expertise. We made love at her place and discussed the doubtful prospects for our reunion. But I was more turned on by the mobility of the car than by her familiar closeness, however grateful I was for her solidarity. I faithfully took my Thorazine four times a day and bugged Hank every few days to take me shopping for a car. I still had plenty of bread in the bank and was old enough to spend it but I needed the support of his authority, his understanding of the world of commerce, his confidence, to be sure I was doing the right thing.

On a lot in Beverly Hills we found a silver 1960 Porsche 1600 Super cabriolet, similar enough in appearance to Jimmy Dean's '55 Spyder that only a sports car freak would note the subtle difference in the bathtub-style lines, the bumpers, the shape of the windshield and the fold-down canvas top. Dean's spirit was following me. The car was perfect. I wrote a check and drove it off the lot.

Now I had some degree of autonomy but I still felt like a pinball in the flashing glass enclosure of Los Angeles. I spent less time with Julie and more on the street, reveling in the freedom of being able to move about at will despite the fact I had no place to go. I kept the top up except at night because the sunlight scorched my Thorazined skin and gave me the feeling I was turning black, like a piece of meat on a barbecue grill. I persuaded Silverman that in my silver car I was ready to blow this town and resume a quiet life in the suburbs of Santa Cruz, taking my medicine scrupulously and putting my imagination to work on paper instead of on other people. Julie would stay in LA for now, working on her own neuroses. I kissed her good-bye, shook hands with Hank, said so long to the shrink, and hit the freeway. From here to eternity. Northwest passage.

Ever since Altamont I'd felt my life was being guided by superior powers, that gods of the revolution were secretly directing my trip through this mythic dimension suffused with meaning most people were forced to ignore because they couldn't use the information, they'd be overwhelmed, but I had been selected and was acting out for the collective welfare some model scenario of new consciousness. It was more than just drugs or ideology or politics—a poetic transformation was demanded, so naturally poets were chosen as the guerrilla vanguard, we were collaborating with all art, as Morgan had exhorted and Julius had encouraged with his civil dramatics, creative saturation on every plane, the world was the poem.

Going public with my revelation had been premature, immature, I vaguely realized as I drove north impersonating Dean in the silver roadster. My big mouth, unable to censor its messages and fight songs and rambling ballads, had landed me behind bars and strapped to beds instead of out in the air where I could spread the word more widely. I knew my performance was being monitored and maybe broadcast, even in the nuthouse, but incarceration was obviously not an end in itself. I was being readied for more important missions. That I'd ended up in a resurrection of Dean's wrecked car after hitching a ride from an incarnation of him in Malibu just weeks before drove home the understanding that my work was serious, dangerous, possibly fatal—he'd crashed at twenty-three—and I should watch each sign for its unwritten instruction. This edge of renewed alertness as I raced up 101 was thrilling, not in some cheap rush that fades in a few minutes but in a continuous current of fresh electricity bathing the brain and the nerves in streams of certainty bordering on fear—a sense that survival hinges on every move, and every move feels inevitable and right. I didn't know what I was doing but I knew I was destined to be doing this, proceeding on a return route to complete some circle.

The top was up on the cabriolet as I didn't want my face to fry, but I could still breathe the rich green early spring landscape's rain-enhanced grasses and the first wildflowers, cows on the San Luis Obispo hillsides looked happier than ever, and birds were darting deliriously through lucid white-clouded blue. The hum of the motor massaged my back and arms and legs as I sat comfortably low, snug in the driver's seat. I was on my own. I reviewed the hundreds of seemingly random signs I now understood as prophetic, setting me on this course from as far as memory could wander.

Walking on the Boardwalk in Santa Cruz one night the previous summer with Julie I'd noticed coming toward us a tall ungainly guy I recalled having seen years before on Hollywood Boulevard—a roominghouse loser who cruised, just browsing in the storewindows and watching the other walkers or ogling the cars that were also cruising, as I was roaming the sidewalks in search of urban reality, human epiphanies to feed my poems, mysterious insight into others' eyes. He resembled pictures I'd seen of Thomas Wolfe, deranged by the intensity of perception, wild-eyed, drunk or high. As we approached each other and passed he looked at Julie and me and raged, "You don't deserve her!" Lonesome souls like him were suffering immense alienation while in his eyes these overprivileged punks were fucking to our nuts' content in clean beds with gorgeous girls even if we did have hair like hippies. He was right, I understood instinctively through my momentary terror, I didn't deserve her. Was he a messenger, following me over the years all the way from LA to tell me, as April had done, that our marriage was a mistake?

Then in the fall while still in school I had this dream: I'm standing in a muddy field amid thousands of young men milling around apparently attempting to form ranks. It's a battlefield and the guys are soldiers, tired-looking, too exhausted to stand in straight lines or come to attention. It occurs to me they are English majors— and captains and lieutenants and sergeants and corporals and privates—a whole division of graduate-student grunts and tenured professors assembling in their filthy uniforms, for what? Marching orders to some POW camp? Shipment into the jaws of some academic bureaucracy from which, once inducted and indoctrinated, there is no escape? I had to bail out of that army. Desert for the sake of sanity. Every conscious and unconscious indication was leading me out of context, suggesting I cut ties to all conventional institutions—marriage, a career in university servitude, wired into the system—and venture into more exposed zones.

Which is what I'd done, only going a little too far into uncharted waters for my own good, sailing totally out of orbit so I'd had to be captured, brought down inside existing boundaries, trained to stay on the edge without going over. I was beginning to get that, even though it was next to impossible not to respond to the pressures of this expanded universe by leaping out of my skin.

Approaching the power plant at Moss Landing, its giant smokestacks and miles of pipes dominating the little fishing harbor, I felt a fresh excitement in returning to this coast, this bay, this territory just beyond the range of Jeffers and Steinbeck and their classic but dated imaginations. The new poetics were postliterary and I was their representative. Waiting at my house now in Rio Del Mar, past the Yale lock and the tracks of the Rum Tum Tugger, would be my occult instructions for carrying on the campaign of pure subversion I'd accidentally derailed by going overt. All I had to do was find the key and read them right and carry them out with original vision.

I stopped for dinner at Javier's, savoring the warm smells and spicy tastes of the sauces and the sounds of the Mexican folk songs in the speakers of the candlelit room, the most beautiful meal since my last stop here with Hank on our pass from Franciscan. It was early, very few diners, and the natural late-afternoon light filtering softly through the latticework of the front windows complemented the cold Carta Blanca bathing my tongue and throat as it soothed the fire of the salsa. Every bite was a soft explosion of flavors, my tastebuds retuned to noninstitutional foods, each taste freighted with waves of association that swept me into the delicious romance of what I'd begun by coming to Santa Cruz in the first place instead of staying back east or accepting my folks' offer of a basement domain beneath their new Bel Air hacienda. No, I'd chosen a home of my own, even if it only proved another point of departure.

My bus, its engine rebuilt at a garage in Livermore and retrieved by Julie, was parked in the driveway. I pulled the silver Porsche in behind it. Early dusk. The day's last birds were running off their riffs as if to welcome me back. No sign of the Tugger; maybe he'd moved on to more reliable providers. The house was cool. Peaceful. Spookily quiet until I put on music—the Temptations, keeping things light with five-part harmonies, contagious bass guitars and Smokey Robinson rhymes, *You got a smile so bright, you know you coulda been a candle, I'm holding you so tight, you know you coulda been a handle,* dance music for teenage romantics such as I was once and hadn't outgrown, and I danced alone, delighted to be back, boogalooing to the Motown beat like Dr. Williams under the influence of a dark Detroit as night dropped behind Santa Cruz just ten miles up the coast. I wasn't going to be able to stay home. I was too loaded with the juice of my new freedom. I had to be with people, connect with my fellow spirits, I couldn't keep this happiness to myself. Something must be happening downtown. I could see if April was home. Or Carolyn Corday. Some cool woman to let me rave. And there was the Rodeo, the local collective unconscious, I'd run into someone I knew, might catch some music, watch the erotic rituals. Or I could drive to the mountains and see if Nona was at the lodge.

It didn't matter. Wherever the roadster took me.

15

Temptations of Prince Valiant

Tooling into town with the top down—night meant no sunlight to blacken my skin—I had the radio on loud listening for directions from the songs, the deejays, even the commercials, you couldn't be sure where word would come from, *whispers of wind in the listening sky*, as Stephen Spender said, and now Stevie Wonder was singing over the air, *I'm wondering, little girl I'm wondering, how can I make you love me a little more than you love him*, as if speaking to me, for me, the wonder spender, way over budget, increasingly amazed by everything, *the spirit clothed from head to foot in song*. I wanted to share the overflow, spill my soul music into a collaborator in the current overthrow, someone whose rhymes and rhythms would complete mine. The Rodeo would be humming with connections later but it was too early for much to be happening there. Carolyn, who'd been some kind of guru to Julie and had locked eyes with me that New Year's morning as a way of inciting my cooperation, Carolyn with her cock-eyed gaze that drove me overboard, who seemed to know me more intimately than I did her, maybe she had come and fucked me once as Julie, I mean they'd traded bodies—Carolyn would be feeding her kid or putting him to bed, a bad time to barge in. The lodge was too far, I wasn't ready for the mountains yet even though I wanted to see Nona, it was too dark up there, too many trees. So that left April in her garage on Riverside Street, right across the river from Carolyn, over the garage actually, she had a studio where she practiced her abstractions and slept on the floor on a Japanese mat. Last time I'd come by, her boyfriend had been there, they were in bed, a tense scene for the few seconds I stayed, but no sweat, he was a pacifist, not the kind to kill you for the intrusion. I didn't care if he was there tonight, I needed to see April, she was the only one to take me literally, see me as the angelic force I was. Our connection was unconscious, we could converse not saying a word, just shooting intuitions from psyche to psyche like jazz musicians without the instruments. Throughout my various incarcerations I'd often had the sensation it was her body I was inhabiting. She was my other.

I pulled up and parked, punched the radio off, got out, the car door shut with a comfortable thump. The arc lamp on the sidewalk a few yards down from her house was buzzing. From across Beach Flats and the river you could smell the bay. Fruit trees were blossoming, a hint of sweetness in the evening air. I walked around the side of the main house and up the driveway to the garage. At the top of the stairs a bare bulb lit the green-painted door. White paint was flaking off the banister. I knocked.

"Come on," April said. It was unlocked. Inside, her oil paints smelled up everything, overwhelming even the smell of the musk oil she always wore and the fresh tea steeping in a ceramic pot. There were fresh brown, green, and yellow squiggles on the big square neo-ex-post-abstract-expressionist canvas-in-progress leaning against the wall. A plastic bag of granola lay open on the floor amid a miscellaneous display of clothes strewn to shape the setting, soften the room's straight lines. She was wearing jeans and a cotton smock, barefoot as usual, and didn't seem surprised to see me. "You look like Prince Valiant," she said remarking on my new face.

"Actually I'm an escapee from a García Lorca look-alike contest."

She laughed briefly. "Bob's going to be here any minute." Bob was the pacifist physicist.

"Maybe we can have a metaphysical fist fight."

"How did you get out?"

"I tricked my shrink."

"Really, you should be gone when Bob gets here. He was very upset last time. He cried after you left."

"Maybe I should have stayed."

"I'm not kidding. Let's not have a scene, okay?"

"Then come with me—for a walk or something. I need to be with you. There's so much going on."

She gave me that spacy gray-eyed longing know-it-all look, omniscient and indifferent at the same time, hungry for love yet above desire. She wanted to join me, would but couldn't. I wish you could just be cool, said the look.

Footsteps bounded up the stairs, the door opened, and in came big gentle brainy Bob, six feet tall and even darker than me—he could pass for black if his hair were nappier. "Oh, April," he half-whined, half-sniveled. "Not again."

"Come on in, Bob, we can talk," I said. A gracious host.

"I can't do this," he said, turning for the door.

"Wait," said April, chasing him onto the landing, down the stairs, their footsteps shaking the garage, her voice trailing into the street.

After a minute or so I heard two car doors slam, one after the other. An engine started and the sound pulled away. April was gone, just like that. I paced the small space, stepping over her stuff. Rinsed out a funky mug in the bathroom sink. Poured myself some tea, still steaming in the pot on the floor next to her sleeping mat. I held the mug under my nose, breathing the spearmint spirits, staring at the painting, a hideous muddle of wormlike shapes writhing pointlessly or possibly trying to wiggle out of the picture, climbing over each other, struggling, not getting anywhere, mired in some oily bog from which there was no escape. I marveled at the seriousness of April's commitment to painting, figured she must have some deep vision to see meaning or beauty in such a composition. It was clear the form was intentional, each stroke deliberate, a mess with a guiding intelligence, reflecting the mess of the room, creating a dialectic with the environment. I sat on the mat and sipped the tea. Then I lay down, enveloped in her smells. Spearmint, musk, her pungent female odors pressed into the sheets and mixed with her lover's sweat, all wrapped together with the overriding strength of the paints were making me dizzy. I turned off the lamp. A shaft of light from the streetlamp angled in through the front window, catching a corner of the canvas. I took off my shoes, then my shirt and pants, and crawled naked into the bedding reeking of her essences. All that was missing was her flesh, her breath, the cool dialogue that sealed our sex.

Then I was waking up. It was still dark, I had no clue what time. The embrace with April had been imaginary. She wasn't coming back—not soon enough, anyway. I put my clothes on, left the light off, stepped carefully through the obstacle course, outside and down the stairs. I felt as if I were leaving a sweet late fuck, slipping off into the dawn while she slept. But there was no her, no fuck, no dawn. I needed the touch, the trust, the naked connection, sexual or not. I was dying for some kind of oneness.

I drove the car across the Riverside Bridge to Carolyn's place in Beach Flats. I hoped it wasn't too late. A light was on inside. I knocked.

From behind the door came Carolyn's voice, pitched low. "Who is it?"

"Prince Valiant," I said.

"Who?"

"It's me, Stephen the K."

She opened the door a crack, gave me a long skeptical look, and let me in. "I thought you were in Los Angeles."

"I was, but I got out. I made a getaway disguised as James Dean. Want to see my new car?"

"No. Shh. Keep your voice down, Siddhartha's asleep." She motioned me over to the low couch. "Want some tea?"

"Sure." I watched her walk to the kitchen and return minutes later with the teapot and mugs and honey on a tray. She was large, big breasts and hips like an exaggerated version of Julie, but moved with the grace of someone lighter, sure of her steps and the flow of her own motion. She had on a loose cotton sweater and baggy bell-bottoms. Casual. She'd been reading. A paperback copy of *Black Spring* lay open face-down on the cable-spool coffee table. This was to be a black spring, a Harlem Renaissance for the whole country. She was tuned in. The bungalow smelled of jasmine incense, Carolyn's favorite flavor.

"So how are you doing? Feeling better now?"

"Good. Really good. It's great to be out of there. Coming back north is a bath, you know what I mean?—like, what a relief." Her face was seasoned, serene, which made her crossed eyes seem even wilder, her thick lips even more sensual. "I'm glad you were here." I wanted to bite those lips.

"Oh yeah? How come?"

"Where's Kevin?" Since his nervous visit with me at Franciscan, I'd seen neither Kevin nor Carolyn, didn't know what their status was, maybe I shouldn't have brought it up but I didn't want another scene like with Bob at April's. Boyfriends.

"I have no idea. Why?"

"I just . . . I didn't know whether . . . Are you guys . . ."

"Yes, we're still lovers," she said to me, looking me straight in the eye with one of hers. Then she poured us each a mug of tea. "Honey?" I nodded, hooked, as she spooned a golden dollop into my mug. Lovers. Honey. I thought of Lenore Kandel's great lines *My cunt is a honeycomb, we are covered with come and honey.* She stirred in the honey, set down the spoon.

"Carolyn . . . " I took her hand.

"What are you doing?"

"It was you one of those times, wasn't it?"

"One of what times?"

"You know. When you came over as Julie."

She pulled her hand away. "What do you mean?"

"When you came over as Julie and we fucked."

She looked at me a long time. "You're really strange, you know that, Stephen?" She was sitting on a pillow on the floor so I couldn't get next to her without leaving my seat on the couch. I was trying to keep cool, but those lips, those eyes. "You're married to Julie. She's your wife. I've never fucked you and I'm not going to."

"Julie and I aren't getting back together. I don't deserve her."

"Well, I guess that's between you and Julie." She took a sip of tea, still looking at me cockeyed. Was I reading into her signals, or did she want me? I wanted her. I wanted to be rocked in her calm strength. We'd done it before, I was sure. I needed her healing power. "Crazy is fine, but don't be stupid, Stephen."

I got up. She got up. I walked around to her. She backed up, held me off. "Carolyn," I said. "Come on."

"Forget it, man. I shouldn't have let you in. Time to go now." She took the offensive, grabbed my arm and led me to the door. There wasn't much I could do, it was her house, she'd taken control. "I won't support this weirdness," she said, shoving me out the door. "Come back when you've got your trip together." She shut the door behind me. The lock clicked.

Shit. What was the matter with me? Or was it them? Who wasn't getting their signals straight? I was just doing what Stevie Wonder said, *make you love me a little more than you love him*, had I lost something in the translation? I was lost. Rodeo sort of rhymed with radio. Maybe I'd get some clearer message there.

The first summer I was in Santa Cruz I accidentally discovered the Rodeo one night when I walked out the back exit of a bookshop into a mirrored barnlike room with a fountain in the middle and plants hanging all over the place. A handful of people were scattered at the tables gossiping over cups of coffee or reading a magazine or deep in discussion over beers. The fountain room led into an even bigger barn, as I learned later a hotel carriage house, with a long deli counter at the back and a small bandstand in front and a whole wall of little windows along the street, which was the front way in. The other little room off the mirrored barn adjacent to the bookstore was a cavelike corner between the two larger rooms with a giant pink nude on a bearskin over the bar and wild boar heads and steer horns on the walls, no windows at all. Nothing was happening here but I liked the atmosphere, nice and funky, with chess players and tea drinkers and university people and mellow bikers and mountain boys with beards and cowboy boots. In the year and a half since, the Rodeo had turned into the hottest down-home hanging-out spot in town, with solo acoustic acts during the week and boogie bands on the weekend, everyone went there to meet friends or dig the crowd. The staff consisted of hippie busgirls clearing the tables and tackily glamorous jaded waitresses and bouncers who'd be happy to kill you if necessary and a big black manager named Eugene who ran the place with genial authority, keeping things cool when the folks got over-amped. I'd often come by here when I couldn't stay home but had no place else to go. Like tonight. A weeknight, Tuesday or Wednesday, I'd lost track, it was all eternity to me. The time, I saw on the clock behind the deli counter as I walked in, was nine-ten. Possible straight. Jack-queen-king, I drew in my mind's hand. I couldn't lose.

No live music was evident, but a lot of tables were occupied and there was an edge in the air, high expectation, a cacophony of noisy conversations. I missed my boots. Street shoes just didn't ring on the wood floor with the same percussion, didn't have that rap of power I dug in Julie's heels, and in my Fryes before City Prison. Desert boots were boots in name only, more like white man's moccasins, a soft rubber tread for the city. I walked to the back and ordered a dark draft.

As I came out of the bar with my beer a voice from the corner called, "Hey, Marlon, Marlon Brando." It might have been one of the cats from the lodge, Jesse or Dirk or Spider, or some smartass stranger razzing me for my style, but I just nodded and kept on, into the big room where the light was kinder, a soft yellow reflecting warmly off the green walls. It felt as if everyone was here for a reason. As I stood in the bar doorway surveying the main saloon Randy Chatsworth walked up. Last I'd seen him was in the Cowell coffee shop right after Altamont when he was totally freaked. Tonight he seemed lighter, much less edgy. "How's it going?"

"Great. I just got out of the nuthouse in LA. What's been happening here?"

"Yeah, I heard you'd flipped out or something. Glad you're back. My house burned down. I lost all my stuff—manuscripts, everything." He looked as if it had done him good, evaporated all distractions. Down to essentials.

"Far out, man," I said. "You look great. Congratulations." We both laughed. Looked one another in the eye and laughed some more. We knew the joke was on us but what the fuck.

"How come they put you in the nuthouse?"

"Beats me. I think I was seen in too many places at once. Playing the role of the Pony Express. Too many messages, too much news. I was like some kind of radio. A poetry spill in motion. Messing with people's imaginations."

He nodded. "Heavy." Randy's hero was Faulkner, he talked about him all the time; he'd already written a couple of novels invoking the master, and now those books were ashes, like all the grass we'd smoked over the last year and a half. We were both starting over. Stoned. I on Thorazine and herb tea and beer and adrenaline, he on what I had no idea but he was clearly high. Like me, looking for a connection, and here we were, talking to each other like co-conspirators. Maybe he was my source. I hoped not. Much as I liked him to sip a pint with and stir the breeze, he was too overwrought most of the time to be trusted. I needed somebody lower-strung. "You just get here?" he asked. I nodded yes. "The booked entertainment flaked, some folk singer, and people are hot for music."

"I thought it felt a little jumpy in here."

"You should get up there and do your Dylan Thomas imitation."

I had a jukebox memory for Thomas's poems from listening to his records over and over, could reel off all of "Fern Hill" and many others on request, which I did now and then to entertain literary friends. Randy had been impressed one night by such a performance. "No thanks. Bob Dylan maybe. Or James Dean: I could just stand there looking cool and moody. Actually I'm laying low. Watching the show. Great bunch of people, huh?"

"Unbeatable."

Through the cigarette smoke and cheap perfume and coffee steam and beer vapors I drank in the shapes and textures and rhythms of the room, a saloon Toulouse-Lautrec would have loved, waitresses moving gracefully among the tables with their trays, long hair everywhere, outdoor skin in all its shades of brown, long dresses, short skirts, denim and leather, colorful cotton shirts, musical language, laughter and flashing eyes. So good to be north, back to the country roughness, a slower unfolding than LA's but no less miraculous. I recognized some faces, a continuous turnover of fresh ones among the regulars, but more than that I felt at home in the vibes, way more than I had down south. This was extended family.

"Catch you later." Randy peeled off to talk to someone else and I circled the room in search of a table on the far side, by the windows. From against the glass wall I could see everything. I sat down near the little corner exit. Some musicians came in that way, it was nearer the stage than the main door, and strutted to the bandstand with their instruments, hurriedly setting up, plugging in their amps. People applauded, yelled encouragement, even though nobody seemed to know just who these five guys were—the excitement level made it feel historic, like they were some legendary group under cover, they couldn't say who, it would cause a riot. They took the stage as if they belonged there, tuning their guitars, and people in the audience stood up, waved their beers, whooped, stomped, ready for transport on the magic strings, begging to be carried away. As the phantom band tuned up, Eugene approached the stage, totally in command, and said something to them I couldn't hear, motioning that they should unplug their stuff. The crowd was agitated. Eugene took the mike and announced that only acoustic music could be played weeknights, sorry, these guys weren't scheduled, come back on the weekend for rock'n'roll. Some big drunk in back, probably a biker from out of town—no local would have done it—yelled, "That sucks, man, we came to get down," and threw an empty beer glass that sailed in slow motion across the room and crashed against the bandstand, just missing the manager. Three Rodeo goons, bartender-bouncers, converged and pounced on the drunk and started pounding, which provoked a guy at another table to intervene, or try to, before he was pulled off and fists were flying, chairs and tables falling over, women screaming and men shouting and people scattering in a scared tumble. I left my beer half-drunk on the table and made for the corner door. This wasn't my idea of enlightenment. Cops were pulling up on Front Street as I headed for my car.

What the fuck was going on? I felt responsible. Everywhere I went people got weird within minutes of my arrival. I'd seen some standoffs in the Rodeo before, scuffles, drunks hustled out, but never a glass thrown, never a brawl. As I pulled away up Front Street toward the post office I could see things had settled a little already, police were escorting two or three guys into some waiting cars and through the saloon's front windows I saw cops talking to people and others arranging the tables. I wanted to know who the band was, really, why they'd tried to hijack the place, what had got the patrons so excited. I needed a mellower scene, some solid ground. Where now? Not home. The cottage in Rio Del Mar was cold, it had been empty too long, all I'd do there would be bounce off the walls. I drove out River Street and proceeded across Route 1 to Highway 9, following the road upriver and into the trees. On KDON the Temptations—minus the lead voice of David Ruffin, who'd split from the group for mysterious reasons and left them without the soul of their sound—were singing their latest hit, "Cloud Nine," an antidrug diatribe aimed at the ghetto, or maybe at me, the nine rhymed with the highway as I swung the roadster smoothly around the curves. *You're a million miles from reality*, intoned the Temps, *doin' time on Cloud Nine*, but I was sailing, the headlights sweeping a clean path before me, purple-black branches of the redwoods skimming by overhead with stars peeking between, rain-enriched river below on the right, my lungs sucking in the pure forest air for the first time in months, smells of spring mingling with the car's exhaust trailing behind me in a heady cloud. Love Creek here I come, Nona or no Nona, it was worth a spin through the hills to see where the night led after all these false stops, detours, small fiascos. Fingers of wind caressed my naked face, Prince Valiant pageboy flying. Please be there, Nona, somebody be there, please.

Lights were on in the big house at the lodge, but no car was parked in front. I pulled around back and saw the silver BMW. Maybe my luck was picking up. No other cars, and the cabins were dark, no sign of anyone else. I parked next to Nona's car, killed the lights, shut off the engine. In the kitchen I could see her moving around, red hair loose, a bright oasis. She must have heard me pull up, because she came to the window and looked out. As I walked to the back porch I felt a rush from the damp smoky air, the deep cool nighttime forest oxygen lifting its wings in my brain. I knocked. "Hi, Nona. Remember me?"

"My goodness," she said, opening the door. "Stephen! I've thought about you. I've been wondering how you were. Are you all right now? Your wife said you were in the hospital."

"I'm fine. Everything's better." I stepped inside.

"Let me give you a hug." Jesus. Even this polite embrace shot bolts of electricity through my body as she pressed herself gently against me. She seemed so calm and warm. More grounded. More sure of herself. "Come in, come in. Can I offer you something? Wine, juice, coffee, tea?" The kitchen looked more lived-in. A fire was going in the woodstove.

"Tea, I guess. Thanks. Or whatever you're having."

"I'll boil some water. Please, sit." She was wearing jeans and a soft wool turtleneck sweater, gray. Lace-up moccasins covered her calves. Something had happened. Her style had changed. "So much has happened since you were here," she said as she set the teapot and two stout coffeeshop-style mugs on the table.

"You look so different. What's going on? Where is everybody?"

"Oh, it's quite a story. And it's sort of sad. But maybe it's all for the best. I guess it must be," she added a little wistfully, pouring the hot water into the pot. "Would you like to smoke? Some grass, I mean." Am I hearing things, or did she just offer me marijuana?

"Sure." I watched her face, awaiting further word on her transformation.

From a small ceramic crock on the table she tapped some grass into a rolling paper, skillfully twisting up a number and sealing it with a lick of her wet tongue. She'd had some practice at this procedure. "You see, I've split up with my husband. I'm living here for now, but we're selling this place. I had to ask everyone to leave. It was very upsetting. But Barry won't support my plans for the lodge now, and I don't have the resources to do it myself." She lit the joint, inhaled and passed it to me. The fire snapped in the stove. "You know," she said, letting out the smoke, "that night when we smoked the hash—your lunar hash, remember?—that night was very important to me. I realized, eventually anyway, that I could experiment a little without being irresponsible. I mean, I don't have any kids, I can test my boundaries without putting anyone else at risk. Or that's what I thought. But I was right. I was suffocating in the suburbs. As a wife—a certain kind of wife. I didn't realize how limited, how constricted my life had become. Barry's so straight. I felt more at ease with the people up here—you and Tanya and

Jesse and the others—than with our social friends in Saratoga, Barry's friends, the professional set. Very nice people, really, but just . . . closed. Uptight. They could only loosen up by getting drunk. The more time I spent up here, the less I felt connected with my life on the other side of the hill. Then one day Tanya offered me—you know, after I'd discreetly expressed some interest—she offered me a tab of LSD."

The sound of those three letters combined with the smoke sent a surge of strange energy through me, a lucid sort of vertigo or nausea. Excitement. I could taste the acid, feel it coming on. "Far out," I said. "I guess you took it."

"I did. But I made the mistake—maybe it was a mistake, but maybe not—of taking it at home instead of here. It was a Sunday afternoon, a beautiful late January day, and I thought the acid might give me a new insight, help me understand Barry better, or something, I don't know what I was thinking, really, just that I needed another view of things, you know? Another perspective." She laughed, or rather giggled, maybe a little embarrassed. "I guess I got more than I bargained for. You know what I did, Stephen? Once the drug came on, I saw so clearly what an oaf he was, I couldn't face him, couldn't relate to him at all. I locked myself in the bathroom, horrified. What had I done to myself? I mean by marrying him. I curled up on the bathroom floor and just lay there hallucinating. My life was completely wrong. My whole subconscious came rushing up to show me what a horrible mess I'd made of it. Not that it didn't have its grace notes. I mean the lodge and everything. But I'd compromised so much, what would be left if I went on like this? I told Barry just to leave me alone, I'd be all right, it was something I ate." She laughed. "It really was. And when I got up the courage to come out, he'd gone. A golf date, I think. I looked around our house and everything seemed completely grotesque, pathetic, so ridiculously sterile, all that stupid furniture, that silly art, I felt no relation at all, it was totally empty, and there was something terrible in that emptiness, that imitation of safety. I realized it was wrong for me to be there, that I had the choice to change. It was almost as if I had to change or be resigned to hating myself as well as my pitiful husband." She paused, poured tea for both of us. "I'm sorry. I hope it's not too strong."

"Not at all." I wasn't sure if she meant the tea or her story. "It's a great story, Nona." Almost as wild as mine.

"There was just no way I could keep living like that. So that night, feeling very tender and vulnerable—opened up, pleasantly fatigued after my trip—I told Barry how I felt, or tried to tell him, tried to explain how I didn't fit in that setting, how I needed my own life. He became very abusive, called me ugly names, told me I was out of my mind, that I'd been ruined by my hippie friends. But by then it didn't matter. The next day I packed some things and came up here. We're getting divorced. And now I have to give up the lodge. It's heartbreaking to lose this place, but going on that way was too high a price to pay. All he wanted was an ornament. A cheerleader for his career. I'll find a little house to rent in the mountains, look for a job on this side of the hill. It's a whole new life now." She sipped her tea. "A whole new life."

We were sitting in the same places as Thanksgiving night. It felt as if we were simply continuing the same conversation. Except that we'd both had breakthroughs, we'd exploded old selves and shed them. "It's like we've been on the same trip, Nona, through separate but parallel universes. Space travel, inside. Mental travel. And here we are now just like last Thanksgiving—god, how many miles and lives ago was that?—picking up where we stopped. Full circle. That must be what brought me here, some kind of orbital gravity. It's amazing."

"It is," she said, passing me the roach. I took a toke and we both drifted. Her story spaced me out and sobered me up at the same time, pulled me out of my own adventure and into hers for a minute, our trips mingled, intertwined, and the braid we made temporarily steadied me, as if this was the most stability I could hope for, this mirror of my crisis, this opposite equal to balance my high-wire act. Plunging together through the same unknown. Flying. "Would you like to see where I live?"

A shudder rolled through my guts. She was looking me in the eyes. Was I dreaming, or what? I swallowed my joy and fear. "Okay."

I followed her through the dining room and up the great wooden staircase, the lodge's huge solitude reverberating around us. Her room was in back, in the corner above the kitchen, looking out over the cabins. Standing by either window you could see the outline of the big trees black against the sky. Inside, soft light came from a little table lamp next to the bed. It was simple in there, and it smelled good, a blend of her fancy soap and traces of smoke from the stove below. Furnished with the lodge's best. Old-fashioned solid woodworking. A fine oak dresser. A high-backed rocker with handcarved armrests. Four-poster bed, heavy wool blankets, white sheets and fluffy pillows.

"This is it," she said. "My palatial headquarters."

"This is it." This is it. That was all I could think. We stood there, hands in our pockets. Listening to the silence of the lodge and the night beyond, thousands of little hums and rustles echoing through the house, air currents, spirits in the dark. It was warm up here, comfortable, just upstairs from the stove, I could feel the soft heat coming through the floor. Clear heart redwood. That burgundy glow. This perfect place. I didn't know how to proceed. I needed her to lead me. "Nona . . ." I took a step in her direction.

There was a sound downstairs—the front door opening. She tensed, turned toward the sound.

"Nona?" a man's voice shouted.

"Oh my god, it's Barry."

Fuck. "What should I do?"

"Nona?" He was coming up the stairs.

"Nothing," she said. "Let's just meet him."

A tall good-looking man in his middle thirties or so, curly dark hair cut short, big shoulders, probably played high school football, appeared in the bedroom doorway. He looked at me, a 120-pound longhair, and all he could say was, "Who the hell is he and what's he doing here?"

Nona was incredibly cool. "Barry, I want you to meet Stephen. He used to rent one of the cabins in back, and he was away for a while, and he's just stopped by this evening to say hello. Stephen, Barry—my . . ." She trailed off.

"How's it going?" I nodded. He didn't extend his hand.

"Nona's a great lay, isn't she, Steve?" I wish. If he'd bothered to look, he'd have seen the bed was untouched.

"Why do you have to say something like that?" She was hurt and furious. "What are you doing here anyway? I thought this was still my place."

"That's a joke. You're only staying here with my permission, whore. I know all about your drugs-and-free-love so-called revolution. You're just a bunch of bums."

"What do you know about love?" she cried.

"Or drugs," I couldn't help adding.

He lurched and grabbed my hair. "You little punk." Pulling me toward the door. "Get the hell out of here." He gave me a shove out into the hall and toward the stairs. He smelled like a cocktail lounge. Nona tried to intervene but he pushed her back in the bedroom. I was powerless. Words wouldn't work on this guy. The drama wasn't mine. He was directing.

"It's okay, Stephen," Nona said over his shoulder, "Go. I'll be all right."

Something was happening here so much scarier than my private odyssey, so beyond my control, I felt humiliated, ashamed to be witnessing their nightmare. And yet I was: I was here. The only way out was out. "I'm sorry." I wasn't sure which one I was speaking to. "I'm not here." I turned and stumbled downstairs and out the front door, circling the building to reach my car. I couldn't deal with this scene, the voices shouting upstairs, it was more distressing than the brawl at the Rodeo, more destructive. We'd been so close to peace, communion. Now I was exiled again. Nona was up there with the man who'd end in her bed, I knew. Or worse. How could this happen? It was beyond me, outside understanding. I turned the key in the Porsche, the engine started and I was gone.

16

Anarchists Fainting

So much for Prince Valiant. I didn't sleep that night. For three or four days I was agitated, restless, I spent hours driving aimlessly around the county as I had in LA, driving itself a kind of therapy, unable as I was to focus on anything else, listening to Cocteau-radio poetry cleverly disguised as pop music, driven by desire for some connection that wasn't there, some human contact that could hold me, still me, make me feel some relation to a meaning, rescue me from these rapids I was riding. Despite the regular blasts of Thorazine I couldn't contain myself, was charged with jolt after jolt of excess electricity, energy, out-of-control awareness, I knew too much, couldn't carry on a conversation, had to keep going, moving. On the street downtown one afternoon I bumped into Kevin Bannister—a likely candidate to be my ally— but I couldn't stand still long enough to talk with him, and he was perplexed, shouting after me, "Where are you going? What's your hurry?" I couldn't answer. I didn't know. Who would understand my coded overtures? Maybe my old friends at Franciscan. I decided to stop by there.

So what if it was night. Visiting hours were for visitors, and I wasn't visiting anyone, just stopping by to say hi, see some friendly faces. I walked through the big door onto the ward like a veteran of foreign wars, expecting a welcome, but the patients were different. Indifferent. They didn't know me. I joined a few of them in the living area gathered around a television set. A nurse intercepted me, asking what I was doing. I explained that I was an alumnus just checking in for a little reunion, I wasn't visiting, my car was outside, I was in a hurry, I had no agenda, where was Lightning Leo? She retreated to confer with a colleague and I noticed on the little stand where the portable record player stood was a soothing blue-and-green album cover with a picture of a composed clean-cut young man with a neatly trimmed mustache, sympathetic eyes turned skyward—Mose Allison, *I don't worry about a thing.* I picked up the foot-square cardboard cover. There was no record inside. I studied the photo of the singer, that relaxed ambiguous expression. Flipped it over to check the liner notes, but my eyes were fucked, the words were a blur. The titles of the songs were in bold type, which if I strained I could make out. *I don't worry about a thing. It didn't turn out that way. Your mind is on vacation. Let me see. Everything I have is yours. Meet me at no special place.* These were my songs, the titles describing different stages, aspects of my odyssey. Had I, drawn here by some psychic magnetism, discovered the key to my relief, my liberation? I held onto the record jacket as a talisman, a square foot of security. The first nurse returned with a psych tech, they ushered me into a room, told me they'd spoken with Dr. Hopkinds, and asked me to lie down. A nurse I knew from before, Marilyn, who looked like Doris Day, came in and welcomed me back, told me to make myself at home, keep my voice down, people were trying to sleep, but I kept talking, asking about inmates I remembered, making up accounts of where they must be if they weren't here, demanding to know what had happened in my absence, what I had missed, all the while clutching the cardboard square, *I don't worry about a thing.* After a while they left me alone but I kept the monologue going, reviewing for them my travels since I was here, blending my story with those of my missing associates from the ward, constructing another scrambled epic for the record. I felt good and safe in the hospital room with Allison's assurance. Mose, my guide to the promised land. All I son. I am the son of all. Everyone's son. I'm taken care of. Only much later did I learn the full refrain: *I don't worry about a thing 'cause I know nothin's going to be all right.*

Soon Marilyn returned and relayed a message from Hopkinds: If I didn't quiet down they'd have me removed to County on a 72-hour hold. Whatever. I didn't know what that meant but I was giving up control, not setting out on any more excursions in search of the keys to new enigmas, just flowing with the knowledge I was covered.

Some time after that two white-coated men arrived at my door with a gurney, instructed me to lie down on it, strapped me down and wheeled me out of the ward, along the hallway, down the elevator, through emergency, a precise reversal of my journey New Year's Day, retracing my steps backward in a way that must mean this whole movie is being rewound, I'm going to come out the other end untouched, it was a dream on fast forward, everything imagined including this, as they folded the wheels under me and slid me into the back of an ambulance, secured the gurney, and rolled out of the hospital loading zone headed for who knows where.

I don't worry about a thing.

After a short ride I was unloaded into a dank facility where a bald man who bore a disturbing resemblance to my uncle Milton and seemed hostile to my hair asked me a series of stupid questions— name, address, date of birth, and so on as if any of it mattered —and wrote my answers on a form attached to a clipboard which he then asked me to sign explaining that I was agreeing to admission here, Santa Cruz County General Hospital, under 72-hour observation. I signed. Then he turned me over to the head nurse, a pale-faced hag with dyed black hair who reminded me frighteningly of the overbearingly nice and insincere mother of a girl I'd dated in high school, Shannon McCleary. Mrs. McCleary took me by the elbow and led me briskly through a dingy green area where patients wandered in zombified states of surly semi-oblivion, snarling at me as I went by or making aggressive comments I didn't get except for the tone, maybe they were aimed at McCleary and pitched at a subvocal level only the paranoid could hear. McCleary with her hideous madeup face and fake compassion steered me into a private room where a kind enough looking psych tech was ordered to put me in restraints. As he fastened the straps to my wrists and ankles I asked them both what was going on, but all McCleary would say to me was 72-hour hold. She left the room for a minute and returned with some liquid medication in a small paper cup. What's this? I wanted to know. Thorazine, I was told. She held the cup under my nose but it smelled so foul I turned my head. Why can't I take a pill? I asked. Drink, she ordered. Or we can give you a shot. I drank, practically gagging, as the attendant held me by the shoulders. Then they both left the room, locking the door behind them. McCleary took one last look through the little wire-screened window, flashing a malicious sneer. I still had the album cover, they'd left it leaning against the foot of the bed. Mose looked up over and past my left shoulder, bearing that serene demeanor. *I don't worry about a thing.*

Strapped down, drugged, stuck shit-deep in this miserable bummer, I wondered if I could endure the latest round of degradation, the worst of all possible recapitulations of everything I'd been through in the last four months. As the medicine took me over my arms and legs went dead and I felt myself being sucked into one of those whirlpools the bathtub makes when you pull the plug and the water goes twisting down into the dark plumbing, pipes of the psyche whose walls were painted with scenes, illuminated by phosphorescent slime, of rock stars plunging their guitars into wild bison and flying breasts and giant dicks held hostage by hijackers dressed as mummies, nurses wrapping them with white tape, hippie werewolves brandishing Buck knives, baseball players with huge hypodermics, electric typewriters wired to the fangs of babbling Draculas in black tuxedoes, a vast array of tortures to make me talk just when I thought I'd told everything, but it was never enough, I was locked in and sinking deeper into this swirling sewer of horrifying associations until the drug kicked all the way in and I went under.

In the morning another psych tech, who told me his name was Louie and who looked Latino, undid the straps so I could use a urinal. He took the pee away and returned with breakfast. I wasn't hungry, but he encouraged me, watching me chew the toast and pick at the scrambled eggs and sip the juice, which I think was spiked. When I was finished he refastened the straps, but not so tight. *Uh Louie Louie, oh no. I said uh we gotta go, ai-yi-yi-yi*, my autonomic soundtrack wailed silently as he left the room and locked up. I lay there too limp to cry, trying to will some feeling into my limbs, inject some strength from my adrenaline reserves, get back into my body. I pictured Houdini slipping out of his chains underwater, imagined myself again to be Steve McQueen, prisoner of war with a head for great escapes, focusing all my ingenuity on wiggling free of the straps. McQueen for a day. Not that I was going anywhere, I knew I couldn't get beyond the locked door, the grilled window, but I needed the dignity of movement at least, some minimal liberation. I invested hours—I had nothing else to do—in a slow squirming dance to shed my bonds, eventually getting one wrist free, then the other, then the ankles, still lying there so as not to attract attention but enjoying the satisfaction of having accomplished something, knowing I wasn't totally powerless, victimized by my keepers. And then McCleary was back, asking why I was out of restraints, ordering last night's psych tech to hold me down, pouring the horrid liquid into me. She told the psych tech to secure the straps and split—she had other victims to attend to. Sorry, he said to me, he'd try not to make them too tight if I promised I wouldn't twist loose again. He told me his name was Chris. Saint Christopher? I mumbled through what seemed to be the mouth of my psychotropic swamp, a body bogged in depressant. Yeah, he grinned and nodded, Saint Christopher.

Later that afternoon Chris came back with a gift for me—a medallion about the size of a quarter hanging on a cheap chain. One side bore the familiar image of the big man carrying the child across the water. I couldn't read the inscription but I knew it from my old medallion, wherever it was: SAINT CHRISTOPHER PROTECT US. He turned it over. On the other side was another image that resembled me before my famous shave, a bearded hippie with a suffering face and his hands together under his chin. The words were blurred. Chris read to me: SAINT ANTHONY PRAY FOR US.

When Hank's face appeared at the little window I thought I must be delirious. Two and a half days in restraints had convinced me my case was lost, I was missing in action, I'd never be heard from again. They had me stashed away where I'd never be found. I'd signed myself in. Something had gone wrong, there'd been a setback, I was being sacrificed. With the Siamese saints around my neck I accepted what was coming, resigned myself, began to have faith in fate. Then Hank appeared, the door was unlocked, opened, the straps undone. Hank was his usual matter-of-fact self, routinely coming to my rescue, it was simply part of his job, no big deal really. He assured McCleary he and his companions could handle me. With him were two goons, Big Al, a black man the size of a tank in a crisp white nurse's uniform, and Bronco, a small skinny blond guy in street clothes with a north European accent, Danish maybe. An unlikely escort service to replace the familiar posse that had almost blown it the last time they'd tried to abduct me. Al I figured must be for power and Bronco for speed in keeping me under control. Hank was the stabilizing element, forever grounded.

Bronco drove the rented car with Hank riding shotgun and Al and me in back. I was grateful to see the sky again, breathe the outside air. A little private plane awaited us at the airport in Scotts Valley. LA bound again, only this time I didn't protest—anything was better than an indeterminate sentence in McCleary's dungeon. I'd never flown in such a small plane before, and the flight felt lighter, much less oppressive with just five people, counting the pilot, soaring up out of the Santa Cruz Mountains, than a commercial jet out of San Jose would have been. Suddenly as we climbed a piercing pain shot through my tooth and Big Al gave me a knowing look, as if to say that's just a sample of what's in store if you try anything funny. A little psychic arm-twisting. I replied silently, Okay, lay off, I'm cooperating already, and the pain subsided. Soon we were cruising over California, down the Salinas Valley, Coast Range below on our right and the Pacific beyond, shining.

By now, Hank told me many years later, he and the rest of the family were wondering if I'd ever come down. Three months of hospitals and doctors and drugs had evidently had little effect on my illness. I had been diagnosed paranoid schizophrenic, a disease that could be chronic, and I'd shown no signs of abandoning my delusions. It's true, I didn't think I was crazy. I was convinced that I'd broken through, had pierced the consensual façade and was experiencing reality in the raw. This was a precondition for poetry—living it, not just writing. So why was I being punished and imprisoned? Why had the revolution ditched me? Where had I fucked up?

It took a month in the Melrose for me to learn the art of obedience. I'd never been very good at taking orders, but between the medication, the structural demands of the hospital's social order, and the vigilance of the staff, I had no choice. The Melrose was a private psychiatric facility conveniently located next door to Silverman's office; he could stop in and check on me here without going all the way to Santa Monica. The Westside mansion had been the home of some thirties-era movie star who'd presumably gone mad in her later years, so this is what they did with her house. Its atmosphere was intimate, personal, less institutional than the average loony bin—at least on the surface—more residential, less antiseptic than Franciscan or St. James, less squalid than either county ward, with softer furniture and an outdoor patio and a volleyball court and a basketball hoop and half an acre of grassy grounds bounded abruptly by an eight-foot concrete wall.

Thorazine-gorged, my flesh couldn't face the sun, but having access to the outdoors, the smoggy but open sky, the lawn and its approximation of nature, I felt at least a simulation of freedom. The one-story Spanish Mission architecture—not unlike the style of my parents' house—gave the place a pleasant sense of rusticity. But the routine was more monotonous and regimented than any I remembered in my other venues. Each day we were herded from one "activity" to another, like schoolchildren, with little breaks in between. Hanging out alone was taboo, you had to socialize, but not disruptively, no poetic discourse to disturb the inmates, everything contained, controlled, imagination was dangerous. Better to shuffle straight ahead, no questions asked, no backtalk, than to tweak the stifled atmosphere with individual vision. It was kindergarten all over again, and I liked it even less now than when I was five. Breakfast, volleyball, occupational therapy, lunch, group, one-on-one with the shrink, maybe a visitor, dinner, TV or reading, bedtime. Report for your pills at the pill counter every four hours. Silverman now had me thoroughly doped up, and the saturation dosage of all these months at last began to have an effect. I was slowed down, still able to associate—cut from one connection to another with flashes of this and allusions to that—but also beginning to drag the baggage of so much drugs, like a fullback pulling just a few more yards with tacklers hanging on. I was more of a broken-field runner, a swivel-hipped zigzagger skilled at bursts of speed and quick reversals, I didn't have the power to carry the weight of a defensive line, it was too heavy. El Silver Man was treating me to a carefully medicated depression, a chemical downer to counter my mania. And part of his prescription was a subtle campaign of signs, publicly posted, literally the writing on the walls, the most memorable of which was a black plastic plaque with white lettering, on a door I never saw opened, that said:

PATIENT HAS THE RIGHT TO REFUSE
ELECTROSHOCK AND LOBOTOMY

It got my attention.

Like a Zen master whacking his student with a stick.

Seeing that plaque was a turning point in my treatment. The sentence stuck in my head, and every time I passed the door I reread it. Through the gloom of my deepening oppression, the physical weight of my drugged bones, and the psychic burden of imposed conformity, the sign shone like a beacon. Its mind-altering ambiguity intrigued me. To those nine words I privately applied all the analytic skills I'd picked up in six years' training in the techniques of the New Criticism, picking the text apart in all its richness, intuiting its ironies, dissecting its multiple meanings down to the syllable, peeling away the layers of their implications. *Patient has the right to refuse electroshock and lobotomy.* In other words, if you don't play by our rules, we're going to strap you down and cut your brain out. We're going to shoot so much juice through your skull you'll never remember what hit you. You have the right to refuse, but a lot of good it will do. We've got the tools, the machines, the wires, the clamps, the precise knives, the goons to restrain you while we do the procedure. We've got the doctors, the locked doors, the institutional discipline, the authority. We've got the guns. You have the right to refuse and that's about it.

Your other option is to play it straight.

I had plenty of time to ponder these revelations. And it's a good thing because they took a while to process. Obviously I wasn't going anywhere. Except deeper into despair of ever escaping. The drama of my so-called psychosis had ceased to be entertaining. The revolution, so flagrantly ubiquitous last winter, had gone underground. No sign of it in this environment. Maybe I'd been miscast. Made a wrong turn. Taken the dead end into oblivion. Whatever had happened, I was on my own. Exiled from history, like an astronaut on a spacewalk with his cord cut. Far out in the dark. Silverman had my number. Fucking drugs. Each day the weight of the medication pressed me further into the floor. Under the thumbs of the dumb staff, unconscious slaves of their own boring emotions. Destiny had put one over on me, lifting me out of the mountains last winter on currents of heroic action, insight, consequential art, only to dump me here. Nowhere. Just another zombie among many. The exuberant anarchy of democratic creation I dared envision as the new world under construction by me and millions of enlightened comrades was a mirage. My brain belonged to the Melrose. On doctor's orders it could be fried or lobotomized. I had the right to refuse, of course. Small comfort, under the circumstances. Earning freedom meant admitting defeat.

One thing I learned about Thorazine was that if you took enough of it for long enough, despite its lobotomizing effects, your eyes began to adjust, you could almost read. Not anything so substantial as a book, but let's say a page in a magazine, a paragraph or two, a poem. Awaiting my daily session with Silverman, in which my progress toward recovery I deduced was being measured by my dullness—a lifeless docility equaling mental health—I browsed through a pile of current magazines. It was in *Harper's* one afternoon that I came across an approximation of electroshock, a poem by Robert Bly entitled "Anarchists Fainting." Bly the blowhard bard who'd been my cellmate in the tank at City Prison, the blubbering Bukowskioid exhibitionist whose own obnoxious noises were a parody of mine, was here in the Melrose addressing me from *Harper's*, speaking to me as "You United States . . ." It was ironic, like "Patient has the right," I was no more united than the country, everything was splitting, had split apart, even the poem exploded in jerky fragments, that's what it was about. Lines leaped off the page, grabbed hold of me, dragged me around the room, shook me upside down by the feet till my brains fell out, made hash of my hash-induced hallucinations, reconstituted and documented my drooping odyssey.

> *Your sons dream they have been lost in kinky hair,*
> *no one can find them,*
> *neighbors walk shoulder to shoulder for three days.*
> *And your sons are lost in the immense forest.*

How did he know? Had he been following me around? Or was it that words were alive after all, that poem-bombs could still be set off in the faces of the unsuspecting? Incendiary messages to burn in the mind. Linguistic insurrection, but on the page.

> *Even at the start Chicago was a place where the cobblestones*
> *got up and flew around at night,*
> *and anarchists fainted as they read* The Decline and Fall.
> *The ground is soaked with water used to boil dogs.*

Your anarchy could be acted out unpunished if you confined your tactics to language and language alone, holding your fire for the right moment instead of just shooting your mouth off whenever the muses moved you. You had to select your targets with care, wait till their eyes saw the whites of your page, and then blam!

> *We look out the window, and the building across suddenly explodes.*
> *Wild horses run through the long hair on the ground floor . . .*

It struck me that I could be as crazy as I pleased so long as I didn't make an issue of it in public, didn't act out every image, restrained my responses, contained my spontaneous creation, conducted myself with subdued propriety, resisted becoming a spectacle. I did have the right to refuse.

> *Our spirit is in the baseball rising into the light*

There was some consensus out there, however pedestrian, and you had to respect it or pay the price.

> *The moonlight crouches over the teen-ager's body thrown from the car*

I was not Dean or Dylan or McQueen, or even my brother Don, though I too had crashed. If speed kills, music heals. Poetry saves lives. Art is an ambulance picking you up in time.

My only way out of the Melrose was to keep it under my hat. I was so bummed by now from the cumulative weight of drugs and imprisonment all these months I had no choice but to give in and go on living as if "sane," as if everything self-evident to me through all these miles of enlightenment were the delusions of a sick young man. As if. I could now come down from this trip, get an honorable discharge from the madhouse, go undercover as a civilian, and be an average guy. I began the final offensive that afternoon, explaining to Silverman how bad it felt to be stuck in here, how I'd resolved to be normal, and I showed him then and for the next several weeks how I could be as normal as the next person, acting just regular, my latest improvisation. I expounded for him my emerging theories of madness as art that escapes the frame, of art as madness that adopts an esthetic, of revolution occurring internally, of mental health as a social convention like driving on the right side of the road—a common agreement for general convenience, even if it was arbitrary. El Silver Man nodded, smiled, agreed I was making remarkable progress. The funny thing was I couldn't write anymore. I was spent, spoken for. I seemed on the surface to be joining the living dead, blending with the rest of the population, and I confess it was depression that made me do it, but I was working on another life.

I adopted a new disorder. I passed over.

Stephen Kessler is the author of eight previous books and chapbooks of original poetry, fourteen books of literary translation, and a collection of essays. Born in Los Angeles in 1947, he has degrees in literature from Bard College and the University of California, Santa Cruz. Following an acute psychotic episode in 1970, he abandoned an academic career to devote himself full time to writing, subsequently publishing his essays, criticism and journalism in many magazines and newspapers, chiefly in Northern California. He was a founding editor and publisher of *Alcatraz*, an international journal, and *The Sun*, a Santa Cruz newsweekly, among other periodicals and independent publishing ventures. He received a National Endowment for the Arts Fellowship and a Lambda Literary Award for his translation of *Written in Water: The Prose Poems of Luis Cernuda*, and is a four-time winner of the California Library Association's PR Excellence Award for *The Redwood Coast Review*, the quarterly literary newspaper he founded and has edited since 1999.

For more about Stephen Kessler, visit www.stephenkessler.com.